Praise
Bon Ap

"A wonderful follow-up to *Let Them Eat Cake!* I was caught up in Lexi's tug-of-war between her charmed life in France with its possibility of romance, and the pull to Seattle where her family and a very special man long for her return. What a perfect story for an evening by the fire or a day at the beach."

— DEBORAH RANEY, author of *Remember to Forget* and *Leaving November*

"Paris, French culture, and pastries loom prominent in *Bon Appétit* by Sandra Byrd, who writes with insight and authenticity about the life of an American student at a prestigious pastry academy."

— RUTH AXTELL MORREN, author of *The Rogue's Redemption, The Healing Season,* and *Hearts in the Highlands*

"Sandra Byrd does it again! If you want a book as sweet as caramelized sugar and as intriguing as a handsome stranger, reach for *Bon Appétit*. Delicious and satisfying!"

— LYN COTE, author of the Texas: Star of Destiny series

"Lexi is a delight, and one can't help rooting for her as she struggles to achieve professional success while seeking the perfect recipe for romantic bliss. *Bon Appétit est très magnifique!*"

— TRISH PERRY, author of *Beach Dreams, Too Good to Be True,* and *The Guy I'm Not Dating*

Bon Appétit

a novel

Bon Appétit

Sandra Byrd

WATERBROOK
PRESS

BON APPÉTIT
PUBLISHED BY WATERBROOK PRESS
12265 Oracle Boulevard, Suite 200
Colorado Springs, Colorado 80921
A division of Random House Inc.

The characters and events in this book are fictional, and any resemblance to actual
persons or events is coincidental.

ISBN: 978-1-4000-7328-3

Published in association with the literary agency of Janet Kobobel Grant, Books
& Such, 4788 Carissa Avenue, Santa Rosa, CA 95405.

Published in the United States by WaterBrook Multnomah, an imprint of The
Doubleday Publishing Group, a division of Random House Inc., New York.

WATERBROOK and its deer design logo are registered trademarks of WaterBrook Press.

Library of Congress Cataloging-in-Publication Data
Byrd, Sandra.
    Bon appetit : a novel / Sandra Byrd. — 1st ed.
      p. cm.
    ISBN: 978-1-4000-7328-3
    1. Young women—Fiction 2. A   Fiction. 3. Bakers—Fiction.
4. France—Fiction. 5. Chick-lit. I. T
      PS3552.Y678B66 2008
      813'.54—dc22
                                            2008013292

Printed in the United States of America
2008—First Edition

10 9 8 7 6 5 4 3 2 1

For Anne and Malgwyn Elmer
For Ann and Kyle Lewis

De vrais amis en France with a true gift of Christian hospitality.

Merci!

Hunger savors every dish.
French proverb

One

*How can a nation be great
if its bread tastes like Kleenex?*
Julia Child

Living in France was my dream, and I was going to make it work. With that goal in mind, I waited nearly two hours to get my *autorisation provisoire de travail,* the temporary work permit that would allow me to take a job at the Delacroix bakery while I attended pastry school.

A bored-looking woman behind the counter beckoned me forward with her finger.

"I need to apply for the APT," I said in fluent French, handing over my paperwork. I had a letter from Luc's uncle saying I would be working at two family bakeries in a neighboring village and town, the student resident permit Luc's mother had acquired for me, and a letter from L'École du Pâtisserie stating I was enrolled in their sixteen-week program from September through December.

"If you are a citizen of a European Union nation, you don't need this." She flicked the papers back at me but paused to look at my identity card. "Lexi Stuart. What a strange name."

"I'm an American."

The room went quiet except for some muttering. I felt like shouting, *Yes, an American. You know, the ones who saved you in World War II.*

Instead, I forced a polite smile onto my face.

"You speak French," the woman said, as if noticing for the first time.

"Oui," I answered. "My permit, please?"

She moved incredibly slowly. Finally, having assembled and stamped all of my paperwork, she handed a card over the countertop. "You do know that you cannot work in France once you complete your school program? You'll have to go home."

I shook my head. "I read that foreign workers are welcome in France." The words dried up in my mouth.

"Welcome? *Non.* But they can be hired. If no one in the EU can be found to do the same job, that is. Of course, we don't have many bakers and pastry makers in France, so I am sure they'll make an exception for you." She directed her sarcastic laugh more at the woman next to her than toward me. The second woman coughed out a laugh, but hers seemed halfhearted rather than truly cruel.

"Here, Lexi," she said, drawing out my name to make it sound like "Leaksie" before continuing. "*Bon courage.* I hope you enjoy your stay in France. This permit expires in six months."

I left, slowly walking to the Rambouillet city center, and stood

by myself at the train station, permit in my purse, shoulders droop-
ing, sensible shoes on my feet. I slumped onto a bench.

I heard the arriving train announced in French, and the suave
melody of the language reminded me. *Lexi! You're in France. You're
living in France. Your dream has come true. One cranky, ill-informed
government worker does not a nation make.*

In spite of everything, I was here. I was breathing French air,
eating *real* French bread, meeting French people. Kind of. I
grinned, remembering a joke I'd read before leaving Seattle a few
weeks ago.

In European heaven, the British meet you at the door, the Germans orchestrate your schedule, the Spanish plan your entertainment, and the French prepare your food.

In European hell, however, the Spanish orchestrate your schedule, the Germans plan your entertainment, the British prepare your
food, and the French will greet you at the door.

Considering my welcome thus far, I could assume I'd landed in
European hell. All I needed to confirm it was an unorganized siesta
and a plate of fish and chips followed by a lively reading of Goethe's
Faust.

I decided not to worry. I'd make it work.

Thirty minutes later I got off the train and lifted my chin toward
the sun. My village, Presque le Château, was perfect, a tiny jewel on
the necklace of towns that encircled Paris. Old houses, tidily kept,
lined the streets. The air was perfumed with the sweetness of orange
blossoms and bitterness of orange zest. I trailed my hand along the
low stone wall fronting the sidewalk. My fingers and heart tingled at

the thought that hundreds of years before the United States was even a nation, some other young woman may have trailed her fingertips along this very wall, wondering what life held for her.

"Bonjour!" I called to a woman I passed on the street. She said, *"Bonjour!"* back to me. Would that exact woman show up to buy her baguette from me in a few days? In fact, that very woman may become a friend or end up buying baguettes that I *make* in a few months. Or ordering a birthday cake from me in a year! I loved that thought.

When Luc, my boss at the French bakery where I'd worked in Seattle, had first approached me with the idea of swapping places with his sister, I felt both excitement and anxiety. His family owned several bakeries in France and two in Seattle. As they expanded their business, the family members went back and forth between Seattle and France to get experience in both. Luc's sister was coming to the US to work in Seattle for six months or more. Would I be interested in taking her place in France?

Mais oui!

I arrived at Luc's maman's house and pushed open the black wrought-iron gate. Their big stone house was threaded with ivy, and the wooden shutters were flung open, letting in the mid-July sun. As I walked by, I squinted at the windows, unable to see in through the lace curtains. That's how the French were. Beautiful, stylish, but with a veil of privacy between you and the outside world. Intimacy reserved. Since arriving a few days ago, I had not been invited into my host's house. I was starting to fear that what I'd heard was true: I'd never be invited anywhere personal while here.

Come on, Lexi. It's only been a few days.

I walked along the cobbled stone path that led to the cottage tucked behind the house. In the old days, it had housed the bread ovens. Luc's family had transformed it into a perfectly *petite* cottage for his sister. Now it was my home.

I opened the door and walked in. The front room was a tiny kitchen, complete with all appliances, and an eating area with a wooden table for two, painted mustard yellow. Beyond that was the smallest living room I'd ever seen. A fairy room, really, perfectly proportioned, with two soft needlepoint chairs and footstools. I pushed open the windows and inhaled the pepper and spice of the red geraniums spilling over the window box.

I opened my laptop and logged into my e-mail. One new one from my mom, which made me laugh. She was getting ready to visit Italy and said she'd wave when she flew over France. That was it for new e-mail.

My finger hovered for a moment, indecisive. Then I clicked on an older e-mail I'd read several times already.

Hey Lexi,

I know we said good-bye in person last night, but I wanted to send an e-mail to say one last thing. It's hard to believe we've said good-bye for now. I keep thinking of things I want to tell you, but I know living in France is your dream. I admire you for working so hard to make your dream come true, and I want to honor that. Have the time of your life, and keep in touch from time to time. I want to hear what's happening.

Yours,

Dan

Yours, Dan. But the tone was much cooler than the heat we'd felt when saying good-bye in person.

I resaved the e-mail, pushed back the unwelcome emotions it aroused, and shut down the computer. Then I went into my bedroom and kicked off my shoes. I lay on my bed and fell into the deep sleep of the recovering jet-lagged.

When the phone rang hours later, darkness had swallowed the house.

"Hello?" I said, fumbling for the phone and trying to get my bearings.

"Hi, Lex." It was Tanya, my best friend from home.

"Oh. Hi."

"Wow, I'm overwhelmed by the enthusiasm of that greeting," she said.

I laughed. "Just waking up." A slow warmth spread through me. It *was* good to hear from Tanya, but I'd hoped it would be someone else.

I took the phone with me as I went to close the windows, looking jealously at the twinkling lights in the "great house" where Luc's *maman* and *papa* lived. Chattering voices floated out of their windows despite the hour.

"Ready for work tomorrow?" Tanya asked.

"Yes," I said. "Busy day, I think. It's the Fourteenth of July, Bastille Day. A French national holiday, like July Fourth."

"Trial by fire."

I agreed. "Lots of dishes to wash, I'm sure."

"When do you start school?"

"Not till the beginning of September," I said. "That'll give me plenty of time to make friends at the bakeries or in the village and figure out what I'm doing. I hope to make a couple friends to explore Paris with, and scope out what the future job market looks like."

"It's really nice that they're paying for you to go to school while you're working there," Tanya said. "They'll probably want you to stay on."

"Yeah." I hoped! "That's how I know they feel like I have a future here. Otherwise, they wouldn't be investing in me—the tuition and boarding costs."

"Any word from Dan?" Tanya asked, her voice quiet.

"He e-mailed right after I left, and I e-mailed back. He's busy working on a case. His law firm has really cranked things up. And their softball season is in full swing." *I thought maybe you were him when you called.*

"You guys decided there was no commitment, right? Since you were leaving and didn't know when—or if—you'd be back?"

"Yep. It was actually my idea. I wanted it to be open-ended since I didn't know what the future held." At least, that's what I said I wanted.

"So it's okay as it is," she said softly. "I'd better go. Steve is taking me to the lake. We're jet-skiing with some other couples and want to scout the place out and swim a little first."

"Oh," I said. "Right." We said our good-byes and hung up. I sighed and nibbled on a sandwich made from a crusty baguette of the most magnificent bread I'd ever tasted and some stinky cheese.

Then I laid out my uniform for the next day and set the alarm for three o'clock in the morning. It was really quiet, but I just lay there, wishing I could sleep.

When I did sleep, I dreamed Dan was jet-skiing with another woman, and Tanya and Steve knew and didn't tell me.

A few hours later, I could barely force my eyes open. The jet lag should have been gone by now, but maybe a shower would help. I reached for my clock and glanced at the digital display.

Adrenaline shot through my veins. 4:55 a.m.!

What happened to my alarm? I had to be at the bakery in the center of the village by five o'clock in the morning. I knew the bakers would already be there. I pulled my uniform on, brushed my teeth as fast as I could, put my hair in a French twist, and ran out the door. I wanted to make a good impression right away. I wanted to be a benefit to the family and to my colleagues.

The birds whistled, but I couldn't stop to listen. Dawn had broken, but I couldn't pause to look at the sun as it poured onto the village like a runny yolk. Instead I thanked God I had scoped out how to get to the bakery and ran up the street to the village square.

When I walked into the bakery, Luc's mother was there, shouting orders to the bakers in the back and a fawning young woman in the front.

"Ah Lexi," she said, throwing an apron at me. "In this bakery, we arrive on time, all the time." She looked at her watch. I was fourteen minutes late. "Today is a holiday, as I am sure you know. We will be very busy. You help in the front; Odette will show you what to do."

I introduced myself to Odette, who moments before had been sweetness and light to everyone else, but who responded to me with deafening silence.

"What can I do?" I said, putting on my best American cheerfulness.

"That is indeed the question, isn't it?" Odette said, the smile she'd given Luc's mother evaporating. Clearly I wasn't important enough for politeness. It occurred to me that the name "Odette" and the word *odious* were closely related.

Patrons came in and bought their daily bread. Odette jovially greeted each one by name, and I simply smiled and said, *"Bonjour."* They looked at me uncertainly.

I handed over breakfast breads and boxed-up pastries, my stomach growling with each warm chocolate croissant I surrendered. Odette ran the cash register.

The customers petered to a trickle, and Madame came to get me. "Odette can handle it now," she said. "You're here to help me."

I followed her into the back of the bakery, where several men were prepping bread. It was smaller than L'Esperance, where I'd worked in Seattle. Madame and her brother, Marcel, had inherited the family business from their father. Marcel usually worked at the bakery in Provence, several hours to the south. His son, Philippe, managed the bakery in Rambouillet, not far away.

"Clean this up, please," Madame said. Bowls lay everywhere, mixers dripped with chocolate *ganache*, and a huge pile of cookie sheets, stacked like a deck of cards, needed scrubbing.

I nodded cheerfully. Luc had warned me I'd be the low girl on the totem pole.

As I stood in the washing room, cleaning and hanging the utensils, I watched Madame work. She slung dough and barked orders in salty French. The bakers ducked away from her and kept a low, respectful tone when talking to her. I grinned.

"Something is amusing?" Madame stacked another set of pans in front of me. "I could use a good laugh."

"Oh, no," I said. "Nothing at all, Madame."

"*Bon.* Call me Maman. I am the maman of the bakery." She went out back and smoked a cigarette, then came back in to make puff pastry for éclairs. She reminded me of Patricia, her niece, the baker in charge of the pastry room in Seattle. Patricia was here now too in Rambouillet. I'd see her again when I worked a shift at that bakery. I was a floater, a *commis,* helping wherever I was needed with no permanent home.

That thought struck too close.

One of the bread bakers walked by and looked at my face. "You are sad?"

I shook my head. "Tired."

"Ah," he said, and left. A few minutes later, he came back with a chocolate croissant. "To wake you up." He handed me a cup of coffee. "Take a break. Not be sad anymore." He hadn't fallen for my tired talk.

I looked to see if Maman approved, and she nodded. I went out the back door and sat at the picnic table set up for staff breaks.

I bit into the pastry and remembered something I'd once read.

The croissants in France are so light they must be made by angels, and the coffee, so thick and black, by the devil. I sipped my coffee, hot and strong, and agreed.

Church bells chimed the start of the workday. It was eight o'clock in the morning, my first day of work in a real French bakery. It was eleven o'clock the night before in Seattle. Tanya was probably still roasting marshmallows at the lake.

I drained my coffee and went back to the kitchen. The day went quickly as I cleaned the dishes, the back bakery room, and neatened the supplies. At lunchtime, I heard a happy shout.

"Poupée!"

As I turned, I saw Maman open her arms and smile, and ten years dropped off her face. "Are you ready for the celebration tonight?"

"Oui," a little girl answered. "I can't wait!"

Maman gave her a treat and went back to work. The little girl— whom Maman had called *poupée,* or doll, a term of endearment— turned and looked at me. She offered her hand. *"Bonjour.* My name is Céline."

Such perfect manners. Such a sweet spirit. Totally unlike the only other Céline I'd ever known at a short-lived job in Seattle. Little Céline's school uniform was starched, her hair tied back in a neat ponytail with the tiniest pearl studs clinging to her earlobes.

"Hello." I shook her hand. "My name is Lexi."

"Lexi! I like that name." She sat next to me.

She *liked* my name! She didn't think it was strange. Take that, mean work permit woman.

"Are you taking the place of Dominique?" she asked.

Dominique was Luc's sister. "I'm working here while she works in my town."

"In America?" Céline asked, biting into her cookie.

"Yes."

"Do you live in California? I love California."

"No." I watched her eyes droop. Not ready to lose my first and only French friend, I added, "But I live very close to California." *As U.S. geography goes,* I thought.

"Oh, good. That's fine then." She hopped off the stool next to the weighing counter, taking her cookie with her. "Do you know my papa?"

"I don't know," I said. "What is his name?"

"Philippe." She took another nibble out of her cookie.

"No, I don't know him yet."

"You'll like him," she said. "He's *très sympa.*"

I laughed. "I'm sure your dad is very cool."

She laughed too and walked up front to bask in the adoring gaze of Maman and Odette.

I smiled for the first time that day. Céline was definitely *bien élevé,* well-raised, and polite.

A few minutes later Maman came and handed me a list of ingredients. "Weigh these out for me, to prepare for tomorrow."

"Immediately," I said. Then I added, "Céline is a delightful child."

She nodded. "I know. If only I had grandchildren. She is my brother Marcel's granddaughter. She's in the village today for the fireworks celebration tonight. Normally she's in Rambouillet with her father. But school is now out until September, and since her mother died a few years ago, we all take care of her."

I hadn't known Philippe was a widower. I remembered Patricia talking about her brother when she was in Seattle and knew she doted on him. Poor Céline. No *maman*.

"Ah well," Maman said. "Luc is getting married next month, and maybe I'll have grandchildren myself soon."

"The wedding will be very exciting!" I said. Even though I'd had my fill of weddings at home, it would be fun to see a French one. And I had truly begun to like Marianne, Luc's fiancée.

Maman looked at me strangely and walked away.

I shook it off and began to weigh out the butter, *exactement,* according to her instructions.

Out of the corner of my eye I spied Odette, who had been eavesdropping, I was sure. She hung her apron on one of the pegs in the back. The bakery was closing early due to the holiday.

I tried again to make polite conversation. "How nice that your name is embroidered on your uniform!" I said. "I'll have to get that done."

"Temporary workers and floaters don't have their names on their uniforms," she said. "There is no reason for it, as the customers and suppliers, even the other bakers, won't need to know their names, and they don't stay long enough to matter. It's for those who are *permanent.* It would be a great *faux pas* to have it done yourself."

"Oh," I said, busying myself with the butter. I blinked back tears and was ashamed to admit I wanted my own *maman* despite being twenty-five years old.

Odette took a pastry box out of the refrigerator case and readied herself to leave for the day. "You won't be going to Luc's wedding," she pronounced. "It's for family and friends."

And then she left.

I grinned. That was where she was wrong. I knew the bakery would close for two weeks in August, as many businesses in and around Paris did, and that the family was traveling south for the wedding.

I couldn't wait to visit Provence. Odette may not have realized it, but I *was* Luc's friend.

Two

Sacred cows make the best hamburger.
Mark Twain

A few weeks rolled by, and every day after my shift, I plopped down at an outside table at the village café, eating a late lunch, drinking iceless Orangina—though I really wanted a Coke with lots of ice cubes—and trying to look like I fit in. I doodled or read so I didn't look alone. I loved France. I loved the French. Why didn't they like me? Everyone was polite enough—except for Odious—but not friendly.

"*Bonjour,*" I said to the same waiter every day. "*Une salade niçoise,* please."

"Yes, certainly, right away," he said with French efficiency and a brief smile. But there was no small talk.

Maman said very little to me, but one of the bakers let it slip that they all had to do the elbow-busting work of the *commis* before they went to baking school. I held on. School started in September, and I knew that after schooling, pastry chefs made much more in France than in Seattle. So I cut the bread, bagged it, and swept up the crumbs. I kept the front pastry case looking fresh. I wrote the specials of the day on the chalkboard with French-style printing. I kept my uniform clean and my hair neatly tied back.

For all this, I earned a quick, smile-free nod of acknowledgment from Maman and more dirty dishes.

My heart was empty. I never thought it would happen to me, but it did.

I was homesick.

"Tomorrow is your day off," Maman said to me one Thursday afternoon. "What will you do?"

"I'm taking the train to Paris," I said, encouraged by her slight thaw. "I want a new dress and some shoes."

"Bon!" Maman said. "That will be a wonderful day. What girl wouldn't want to go to Paris?"

I couldn't imagine any girl who wouldn't want to go to Paris. This girl had dreamed of it her whole life.

I hopped on the train to Paris and immediately felt more cheerful. Unfortunately, I wouldn't have time to do much sightseeing, due to the train schedule, but I'd still be in Paris. When the train arrived, I got off, had a *café crème,* and walked to one of the secondhand designer shops I'd looked up online.

"God," I prayed under my breath, "Some people might think it's silly to ask You for help finding a dress, but I want the perfect one, and I'm on a budget." I had some birthday money my parents had sent me a week ago, but that was all.

I pushed open the door to a small boutique in the Eighth Arrondissement, one of the more exclusive neighborhoods.

"Bonjour!" the saleswoman called out to me.

"Bonjour," I replied.

She smoothly came alongside me. "How can I help you?"

I put myself firmly in her chic, fashionable hands. "I'm looking for a dress to wear to a wedding in a few weeks. And shoes to match. I want to make a nice, understated appearance. The wedding will be in Provence."

"Bon, I can help you." She bid me sit in the upholstered armchair next to the dressing room while she whisked about the store, gathering items here and there. A few minutes later, she stood in front of me with her choices.

First she showed me a sea green silk dress that hit midcalf and midchest.

"Too low cut for me," I said.

She didn't blink and offered the second dress, peach and classically cut. It would definitely show off my warm skin tone.

"Let's try it." I stood and reached for the dress.

"Attendez!" she said, motioning me back with her hand. "Wait one minute. I will offer you one other." She held up a navy blue summer dress made of linen.

It was chic. It was young. It had polka dots, a white, wide-brimmed hat, and a set of large, long, white beads. I had never dared to wear anything so bold.

"Do you think?" I asked, holding my breath.

"I know," she said with a certain nod. She handed me her choices, opened the dressing room, and closed it firmly behind me.

First I wriggled into the peach. It looked great, but it also looked like something I could have bought and worn at home. I took it off. Next I slipped into the navy. I zipped it up and straightened to my full height before looking in the mirror.

I, Alexandra Stuart, looked French chic. I grinned at myself in the mirror, and heard a discreet knock on the door.

"May I see?" the saleswoman asked.

I opened the door. *"Voilà,"* she said. "It's perfect. You must buy it." She pinched the back zipper, which was the tiniest bit strained. She didn't need to say anything.

"Too many baguettes," I admitted.

"No baguettes this week, and it will be just so." She closed the door behind her, perfectly confident in her professional assessment, and perfectly confident I would take her advice.

And, of course, I did. I let her ring up the purchase, not daring to look at how many euros this ensemble would cost me until it was a done deal.

I "licked the windows" for an hour, as the French call window shopping, and stopped at a chocolatier for a few lush goodies to nibble on as I walked around Paris. I wanted to beat the hours-long commuter rush I'd been warned about, so I hopped on the Métro, took the train back to the village, and strolled home. I hung my to-die-for polka dot dress in the small armoire in my bedroom and settled the shoes neatly under it to await their grand debut.

When I went to work the next day, our customer flow was slow, as many of them had gone *en vacance* for the month of August. I was in the back shelving items when a little voice called out, "Lexi!"

Céline ran into the back, ponytail bobbing. "I came to see you," she said.

"To get a *goûter,* a sweet treat, more likely," I teased her. She grinned, and I saw that she'd lost a tooth. "Did the tooth fairy come?" I asked.

She wrinkled her nose. "What's the tooth fairy?"

"She comes through your window on the night you lose your tooth. If you leave your tooth out where she can see it, she will leave you a euro in return."

"Oh, would you please ask the tooth fairy to come from America and visit me next time?" she asked. "I don't think she knows how to get to France. We only have a little mouse who comes and takes the teeth away. A fairy would be much more beautiful."

I laughed. "I'll see what I can do. Now, why did you come to see me?"

"I'm leaving to visit my grandparents in London, and then we'll go to Papi's house in Provence till school starts. I wanted to say good-bye. And to have you meet my papa." She tugged my hand and led me out to the shop front.

When we got there, I saw Odette talking—*flirting*—with a man who looked about thirty. At a quick glance, he reminded me of Luc, his cousin. He had the same muscular baker's build and the same medium-length hair, though his was not queued in the back. It ended at the bottom of his neck with a couple of light waves.

What were different were his eyes. Luc's eyes always had a "come-on" look in them, flirtatious, challenging, laughing. When Philippe looked at me, I noticed that while he was still very attractive, his gaze was more direct. Kinder.

Odette pursed her orange lips, and Céline said, "Papa, this is Lexi. She's the new Dominique."

I smiled and held out my hand. "I am certain I cannot take Dominique's place, but I'm glad to be here, and thankful to Luc for sending me. It's nice to meet you."

"Ah yes, Alexandra," Philippe said.

Blood rushed to my face. "How did you know my name?"

He grinned. "Luc told me you were coming. You'll work with me at the bakery in Rambouillet too, now and again?"

I nodded. "I'm looking forward to seeing your sister again."

He laughed out loud. "Patricia? You're the first person I've ever heard say that. Patricia is a bit…firm. Opinionated." He lowered his voice. "But Lexi knows our secret, doesn't she, *ma puce*," he said to Céline. "That below Patricia's hardened face lies a heart as soft as buttercream."

Céline giggled and looked at me. "I will see you when you're at my bakery. Don't forget to talk to the tooth fairy."

She ran off with Odette to get a cookie.

"Thank you for agreeing to have me work in Rambouillet," I said.

"Ah, it's not my place to say," Philippe said. "I am sometimes at this bakery, sometimes in Provence, sometimes at the office running the numbers. My father is the real *patron*, the boss, of the family business. He agreed to bring you on at Luc's insistence. Luc said you had promise and that, since we were working in America, it would be good to bring an American here too."

I could have imagined it, but I was paying close attention to every inflection when people spoke to me in an effort to perfect my French, and Philippe's voice hardened when he mentioned his father. I had yet to meet Monsieur Delacroix. Maybe I didn't want to. I hadn't known that Luc had insisted I come.

"I will have to thank Luc again," I said.

"You can do it soon," Philippe answered. "He and Marianne will be here next week."

Maman came up from the bakery to see what I was doing. She said nothing, simply looked at me.

Philippe understood the look too. He grinned and winked. "Back to work, eh?"

I smiled back. *"Alors…"*

"I will see you soon," Philippe said.

"Oui," I answered.

Odette rushed up to Philippe and restarted her conversation until a customer demanded her attention. I watched Philippe politely disengage, take Céline by the hand, and walk out the door.

He was kind. He and Céline were somehow different than most of the other French people I'd met so far.

I walked home that day, running my hand against the long stone wall, tired but feeling like I was breaking through the ice and beginning to find a place here. I saw a car in Maman's driveway, but didn't recognize it.

A few days later, I saw it back again. I peeked through my own lace curtains this time, thankful for the privacy they afforded, and began to feel much more French in that matter. Philippe was putting suitcases into the car's trunk, and Céline loaded up toys and books.

Normally, I am not a kid person. If someone had asked me a few months back what I thought would be appropriate gear for a road trip with a child, I'd have said a muzzle and some restraints. Depending on the kid, maybe pepper spray. But I didn't feel that way about Céline. Maybe it was because she was my first real French friend, despite her young age. Maybe it was something else.

I opened my armoire the next morning and pulled out a clean uniform, pausing to run my finger down the navy dress. Smiling, I closed the armoire door and walked through the misty dawn toward work.

Once inside I was seduced by the warm, buttery air, sweet with dark chocolate and vanilla cream. Odette ran the register, and I pulled the croissants off the cooling racks one by one, then stacked them in the display case. The village bakery wasn't fancy, but it was much more appealing than any small bakery I'd seen at home. The only really lovely bakeries in Seattle were owned by the French—Luc's two and one other that, in my opinion, wasn't even comparable. Instead, we had coffeeshops with cases stuffed with over-processed, overpreserved breakfast breads that tasted like something made by Hostess. Every resident of even the smallest French village would not expect to eat bread more than six hours old. Many of our customers came to get bread in the morning and then again before dinner.

I was getting to know them, but they still hadn't warmed up to me. Maybe it was because my uniform had no name. Maybe everyone knew what that meant. I was the only one in the bakery who had a plain uniform. It felt like a naked badge of shame.

In the back of the bakery, the friendly baker, Kamil, was rolling out dough. He grinned and waved. I waved back. *The angel was making the croissant.*

I looked to my left, where Odette was refilling the coffee machine. She grimaced. I smiled. *The devil was making the coffee.*

A few hours later, I was bent over a large mixing bowl, pouring in the exact measurements Maman had left, when I heard a voice.

"Alexandra!"

I turned around.

"Luc!" I wiped my hands on my apron and went to shake his hand. He greeted me with two kisses on the cheek, French style, and then gave me a hug, American style.

"How are things going?" he asked, nodding around the bakery. He reached for one of my hands, took it in his own, and looked at it. "Red knuckles. Your training has begun," he joked.

Just seeing him dissipated the homesickness I'd felt for days. "I'm so glad to see you. Marianne is here, also?"

"Ah, *oui,*" he said. "Getting a fitting for the wedding dress." He reached into his pocket and pulled out a card. "*La Sophie* asked me to give you this."

I took it from him. It was a business card that listed her as the assistant manager of L'Esperance. A wave of homesickness enveloped me again as I imagined her driving my asthmatic Jetta to work each day. I smiled and slipped it into my pocket. "I'm very happy for her."

"I too am very happy," Luc said. "She is so good I can leave and know things will be fine. You are ready to start school in September?"

"Yes, and thank you. Philippe told me you insisted I come."

"I believe you will do a good job here," Luc said. "You will not let me down. You will be an asset to the Delacroix bakeries."

Hearing him say that made me more determined than ever.

He checked his watch. "*Je regrette* that I cannot talk longer," he said. "I am only here for a short time, and there is so much to do. But I am glad to see my friend happy in France. And now, I must go. I am sure the others will tell me how things are going, and I will see you again when I come back for Christmas. It will be just about time for your exhibition, then."

"Ah, *oui*," I said, barely choking the words out.

He'd see me at Christmas. Luc had called me his friend, yet I was clearly not going to the wedding. No wedding. No navy polka-dotted dress. No good time together, *en famille.* I felt the corners of my mouth tug down. I wondered, fleetingly, what my exhibition was, before returning to the depressing news that there would be no wedding invitation forthcoming.

Luc kissed my cheeks again in good-bye, and I did the same, mechanically. Then I turned away, not letting Kamil see my face, and went back to pouring flour.

All the Delacroix had left town, and the bakery was closed. Even Odette had gone back to her family in Alsace. The village was dead. Everyone who had any money at all was on vacation, and even the little grocery store in town was abandoned with a Back in September sign hand drawn and tacked to the door. I had to take the train into Rambouillet for provisions. I sat in my cottage the first day, stunned, really. I e-mailed Tanya and poured out my self-pity at being left behind.

The next morning when I woke up, I clicked on my new e-mail and found one from her.

> Hi Lex,
>
>   I'm so sorry about the situation. I totally understand what you mean—you thought it was going to be like an exchange student program, where you fit in with the family. But maybe it's more like, well, being an employee. In the long run, even though it's lonely, isn't that better? They'll start seeing you more and more as a baker, not a kid. I've gotta run—am setting up next year's classroom. But I'll pray for you.
>
>   Love,
>
>   T

Tanya was right. I was in France! And I was going to play tourist for a few weeks. Cheaply, yes, but still do it. Tomorrow I headed to Versailles. It had been my lifelong dream to visit the Château de Versailles. I could barely sleep that night, thinking about it.

I woke the next morning and boarded the train. Apparently everyone else had decided to take the train to Versailles too. The

French had bugged out of town, but every tongue and dialect in the known world had gathered for the first time since Babel and swarmed into greater Paris.

At the Château de Versailles, I stood in line for two hot hours to buy tickets to the palace. It took another hot hour to get in. I didn't care. I spent the time in awe of the *château,* the envy of European royalty for centuries, and the focal point of the beginning of the end of the French monarchy I'd studied so long.

It was huge, overwhelming, unlike anything I'd ever seen. During the heyday of Louis XIV, nearly five thousand people wined, dined, slept, and ate breakfast in this one castle alone. I read in my guidebook that one head of state had said the horses of Versailles lived better than he did.

Once inside the castle, it was nose to armpit all the way, surrounded by dusty, sweaty bodies and shrill foreign voices. I hardly noticed. I gazed at the ceilings, enraptured by the swirling, painted frescoes that had taken months to paint. I stood for fifteen minutes looking at the extravagant bed in which Marie Antoinette had given birth and the tiny door to the side where she had tried to escape and retain her head. I walked down the Hall of Mirrors, thinking that Madame de Pompadour had bustled down this same hallway, arranging conquests for the king. Then I came to the chapel installed by Madame de Maintenon, who had married another French king in order to save his soul.

As I looked at the altar, I realized how much I'd missed going to church. I hadn't gone since I'd arrived in France. *I'm sorry I've forgotten You in the bustle, Lord.*

After wandering the gardens and pathways, imagining the king on his horse on the very same trail, mingling with his squealing, flirting courtiers, I trudged to the station and boarded the train home, where I was forced to sit next to a mother and her screaming baby.

Watching the royal city retreat into the distance as the train pulled away, I remembered what a friend had told me. There's no sense at all in visiting anything as stunning as the Taj Mahal if you have no one to turn to and say, "How beautiful!"

Among the throng of humanity squeezed into the train, I felt more alone than I could ever remember feeling.

The next morning, I checked my e-mail again. Seeing my empty in box, I decided to be proactive. I found Sophie's new business card and sent her a note. *How are things going?* I asked. *Have you been getting along with everyone? I'll check back in a few days. I'm going to Paris!*

Almost everyone at home thought I was having the time of my life. I needed to at least try to have some fun. And this was likely the only vacation time I'd see for a while.

I decided to splurge and made a reservation at a Parisian hotel for two days. That way I wouldn't have to rush my sightseeing. Breakfast was included, and I'd feel pampered. I packed my suitcase and looked at the navy dress. I packed it too, sighing. It was the only way.

Once in Paris, I checked into the little hotel and headed back to the Eighth Arrondissement. I took the dress, hat, shoes, and beads back to the secondhand designer shop.

The saleslady remembered me. "Ah, you have returned!"

"I'm bringing the dress back," I said softly.

Her brow wrinkled. "You didn't like it?"

"No, I just didn't need it after all." I didn't want to tell her I hadn't been invited, and that if I wanted to sightsee, I needed the money.

"The wedding was called off, eh?" She nodded knowingly. "That's okay. You visit me next time."

I nodded, knowing there wouldn't be a next time, and handed over the outfit. Then I set off for Nôtre Dame.

I took the Big Red Bus, just like every other tourist, because the Métro was underground and I wanted to drink the city in through my pores. I plugged in the earphones and chose English, thirsty to hear my native tongue.

Paris, the narration said, is stunningly beautiful. They were right. The bus wound through tree-lined streets, past row upon row of three and four story buildings, all similar but not boring. Their sandy exteriors were the color of lightly burned butter, warm and smooth, inviting. Each window was graced with black wrought iron, curling like dark eyelashes and just as mysterious. Window boxes spilled over with a gluttony of flowers. I smiled. This was Paris.

I got off at Nôtre Dame, the most famous church in the world. I recalled watching *The Hunchback of Nôtre Dame* as a young teen, Tanya and I in our sleeping bags in my family room, me dreaming of France, a little Francophile already. Now I was a woman at the very church itself. I swallowed some sorrow and wished Tanya were here to see it too.

The sanctuary was airy, musty, and thick with the history of the city it dominated. The gargoyles grimaced at me, liked they'd escaped the legions of hell. A plaque read, *All distances in France are measured from Nôtre Dame. Nôtre Dame is Mile One.*

As I walked out and waited at the Big Red Bus Stop, I thought about that. It made me sad. The French marked their way from the church, but God was the last person on anyone's mind. The cafés were full to bursting. The churches were empty of anyone save tourists.

I ate an orange *crêpe* to stave off my hunger as I walked down the Champs-Elysées, wind blowing in my hair. Everyone held hands with someone, or had their arm around a loved one's waist. I put my hands in my pockets and kept walking, looking for a place to eat dinner. Every corner had a café, of course, but I didn't want to stop. Finally, I looked at one of the many chalkboards proclaiming today's specials.

- French Onion Soup
- Beef Bourguignon
- Veal with Mushrooms
- Chicken à la Bresse
- Salade

Tables spilled from the café's interior to the patio outside, full of kissing couples and laughing families and friends. I wasn't hungry.

I trudged back to my hotel room, walked up the stairs, and closed the door behind me. And then I cried.

So God, I prayed through ragged breaths, *here I am. Some dream. No friends, no family, no one to hold hands with. I'm working with red knuckles. I'm not going to a friend's wedding. I sold the most beautiful dress I've ever owned so I could sightsee alone. Is this the dream You had in mind for me? Why didn't You tell me it would be like this? I could have saved myself the hassle, gone to some cooking school in the US, stayed with Dan, hung out with my friends, and had a life.*

I waited for God to explain Himself. He remained silent.

I washed my face with a cold washcloth to cool my cheeks. I picked up the phone and ordered a bucket of ice. So what if they knew I was American. I was paying. I took a Coke out of the mini-bar, not caring if it cost $7.50. When the ice came, I poured the Coke over it and slammed the whole glass in one guzzle.

Then I sat, waiting for God again. I wanted to hear from Him. I really did. I thought, *look in the Bible,* but then remembered I hadn't packed my Bible. In fact, I hadn't read it at all since arriving in France.

I opened the drawers of the desk and the bedside table. Nothing. Of course not. The French didn't put Bibles in hotel rooms.

I really wanted to read the Bible. This was the first time in my life I had craved it, and none were accessible. I felt empty.

I looked at my watch and called my dad.

"Hi, Dad!" I said, trying to sound happy.

"Hi, Lexi. What's wrong?"

"Nothing's wrong. I'm just calling to say hi."

"At eight in the morning?"

"Time difference, you know," I said. "I'm sightseeing in Paris. I went to Nôtre Dame today."

"Good, honey, I'm glad you're having fun. I was a little hesitant about you doing this French thing, but if you're happy, I'm happy. It was worth the cost of the ticket."

I swallowed a lump. "Thanks, Dad. I'm doing well. Everything isn't as easy as I thought it would be…"

"Nothing is ever as we expect it to be, Lexi. The higher the expectations I have for something, the more disappointed I usually am. Take all of your expectations and throw them out the window. You're not French, remember. You don't give up."

My sorrow cracked a little, and I laughed. "No, Dad, you're right."

"And you can come home after your schooling if you want," he said, hope in his voice. "I'm sure you could get your old job back at the bakery, at least. Though I don't know how you'd live on it."

We chatted for a few more minutes. He told me Mom was having fun in Italy, and then we hung up. I brushed my hair, revived by the pep talk, and reapplied my lip gloss. Then I walked back down the road to the café. It seemed friendlier now, and everything on the menu looked great.

I ordered and asked God to bless my meal.

"Bon appétit!" my waiter said.

I grinned. *Bon appétit,* indeed. Dinner was delicious.

I walked back to the hotel, looking at the Eiffel Tower twinkling in the distance. I didn't feel like visiting it alone.

I spent the next day strolling the streets of Paris. I visited an outdoor market just to have someone else to talk with. I walked all the way to the St. Michel neighborhood where the bookstores were and bought myself a French Bible. I drank another $7.50 Coke. Restored and refreshed, I was ready to head home.

The train ride back to Presque le Château went quickly. Once it arrived, I rambled back to my cottage, re-technologized, and checked my e-mail. Sophie had written back!

"Dear Lexi," I read aloud. "Life is great here, the car is fine. No new piercings!" Then I read silently until I came to the end. "Oh, guess what? We hired someone to take your job. He's had some pastry training at a community college and is picking things right up. I know you won't mind, now that you're a Parisian. He doesn't have your creative touch, but he's a hard worker, and he's so thankful to have the job that he does just about anything, and I know he won't quit. And Margot likes him! So that makes all of our lives easier. Mine, especially, because we are now fully staffed."

It sounded...final. *Scarily* final. I took a couple of deep breaths to steady myself and tried to process what this meant for me. The only thing that came to mind was a line from a hymn sung in my mom's old church.

"No turning back, no turning back."

Three

*Bouillabaisse is only good because it's cooked by the
French, who, if they cared to try, could produce an
excellent and nutritious substitute out of cigar stumps
and empty matchboxes.*
Norman Douglas

Ladies and gentlemen, you hope to become professionals. I do not graduate people from this *école* who are not prepared for the rigors of life as a French pastry chef. I do not graduate bakers who want nothing more than to bake bread or show up late, do their work, and go home."

Monsieur Desfreres paced in front of the class, all of us at attention, uniforms pressed, chef's hats firmly on our heads. Five long counters lined the room, and eight of us stood at each one. There were no chairs. The first requirement of any chef was the ability to stand for hours on end without taking a break.

I stole a few quick glances at the others out of the corner of my eye. You'd have thought I'd stumbled into the L'École Militaire instead of the L'École du Pâtisserie. It was that serious.

I was nervous and thrilled. It was my first day of school. New month, new life.

Chef tapped the stainless countertop in front of one sleepy-looking young man. "I do not graduate students merely because they have paid tuition or because their *patrons* have paid tuition. In fact, I consider it a service to the patrons if I can tell them at this early date that one of their employees, regrettably, shows very little aptitude toward becoming an accomplished *pâtissier.*" He looked pointedly at the man, who stopped slouching, but the words rang through to my spine.

"En général," he finished, "ten percent of the students who begin this course will, after their exhibition, complete it with honors. Let me make one thing clear—at graduation, you are not a pastry chef. *Mais non.* You are then prepared to become a pastry chef. My name will be on the *diplôme.* You will conform to my standards or it will become clear to both of us that another career path would be a better choice."

He clapped his hands together, gold link bracelet shimmying on his wrist. *"Bon*—let's begin."

I opened the textbook in front of me. Each of us had a locker, and I'd found mine stocked with textbooks, recipe books, the uniforms I'd be responsible for keeping spotlessly clean, and a slip of paper to exchange for soft-soled chef shoes.

I glanced at the others along my counter. They wore the same

black-and-white checked chef pants I did, the white coat with a double row of buttons on the front, neatly starched and cuffed. I swallowed back a bit of homesickness as I put on my chef's *toque blanche,*
the hat with a thousand folds, and remembered the first time I'd
done that at the bakery in Seattle. The journey of a thousand pastries had started with that first step.

The woman beside me looked about twenty-one. She oozed
chic. Her watch had the subtle flash of real diamonds around the
face, but it wasn't gaudy. Her skin was polished and flawless.

"Hello," I said as we got out our materials. "My name is Lexi."

"Hello," she replied, her voice neither warm nor cool. "My
name is Désirée *LeBon.*" She emphasized her last name, and I got the
hint. The LeBon family owned a large chain of high-end pastry
shops in Paris. Everyone knew that.

After that initial snobbishness, however, she was kinder. My
pencil lead snapped at one point, and she quietly slipped me a
mechanical pencil that matched the one she was using. I mouthed,
"thank you," and continued taking notes.

Two haughty-looking men stood at my table, and I noted that
Monsieur Desfreres seemed to favor them, along with men at the
other tables. He stood so close to them, resting his hands on their
shoulders, that at first I worried he might have some unsavory interest in them. But when he stood directly behind me and began lec-
turing again, I learned the reason.

"The history of pastry in France is noble and long lived. It
would not be a stretch to say that the French have developed and
refined the palate for the rest of the world. It's my charge to develop

both your palate and your palette. To teach you to recognize good taste and then to prepare the breads, cakes, tartes, and other products to meet that challenge.

"Some French families"—he glanced at Désirée and cracked what might have passed for a smile if he'd allowed himself such an indulgence—"have been carrying on this noble tradition for centuries.

"I will not hide that I believe men are traditionally better chefs in all areas of food preparation." He looked at the two smug men at my table who afforded themselves not only a smile but a glance of superiority to the women around them.

"And then there are the relatively young nations, with untamed and undeveloped palates." He moved closer to me. I could feel his presence at my back. I kept my head held high, but I was aware that the eyes of the classroom were drawn to me. "They eat things such as…McDonald's. It remains to be shown if such a palate can be developed, and then in turn develop products to meet the needs of France."

He moved away. Désirée flashed me a sympathetic look, and the other woman at the table grimaced in my direction, then looked away. Well, one person showed promise, anyway. I'd see if I could strike up a conversation with Désirée later.

First though, we listened to a long lecture by Monsieur Desfreres on this week's topic: baking history and science. Then we broke into foursomes and went to our work stations, measuring ingredients and comparing our charts.

"Baking is not for the sloppy cook, the person who works by taste. *Non, non!*" Monsieur Desfreres lectured from the other half of the room. "She is a precise art. If we take away some of this, we must add more of that. Otherwise, the entire proposition will fail. This week, we do not look to be creative. We are food scientists. We look to be exact."

The women from my counter stuck together in a foursome—Désirée, myself, one of the woman who had grimaced at me named Anne, and a recent immigrant from Martinique named Juju.

We pulled out our binders of recipes and blank sections in which we could slip our notes, each page encased in a protective plastic sleeve.

Monsieur Desfreres lectured us about the difference between American and European butterfat contents, clearly favoring European, but showing us how to adjust our recipes when using American ingredients. He looked pointedly at me. We spent the morning measuring cocoa powder, cake flour, and bread flour. In front of each of us was a scale, and we measured not by cup, but by weight, which was more *exactement.*

After a lively discussion about the hierarchy in a kitchen and the proper attitude in a hectic pastry shop, we were ready for our first test.

"Look at recipe card number one in your folder," Monsieur Desfreres instructed, making sure we had each tidied up our weight stations. "I would like you to find the ingredients in that recipe, weigh them exactly, and put them in your mixing bowl. After you leave this afternoon, a small team of chefs and I will bake up the contents in each person's bowl. You will notice that the bowls and pans are numbered."

I looked at mine. Seven, my lucky number.

"Tomorrow, when you come to class, you will see the result of your measurement in the form of a cake baked from your bowl."

For so many people in one large room, it was incredibly quiet. I understood that each of us had a work station here for measuring and sorting, but we would also rotate from room to room. The chocolate room, the cake room, the bread room. "Room" was an understatement—it was more like a huge commercial kitchen, beyond anything I had imagined. It was *fantastique.*

I read my recipe card. Four hundred fifty-five grams of butter—European style. I left my station, ran to the cooler, and took out some hunks of butter, then brought them back to my station and measured the exact amount needed. Leaving the butter in one of my small bowls, I took the rest of the butter back to the walk-in. I measured out 535 grams of sugar and put it into another bowl with a number seven on it. Five milliliters of vanilla—French vanilla, of course.

To my left and right, the rest of the women in my group seemed as intent as I was on getting it right. The room was silent with concentration. We measured the ingredients then used our standing mixers to whip the batter together. At the end of class, we poured the mixture into our numbered pans and handed them to Monsieur Desfreres to be baked.

That was it for the day. In two weeks, we'd start eating lunch together too. The cooking school would provide the main meal, the pastry school the bread and desserts. For now, we were allowed to leave one hour early. Most of us had jobs, and I had to get back to the village. I'd be at the Rambouillet bakery tomorrow. I was eager to see Patricia again, and Céline. And Philippe.

I said good-bye to my team members, folded my uniform, and locked my locker. I tucked my baking science and history book under my arm, determined to read that night after helping Odette with the dinner baguette shift.

I wanted to succeed here. I wanted to learn to bake like the French, the pinnacle of artistic cuisine. I wanted to prove to my friends and family that I was as much of a professional as they were. I wanted to belong here too.

I grinned at my cake pan, lined up with the others, ready to bake. I couldn't wait to taste it tomorrow.

The next day I took the early train from the village to Rambouillet, where the school was located. I arrived bright and cheerful, despite the early hour, and changed into my uniform. I fixed my hair, nodding politely to Anne as she dressed beside me.

"How are you today?" Juju asked me.

"Good! And you?"

"Very good," she said. "I did not eat breakfast. I plan to eat cake."

I smiled. I'd had coffee, but planned to eat some of my pound cake for breakfast too.

We walked into the classroom and found our places, waiting for Monsieur Desfreres. The cakes were nowhere in sight, but there were folded slips of paper at our stations. We each opened ours. I watched as Désirée's face lit with happiness, Anne's warmed with a smile, and Juju looked content. I read mine, and my face burned.

> This cake was inedible. Too much butter, weighed improperly. I had hoped to impress upon you that measuring exactly is critical. If we had had an order for these cakes, and had been counting on yours, we would not have had enough. Poorly done.
>
> Chef Desfreres.

I refolded my paper, but that was not the end of the matter. The numbered pans were brought out and set in front of us. While most of the cakes had nicely rounded tops, slightly split and sloping to the edge of the pans, mine was flat. Greasy. Sunken in the middle.

And yet, I knew I had measured exactly right. I knew it.

Désirée reached over and patted the back of my hand with her well-manicured one. "Don't worry," she whispered, "it's only the first week." Then she sliced into her own perfect cake. "Want a piece?"

I am not averse to food therapy. Especially when I only had an hour to recover from my public humiliation and make it to the Delacroix bakery in Rambouillet.

I'd declined Désirée's offer of a piece of her perfect cake, and by lunchtime my stomach was in knots. I walked three blocks toward the bakery and found a small café.

I scanned the blackboard indicating the day's specials, and chose a salad, some bread, and a *crème brûlée*.

I prayed while I waited. *Lord, let me recover from this somehow. Don't let me fail at the school or the bakery.*

My food arrived. I'd brought my small Bible, realizing I always read at lunch and hadn't been good about reading my new French Bible, despite promising myself I would. Mostly I'd been thumbing through it, letting the Bible open wherever it would and hoping for a word of inspiration. The "lucky dip" method.

Not so lucky for me. This is what I came up with: "Wail, O ships of Tarshish! For Tyre is destroyed and left without house or harbor."

Or this one: "Pay your taxes too for these same reasons. For government workers need to be paid."

I knew every word was inspired, but I needed a more methodical way to get through it. But then, God certainly could see I had my hands full here, and He hadn't jumped in to help or even to chat.

I finished my meal and headed toward the bakery, excited to see Patricia again and perhaps Céline, after school.

As I turned the corner I saw the bakery. It was bigger than the one in the village, with gold and black striped awnings pulled up from the large front windows like painted eyelids. I pulled open the door. Only one customer stood inside, since this was the dead spot of the afternoon when breakfast was over and the rush to buy things for dinner had not yet started. While there were no tables to eat at, like there'd be in Seattle, there were many cases for pastry and a dozen kinds of bread.

I waited politely for the customer to finish ordering and then introduced myself to the woman at the counter.

"*Bonjour,* I am Lexi, here to begin work."

She smiled politely. "*Bonjour,* Lexi!" Her name, Simone, was embroidered on her Boulangerie Delacroix uniform. "We have been anticipating you. And you're early! How nice. Let me take you to Patricia in the back." Already, Simone seemed a vast improvement over Odette.

I saw Patricia before she saw me, and my heart swelled with affection for the sassy pirate. She saw me and smiled too before she caught herself and reaffixed the stern look to her face.

"Ah, *bon,* it's Lexi," she said. "Not a minute too soon." She kissed me on each cheek, a gesture of friendship I wasn't anticipating.

"How goes the school? You started this week, *n'est-ce pas?*"

"*Oui,*" I said. "It's going."

"*Bon.* Because the bakeries are paying for the tuition, I am sure Monsieur Desfreres will send a report now and again. My papa is looking forward to meeting you."

Ah, yes. The family patriarch, Monsieur Delacroix. I swallowed. "When will he send a report?"

Patricia waved her hand, as if that didn't matter. "In a few weeks, probably. Come, let's get to work."

She showed me to a station where she'd already made some lemon tartes. "You remember how to candy the lemon slices to go on top, *non?*" she asked with a sly grin. I grinned back. In Seattle, it had been my pointing out the lack of candied lemon slices on her tartes that led her to agree to my working for her in the pastry kitchen.

"Oui, I remember," I said.

"Bon. You will candy the slices and make the dipped chocolate coffee beans for the *mousse au chocolat.* Also, today, I will have you make something very special for Céline. *Les chouquettes,* for her *goûter.* I have a wedding cake order and cannot get to the chouquettes."

I hid my smile, knowing that to smile too often in France is to not be taken seriously. But the fact that she was allowing me to make the *goûter,* which means "to taste," for Céline's afterschool snack was an honor.

I put an apron over my plain uniform and began candying a hundred or more quartered lemon slices. An hour later, I cleaned up and found the recipe for the chouquettes from the big book in the prep room. I mixed the ingredients together, dipped them in large-grain sugar, and put the pan into the oven. If I ever wanted a recipe to turn out, it was this one. For Céline. And for me.

Chouquette Recipe

Ingredients:

12 Tbsp butter, cut into 1 Tbsp chunks
1¼ cups warm water
½ tsp salt
1½ cups all-purpose flour (not bread flour)
4 large eggs
sugar or hail sugar (also called pearl sugar)

Directions:

Preheat oven to 400 degrees.

In a heavy saucepan, melt butter. Pour in water and then add salt and bring to a boil. As soon as the water boils, reduce the heat to medium and pour in all the flour at once. With a wooden spoon, beat the flour into the liquids till the flour is incorporated and the entire mixture is sticky and pasty. It will pull away from the sides and bottom of the pan into a large lump. This should take only a minute or two. As soon as it pulls away and is incorporated, remove from heat.

Take the dough out of the pan and put in a bowl. If you have a standing mixer, you can put it in there and use the whisk attachment. Otherwise, put it in a large, glass bowl and get your mixer out. Beat in the four eggs, one at a time, on high speed. Make sure each egg is completely incorporated before adding the next.

The dough will remain pasty, but will be glossier now, and smooth. Drop lumps of dough onto a cookie sheet, lined with parchment if you like. The lumps should be about a tablespoon in size. Twelve lumps fit well on a standard pan, leaving them room to "puff." Drop sugar on top of each puff. The best kind of sugar to use is "hail" sugar, because it doesn't melt while baking.

Bake for about 30 minutes, watching carefully. The chouquettes will puff up nearly triple in size and become golden brown with slightly darker brown edges. Take out of oven and allow to cool.

Optional: Insert the tip of a Reddi-wip can into them when cool to make mini-cream puffs.

Makes 12–18 chouquettes.

While the chouquettes were in the oven, I went to the front of the bakery to look at the case and see if the coffee beans were completely dipped or half-dipped. I scooted behind Simone, who finished helping a customer and turned to me with a motherly smile.

"The pastries are different here from in America, eh?" she said with obvious Gallic pride.

"Oh, yes," I said. "In every way. The selection," I waved my hand over the dozen or so offerings, "the beauty, the craftsmanship. The taste. Pastries in the United States are often made with…" I struggled for the word. *"Préservatifs."*

A look of horror crossed her face. *"Les préservatifs?"*

I nodded. "Yes."

Her face drained of color. I smiled weakly and went to the back to check on my chouquettes.

How strange. Of course, I didn't agree with putting preservatives in baked goods either, but it wasn't as horrifying as she seemed to think. Sometimes the French took this food thing a little far.

I opened the oven and reached in with my well-protected arm to pull out the pan of chouquettes. I knew the bread bakers would soon need the oven to bake the evening batch of breads so they would be available when people stopped by on their way home from work.

Holding my breath, I banished thoughts of my greasy pound cake and pulled the pan out of the oven, setting it on the counter. I put the chouquettes on a cooling rack and, a few minutes later, popped one into my mouth.

Perfect! I smiled, put two on a plate, and walked into one of the cool rooms where Patricia was icing and assembling the wedding cake.

"Voilà," I said, passing her the plate.

She ate one, then the other. "A little eggy," she said, "and they could use more sugar on top. But good enough for a child's *goûter*."

"Merci," I said, backing out of the room. I knew from working with Patricia that was high praise.

I piled the chouquettes on a plate to wait for Céline. Then I busied myself dipping coffee beans into slick, inky chocolate.

"Lexi!" A young voice ran through the front of the shop and back to the bakery.

"Hey, Céline!" I said. "I have something special for you." I held out the plate of chouquettes.

"Merci," she said, popping one into her mouth. "Mmm, very good. My favorite." She took another one and set her school bag on the floor. Then she ran back to see her *tante* Patricia.

A few seconds later Philippe walked in and smiled at me. He let his kindness shine.

"Bonjour!" he said. "How is the new chef doing?"

I grinned. We all knew I was not yet a chef. "Good days and bad," I said. "Mostly good."

"What did you do for your weeks off?" he asked. "Conquer Paris?"

If only he knew!

"I did visit Paris, but only for a few days."

"Did you visit any museums?" he asked. "The Musée d'Orsay?"

"No, not yet." I hesitated. "The Musée d'Orsay is at the top of my list. I love impressionist art."

Philippe walked over to the peg board where the evening's orders were posted and took off some slips and a few phone messages. As Monsieur Delacroix was not in residence, Philippe was in charge, and he walked like a man confident in his domain. I found it appealing.

He walked back toward me. "Then why haven't you visited the musée yet?" He looked at me, so genuinely interested, not just making small talk. I felt I should tell him the truth.

"When I went to Versailles, it fulfilled a lifelong dream. I loved it. But there was no one to talk with about it, and it cut into my happiness. I'll have a friend at school—I already have one woman in mind—and then go places with her and share the experience."

"Ah," he said. "That makes perfect sense. Happiness shared is doubled and sadness shared is halved, we say." He smiled again and as he did, he looked younger and sweeter.

"Yes," I agreed. "That's exactly what I mean."

Céline came running back into the room, pulling Patricia along with her.

"Taste the chouquettes, Papa," she said. "They are *délicieux.*"

Philippe bit into one. "Very good," he said, "if a bit eggy." He looked at Patricia. "You've been out of practice in the United States."

Patricia, to her credit, said nothing. Céline was too busy stuffing her mouth to correct her father. I looked down and promised myself I'd practice more and feel okay that I was, as of now, imperfect.

Patricia took Céline into the office so she could work on her homework until Philippe was ready to take her home. Philippe went into the bread-baking room and got the crew ready for the final push of the day, after which, I was sure, he'd join Céline in the office and answer his phone messages. I got back to dipping coffee beans.

About an hour later Simone slid by me. She smiled nervously in my direction, not making eye contact, and went to the cool room, where Patricia had returned to the cake.

A few minutes later I heard a roar of laughter. It was Patricia! Simone glided by and glanced at me again, looking very relieved. She gave me a genuine smile. I didn't know what had happened, but I was glad to see her relaxed toward me again. I had enough stress and few friends here.

After placing the beans into a lidded bin, I cleaned up the area and prepped the butter for the next day's baking. I measured carefully. Extremely carefully.

What went wrong today? I allowed myself to think about it for the first time all day. I was so exact. Could I have used the wrong butter? But I didn't see any American butter in the cooler, and even if I had, it would have been drier, not greasier, as American butter has a lower fat content.

My failure was especially painful because cakes were my specialty. I liked baking them best and prided myself on their success.

I took the garbage to the commercial waste bin in the back, and as I did, I noticed a chalkboard on top of the bin contents. It looked like the ones I'd seen in every café and even here in the bakery. Two hooks at the top held a black plate that listed the day. There was a plaque for each day, *dimanche* for Sunday, *lundi* for Monday, and so on. I pulled it out and set it aside. It looked used, but in very good condition.

I went back into the bakery and saw there was a new chalkboard up front with today's specials written across it. The one by the waste bin must have been an old one. I'd ask Patricia if I could keep it.

I glanced at the clock. It was nearly time for me to take the train back to the village. Tomorrow I'd be in Rambouillet for school, and then I'd work at the village bakery for the rest of the week.

I untied my apron and went back to the cool room. Patricia was grinning.

"I'm leaving soon," I said.

"Bon," she agreed. "Working at the bakery in the village this week, then here all next week, right? We have special orders next week and can use the extra help. The village bakery is a bit slower."

I'd noticed. I preferred working here anyway.

"I found a chalkboard in the garbage bin. May I keep it?"

She shrugged. "Sure. Maybe you can use it to write down French words."

I cocked my head, not understanding. "Have I made a mistake?"

She grinned again. "Do you know what *faux amis* are?" she asked.

"Oh, yes." I'd learned about them in French class long ago and tried to keep up with an ever-growing list. "They're false friends. Words that sound similar in French and English but have a very different meaning."

"Bon," Patricia said. "I think there is one false friend that you are not aware of." She handed me a piece of paper.

Preservative—ingredient that delays or retards spoilage

Préservatif—a condom, used to protect from disease or pregnancy

My face went cold. "Oh no! I told Simone we used *préseratifs* in our pastries at home. No wonder she was horrified!" And no wonder I had heard that burst of laughter from Patricia.

"Oui," Patricia said. "I explained *faux amis* to her, and she was very relieved to hear your baking practices were not as barbaric as she feared."

"Should I talk to her about it?" I asked.

"Non, she's very old-fashioned. I think to bring it up again would be embarrassing. But, Lexi," she said to me, "thank you. I have not had a laugh since I got back from Provence last month."

If we'd been friends, I'd have asked her what was wrong. But we weren't really friends, and I knew better, now, than to get too close too soon. However, I had never seen that vulnerable of a look on her face. She ducked away and went back to work.

"I will see you next week, Lexi," she said softly, a kind but definite dismissal.

On my way out, I passed the office and looked at Céline bent over her book. Philippe sat with one hand on her head and one on the phone, speaking vigorously and with emotion, like most Frenchmen.

I hoped he hadn't found out about my *faux amis* mistake.

On the way to the train, I thought about the mistakes of the day and about false friends. Something bugged me. It wasn't the mistake, it was the phrase.

It suddenly struck me there might be other kinds of false friends I hadn't recognized.

Four

Bread deals with living things, with giving life,
with growth, with the seed, the grain that nurtures.
It's not coincidence that we say bread is the staff of life.
Lionel Poilâne

T he next day at school, thankfully, was uneventful. We spent a lot of time measuring things and took a written test on baking science. I had plenty of my own pencils, and I aced it. So did everyone else in my foursome, and we congratulated one another on being so fine. It was a good start to the week. I meant to ask Désireé if she wanted to visit the Musée d'Orsay over the weekend, but a flier on the bulletin board caught my eye, and I stopped to read it. While I did, she slipped away for the weekend.

Learn English

Want to practice your English speaking skills? It's proven that those who have excellent bilingual skills have more business opportunities. Perhaps your hotel/restaurant/bakery will have an international clientele. Perhaps you'll travel overseas to work.

Please call the Anglican Church of Versailles and ask when the next English practice group meets.

I jotted down the church's phone number. Anne sidled up behind me. "Need to practice your English skills?" she teased.

I laughed. "No. But I've been meaning to go to church, and, well, it might be nice to be in a church that speaks English. Kind of homey."

Anne unwrapped her apron and headed toward our lockers. "Not me," she said. "I'd like to practice my English but not on Sunday. I sleep on Sunday."

An hour later I'd taken the train back to the village and presented myself to Maman.

"How goes the schooling?" she asked as she bustled about in the back.

"Bon," I said, wondering when the family would get a "report card" on me, and what it would say.

Maman pointed to a stack of dishes. "After you're finished with these, you can make some *goûters* for the front. The kids will be out of school at three, and we need some chouquettes. I hear you can make them. Easy on the eggs. Measure exactly—the same weight of eggs as water."

"I will."

"And then," Maman said, "you can mix up the dough for the *biscuits*. I have left the recipe in the back. Bring a chouqette to me and to Odette before setting them out."

I sighed. Great. Odious would pass judgment.

I made both batches, the chouquettes and the sable biscuits, or cookies, and let them cool. First I brought a plate to Maman. She bit into a chouquette. "Nice," she said. Probably her highest praise. "Céline says you make good chouquettes, and it takes a light hand. She should know a good one. In spite of her supposed dislike of pastries, she's been eating good baking her whole life."

Maman bit into the sable cookie. "All right. Next time take them out sooner and let them finish baking for the last minute or two on the pan. It'll be fine here in the village, but in Rambouillet too many would go dry too soon, and we'd have to throw them out."

Maman turned back to her work, muttering that if she had her own grandchildren, she'd make the *goûters* herself.

I brought the samples to Odette.

She bit into the chouquette, leaving a waxy orange print on one side. "Mmm. It figures you'd make a perfect chouquette."

Wow! I tried not to faint.

She finished it off and tasted the sables. "Too dry. You have to do better than that."

I couldn't help myself. "Maman said they were okay, just take them out a bit sooner next time."

"Of course," Odette said. "You're free labor. She's not going to be hard on you. But when you start costing the bakery money, they'd better be perfect."

I set the plate down. "What do you mean, free? I have my stipend, and they're making a big investment in me at school."

Odette laughed. "That's no investment. In France, each employer has to set aside one percent of his payroll for training for his employees. It must be spent each year. It doesn't matter if it is spent on me, you, or anyone else. For a new employee, they'd have to pay the training and a salary. You are cheaper. It means nothing."

The door jingled open, and Odette turned to the customer. I quietly put the sables and the chouquettes in the section for after-school snacks.

It means nothing. It did not mean I would have a job here when I was done, because Maman wanted Dominique back home. I may not even pass my course, which would mean I wouldn't have a job anywhere in France. I'd be letting Luc down, of course, but it turns out I'm a rather cheap experiment, since my labor cost them almost nothing.

My job in Seattle, of course, had been filled.

I got up early on Sunday and put on a summer dress, but took a sweater with me. It was already cool in the mornings even though it wasn't yet October. I picked up my newly purchased French Bible and grinned at the incongruity of bringing a French Bible to an English church.

After the short trip to Versailles, which lay in the same district as the village and Rambouillet, I followed the map I'd drawn at home and soon pushed open the large wooden doors to the churchyard.

I looked at my watch. I hadn't wanted to be late, and so I was early. I walked slowly, past the climbing rose vines still in bloom, though their leaves were beginning to turn wine colored with the melancholy of autumn. When I walked in the church door, I saw a long table with pamphlets and an order of service. A lovely woman extended her hand in greeting. By the name on her tag I could see that she was the vicar's wife.

"Good morning," she said, and for a moment my brain was stunned. It quickly shifted from French into English. How could I have been so surprised by my mother tongue?

"Are you new here?" she asked.

"Yes, I am," I said. "I'm here studying and working. From the United States."

"We're so glad to have you." She pushed a piece of blonde hair behind her ear and continued in her lovely British lilt. "Please make yourself at home, and be sure to sign the visitor's card so we can contact you."

I nodded, took my paperwork, and walked into the church. It was small and would hold perhaps one hundred people. When I'd called to inquire about service times, they told me English-speaking worshippers of all nationalities and denominations came together here. There were not many English-speaking churches in the area.

Part of me felt foolish for coming all this way to attend an English church. Most of me was just glad to drink in my own language for a while and concentrate on God instead of verb tense or noun gender.

I walked nearly to the front of the sanctuary and sat down. The worship band practiced on the front platform. I was thrilled that I recognized the songs, and my heart soared as I sang them, silently, inside.

An elderly British woman doddered in and sat near me, her son behind her. He loudly honked his nose into a handkerchief every few minutes. They left plenty of "personal space" between me and them.

Several families with kids came in and sat around the church, but not in my row. I looked straight ahead and read the various papers in the pocket of the pew ahead of me so as not to appear as uncomfortable as I felt.

A moment later a lovely woman in a lime green suit that perfectly set off her nut brown skin sat next to me. Not by me. Next to me.

"May I sit here?" she asked in prettily accented English. "My name is Buki."

"Oh, yes, please," I said, thankful not to feel like a pariah anymore.

The worship began. To my right, the British woman stood quiet, propping herself on her cane. She made no outward motions but her eyes were closed. To my left, Buki rocked out, lifting her hands, and shouting, "Thank you, Jesus!" I grinned. Her faith and enthusiasm was viral.

After the worship came a sermon on John 1. Quite decent, as the British would say.

When the service was over, the congregation mingled, and the vicar—or pastor, I wasn't sure of his title—came to meet me. He appeared genuine and earnest.

"Hello," he said. "My wife says you're new here."

I nodded. "Yes, I'm here to study baking."

He smiled. "What a place to study—the best. And how wonderful that we've just started John. It's a book full of food images. Food for the body and food for the soul."

He invited me to come back each week and moved on. I had just turned around to pick up my things and leave when I got the shock of my life.

Philippe!

He looked just as shocked to see me as I was to see him. I could barely concentrate as he moved in my direction. I heard someone call out.

"Lexi!" Céline raced toward me.

Philippe came up behind her. He cleaned up nice in khakis and a fashionable, collarless button-up shirt. His wavy hair was slicked back.

"What are *you* doing here?" I asked in English, not having turned my brain back to French.

"You mean, what's a baker like me doing in a place like this?"

"You know English pickup lines!" I exclaimed.

"Were you offering it as a pickup?" He grinned.

I blushed. I *hated* that I blushed so easily. He kept talking to allow me, graciously, to avoid answering.

"My wife was from London," he explained. "I met her while on holiday one year, and I became a, uh, Protestant while living there." He grew uncomfortable.

"You mean a Christian?" I said, breaking the discomfort. I knew from my studies it was taboo in France to discuss your religious faith with someone at work. We weren't at work, but we worked together.

"Yes," he said. "I became a Christian in England. We eventually moved back here, of course, so I could work for my father. But when Céline was born, Andrea wanted her to be equally comfortable with English, so we came to church here, the only English-speaking church in the area. And have come ever since. They were a great support to me a few years ago when Andrea passed away."

"I'm sorry," I said.

He nodded. "Thanks."

"Come *on*." Céline tugged at Philippe's hand. "Let's get our coffee."

"Coffee?" I asked.

"More like milk and sugar with a splash of brown for her," Philippe said. We walked upstairs to the coffee room.

After standing in line to get our coffee, we sat at a long table. Céline drifted away to talk with a friend, but another woman came and sat very near to Philippe.

"Who is your friend?" she asked, looking at me rather pointedly.

"Oh, Lexi, this is Gabby. Gabby, Lexi."

"Lexi. That's an unusual name." Gabby sipped her coffee.

Would I never hear the end of that? "It's a nickname for Alexandra," I said. Never in my life had my name been questioned so often.

I waited for Philippe to explain that we worked together, and that I was here at the sponsorship of his company. But he said nothing. In fact, he seemed to take pleasure in withholding any further information from Gabby. Perhaps she lived up to her name. I suppressed a smile.

"I'd best get going," I said. "I've got quite a bit to do this afternoon."

Philippe nodded, looked like he wanted to say something else, and then decided not to. I gathered up my purse and returned the coffee cup to the small service window. Philippe was already talking with another man, but he waved at me as I left.

"See you at work," he said loudly, unnecessarily so, perhaps.

"Yes, see you then," I agreed.

Gabby pretended to be intensely involved in her current conversation, but I saw her look at Philippe, then me, appraisingly, out of the corner of her eye.

I felt a small twinge of self-satisfaction. It was so rare I held any trump card at all in this country!

"How was school this morning?" Patricia asked as I walked into the bakery after class.

"Fine," I said, not wanting to complain. Even if I was cheap labor, I appreciated getting to go to school. "We're still not doing any real baking, just testing, science, prep, history. Next week we start baking in truth, with breads, then *macarons, petits fours,* and small pastries."

"I know," Patricia said authoritatively. "After class you'll come here or to the village and make the same things you're learning in class, all week. I have some simple pound cakes for you to make today. Let's go."

She walked me toward the kitchen where she'd set out a plastic-covered recipe. I recognized it immediately. It was the same recipe I'd failed the week before in class.

"Please make six of these," she said. "Call me as soon as you're finished."

I hadn't eaten lunch yet, but that didn't matter. I got to work on the cakes right away.

I weighed the ingredients out exactly and beat them just enough to mix everything but not enough to whip too much air into the batter. I didn't want holey cakes.

The baking team in the next room was made of young and old, and one of the younger men turned on a radio station that played French pop. It picked up my mood.

I noticed the light was off in Philippe's office and the door was shut.

I walked by the oven every ten minutes, looking in and praying the cakes wouldn't be burned or flat or greasy or anything else. I cleaned the dishes in the sink and wiped down the labels on all of our spices. I repacked the chocolate tubs.

Finally, it was time. I took the cakes out of the oven.

Perfect!

I let them cool, and when one was ready, I brought it back to Patricia, who was in the cool room whipping up icing for yet another wedding cake. Next to her sat a pot of tempered chocolate and some leaf stencils.

"Here it is!" I said, offering it to her. She looked at it, sniffed its baked butteriness, and broke off a piece.

"Good," she said. "Not greasy. Have Simone package the rest for the front."

By that comment I knew Monsieur Desfreres had reported on my failed attempt. Patricia turned to her work, but just as I was about to leave the room, she called me back.

"Have you made chocolate leaves before?"

I set the rest of the cake down. "No, I haven't."

"Are you in a good mood?" she asked.

I looked at her questioningly. "Yes."

"You cannot temper chocolate or work with it if you are upset, angry, or dull. It will cause the chocolate to bloom. The chocolate can sense your mood."

I nodded. I didn't know how I felt about that, but I had noticed that my recipes came out better when I was cheerful.

She showed me how to temper a bit of chocolate in a small, controlled pot and then paint the chocolate over a leaf stencil on waxed paper.

"You try it," she said, as her chocolate cooled and hardened.

I took a deep breath and melted the chocolate, stirring the bits until it tempered. Then I painted a leaf, and made some swirls and strokes with the brush to imply veins. When both of our leaves had dried, I thought mine was the better of the two.

"You can see how my chocolate has a bit of white on it," Patricia said. "It is not glossy and smooth. This is not a good day for me. I am tired of doing wedding cakes."

Tired of doing wedding cakes? *How about I do the wedding cakes and you do the dishes?* I thought. But then the idea of being in charge

of the most important cake in anyone's life scared me, and I men-
tally backed off.

"Your leaf is adequate," she said, breaking it off. She handed it
to me to eat and bit into hers. "I am going to have a cigarette."

She walked outside and sat at the patio table, and I went back
to the bakery, nibbling on my chocolate. I'd noticed this morning
that my pants pinched a bit. I'd have to lay off the baguettes. Tanya
had asked how I planned to keep my weight down in France. My
mother bought me *The Bible Times Diet*.

"Mom!" I'd said. "Really. What's in here? The John the Baptist
diet—you only eat insects and wild grapes?"

"Or the Elijah diet," Tanya had chimed in. "You only eat what
birds deliver in their beaks."

The three of us had laughed. I missed them, and looked out at
the helpful, but not friendly, Patricia. I know why French women
don't get fat. They smoke.

She came back into the kitchen and motioned to me. "Make ten
chocolate leaves for this wedding cake. I will finish icing it, and then
we will arrange the leaves on top with some acorns made out of
chocolate ganache. It's to be a three-tiered, autumn wedding cake."

She showed me how to temper white chocolate and streak it
through the leaves as they dried. I used three small brushes. The
leaves turned out great, and I stepped back with a sense of accom-
plishment—a thrill, really. I helped make a cake for someone's wedding day! A cake that would be in pictures for years to come.

Céline burst into the kitchen. I was surprised to see her. *"Bonjour, jeune fille,"* I said.

"I am *not* a little girl," she told me. "I am a rather big girl. With another loose tooth. Have you talked with the tooth fairy?"

Patricia shot me a strange look.

"Lexi says Americans don't have a mouse to come and get their teeth, they have a fairy, which I think sounds much prettier than a mouse."

"Ah, *bon*," Patricia said, smiling in my direction for the first time. I had found the key to Patricia's heart—Céline.

They walked toward Philippe's darkened office and turned on the light.

"Will you get me a *goûter*?" Céline asked me.

"Of course!" I went to the front of the bakery and picked out two cookies and a chouquette drizzled with chocolate, then brought them back to the office, where Patricia was getting Céline settled.

Céline sighed. "I wish my papa was here, but he had to go to Provence today to bake while Papi came up here. So I am staying at *Tante* Patricia's."

"My father is looking at a site for a new bakery in Versailles," Patricia explained. "It would be the largest, most expensive bakery we have. The flagship, as I think you say in English."

"Versailles is where my church is," Céline announced through a bite of cookie. She looked at me. "But you know that. It's your church too."

Patricia turned on her heel. "You went to the Anglican church in Versailles?"

I nodded. "Yes. I saw a flier at school. It's the only English-speaking church around here, right?"

"Right." Patricia nodded. "So you saw Céline and Philippe there?"

"Yes."

"Ah yes, I remember. You are a Protestant, like them," Patricia said. "*Bon*. Please prep some apple slices for *tarte tatin* before you leave today. I have a special order for five for tomorrow, and I will have to make them as soon as Céline gets to school. Philippe will not be back until Friday."

She left, and I was alone with Céline.

"She's mad because she had to leave her boyfriend in Provence," Céline announced, licking chocolate off her fingers. "She saw him at *Oncle* Luc's wedding, and Papa said she's been as lovable as dried bread crust ever since."

The reluctance to make wedding cakes made a little more sense.

"I don't know why you want to be a baker," Céline said. "I think food is boring."

"I heard that. But you don't look bored," I pointed out, watching her lick her fingers.

"*Eating* food isn't boring. *Making* food is."

"I'll bet I can change your mind," I said. "Come with me to slice the apples, and I'll show you."

We walked past the bread-baking room, where the others rolled dough in preparation for the dinner bread rush. Once in the prep room, I pulled out a large sack of fresh apples.

"Nothing is as good as an apple in September," I said. Céline wrinkled her nose. "I told you we'd have fun, didn't I?"

She nodded, grinning her gap-toothed grin again. "How?"

"Pick an apple," I told her. She did, and handed it to me. "Pick another one."

I peeled each apple, leaving them round. "Now, I'm going to cut out some holes for eyes, a nose, and a mouth." I carved into the apples, then went to the spice shelf and picked out four whole cloves. "Put one of these into each eye socket," I instructed. She did, giggling.

I selected about twenty pieces of the long grain rice we usually ground for rice flour. "Put ten in each mouth, for teeth," I said.

Céline popped them all in, and we stared at our creations. "Now what?" she asked.

"Now we wait." I put them on a shelf next to the ovens, where they would be constantly exposed to dry heat.

"How long do we have to wait?" Céline asked.

"Till your papa comes home on Friday," I said. She clapped her hands and laughed.

Patricia, walking by, barked out, "Get back to slicing apples. I have orders to fill."

But I saw her softened face as she left us in her wake. I set about peeling, coring, and slicing twenty pounds of apples.

Friday morning I got up, having made it through the week, excited to have been at the larger bakery in Rambouillet but knowing I'd be back in the village for a few days the next week. And we were baking at school soon! Breads, the backbone of every Western culture, especially French.

I glanced at my new French Bible, sitting patiently on my kitchen table. "I'm sorry, Lord," I said. "I don't know how I have the best of intentions on Sunday and then the whole week gets away from me."

I determined to figure something out for accountability.

I stood near the table, quickly checking my e-mail before leaving the house. There was one from my mom, home from Italy, describing their new house and asking if I'd be home for Christmas.

No, I thought. But I didn't tell her yet. Frankly, I wasn't sure where "home" was.

There was also an e-mail from Tanya.

I'm spending Thanksgiving with Steve and his family, she said. *I think it's getting serious.* I already knew it was serious. I might be making chocolate leaves for her cake before another year passed.

And then there was an e-mail from Dan. My heart did a double beat.

The subject line said, "Hi, Lexi!" I sank into my chair to read the rest.

How are you? I've been really busy at work, and of course our softball season lasted all summer. I've thought about you quite a bit, but not knowing how things were going for you, felt like I didn't want to interrupt. I walked by Blue C the other day and thought of our sushi date. I was going to go in, but then I thought, nah. No one to give me a refresher course on how to use the chopsticks. Maybe if you come back, we'll go again.

Anyway, I am going to be flying through Paris in November. I think I mentioned that my sister is doing a year abroad in Belgium. Well, she fell in love with a Belgian guy, and they are getting married there. I thought, if you have the time,

maybe we can meet up and you can show me the sights?
You're probably an old hand by now. If you don't have time,
or have found your own Belgian guy, don't worry about it.

Talk with you soon.

Yours,

Dan

I still felt something. As much as I'd thought I wanted those feelings to be *passé*, they were not—and I wasn't sure I wanted them to be. I wished I didn't still feel his hand over mine at Blue C as I showed him how to work the chopsticks, but I did.

I took a deep breath and shut down my laptop. Then I ran to the train so I wouldn't be late for school.

Once there, I kept my mind on my work as best I could.

Anne leaned over to me. "Everything okay?"

I was surprised, since she hadn't initiated conversation before. She moved over to work more closely, which was fine, since Désirée was chatting up Monsieur Desfreres.

"Yes," I said. *Not at all,* I thought.

She made light conversation throughout the day, and I tried to respond, wondering if this was a change in our relationship and if I understood what was happening in any of my relationships. Or within myself. I was glad it wasn't a day to work with chocolate, because I was sure anything I touched would have seized.

After the distracting day at school, I walked to the bakery. I tied on my apron and went into the back. Patricia showed me a barrel of apples and told me that I should peel, core, and slice them.

"Philippe is here," she mentioned, tossing her head toward the office. I saw the light on, and Philippe talking with an older man. Her tone was casual, but the look in her eyes was intense. I glanced from Philippe to the older man.

"My papa," Patricia said, answering my unspoken question.

The *patron*—the big boss, Monsieur Delacroix.

I got to work, and a few minutes later, Philippe and his father came out of the office. They headed straight toward me.

Phillipe smiled, friendly and encouraging. "Lexi, this is my father, Monsieur Delacroix."

Monsieur Delacroix held out his hand, and I shook it. "Pleased to meet you," I said. "Thank you for allowing me to come and study, and to go to school."

"Certainly. Luc's idea," he said. "Time will tell if it was a good one or not." He wasn't rude when he said it, just matter of fact, like his sister, Maman.

I turned back to slicing apples, and he walked up front with Philippe. Soon, I heard him leave the bakery, and the atmosphere felt like it'd exhaled a collective breath.

Philippe came back to the prep room holding a shrunken apple head. "Is this the kind of thing you sell in America?"

I laughed. "No, it was for Céline."

He smiled. "I know." Then he held something out in his hand. I saw Patricia peeking her head around the corner. "I picked these up—I hope it's okay. You've been so kind to Céline, I wanted to return your kindness. Can you go?"

Musée d'Orsay

*Entrée le
Dimanche*

∾

Sunday
Ticket

I took them in my hands and accepted his offer, which brought
a big smile to his face and a blush to my cheeks. He was even more
attractive when he smiled.

I spent the rest of the day wondering if the invitation was only
to pay me back for my kindness to Céline, and if it mattered to me
either way.

Five

> *There are people in the world so hungry that God cannot appear to them except in the form of bread.*
>
> Mahatma Gandhi

I recognized the car when it pulled into Maman's circular drive. I'd been watching out the window and suddenly felt anxious when I saw Philippe get out and open the gate before driving in. Why I was nervous to visit a museum with two new friends who I'd already seen in church today, I didn't know.

Before I stepped back from the window, I looked up at the big house. It was barely perceptible, but I saw it. A lace curtain was drawn slightly aside to view the driveway, then dropped back into place.

Both Céline and Philippe came up to the door to greet me. "Can we come in?" Céline asked. Her father shushed her.

"Sure," I said.

"I want to see if it's any different from when Dominique was here. Dominique is my cousin, you know."

"I know," I said. I let them in, glad that I'd tidied up a little.

Céline ran into the living room and plopped herself down on one of the chairs. Philippe pointed at the chalkboard hanging on my kitchen wall. "I recognize that," he said.

"Yes, it's from your bakery."

"My father's bakery," he corrected. I nodded, picking up the barb in his tone.

"Yes, your father's bakery," I agreed. "It was in the garbage in the back, and I pulled it out and asked Patricia if I could keep it."

He smiled and read what I'd chalked in.

"No baguette?" Philippe asked.

- Salade
- Cream of Garlic Soup
- Chouquettes

~Jean 3~

"Non," I answered, not explaining. Friend or no, some things a girl kept to herself.

"Jean 3?"

"Since the pastor's teaching through the book of John at church, I'm reading along."

"Ah," Philippe said. "Menu for the body *and* the soul."

I nodded.

"Bon," Céline said, apparently satisfied I hadn't changed too much. "Let's go." She looked at the board. "Chouquettes?"

"I'm practicing at home. Next week I leave them behind to make macarons and petits fours," I said.

"Mmm," Céline said as we left the house. Philippe opened the back door of his car for her, then opened the passenger door for me before walking around to his own side.

Before he could get in the car, Céline said, "Odette calls you a chouquette."

"Oh," I said. "That's nice." She must really think I made them well.

"No, it's not," Céline insisted.

"Why not?"

"If you call someone a chouquette, it's because they think you have nothing up here." Céline tapped her head.

Still Odious.

Philippe carefully pulled out of the driveway and drove in a restrained manner all the way to Paris. I was amazed. Luc had told me all Frenchmen drove like crazy people.

The three of us chatted along the way, uncomfortably at first, circling like birds around topics but never landing, then becoming more relaxed. After forty-five minutes, we pulled into a parking lot near a bridge over the Seine River.

Philippe opened my door and Céline's. We walked up the stone stairs from the water's edge to the busy street above and stopped across from the entrance. As soon as we reached the top, I gazed at the Musée d'Orsay. Various families and street artists were scattered about the grounds like confetti, some sitting, some standing, several eating a quick meal from a cart.

I love impressionist art. I like the idea that the borders are blurry, and that everything in life isn't as crisp and clear as we think it should be. This, to me, was the most important place I wanted to visit in Paris.

"Coming?" Philippe asked, ready to cross the street.

I grinned. *"Mais oui!"*

As it was early autumn, the lines weren't too long, but as it was Sunday, there was a small crowd. We stood in the queue, chatting while we waited to get in.

"Have you ever been here?" I asked Céline.

"But of course!" she said. "I think it's boring."

Philippe looked at her. "You won't when you're older."

"I'm glad you came," I told her, and she smiled, happy to be wanted. She reached for my hand and put her small one inside of it. We talked about art and artists. Once inside we wandered the long marble halls full of artwork. I looked up at the glass ceiling, light tumbling through the panes of glass like water, splashing on the tiles and the artwork below. Bleached white sculptures, flat and unglazed, commanded the floor—a woman on horseback, hair trailing behind her like the horse's tail; a bronze, headless man, muscles flexing. I felt his energy.

We headed toward the first floor. Intense art students squatted and sat on the floor, hair in their eyes, lead in their hands, deep in thought as they sketched page after page, imitating the masters.

"Do you want to see my favorites?" asked Philippe.

"Of course!"

We walked up another floor till we reached the pointillists.

"When you step away from the paintings, you see nothing but blend, like any other impressionist," Philippe said. "But when you get closer, you can see there are actually no brush strokes at all. Only tiny dots. They blur in the eye from a distance."

"So very beautiful," I said.

We walked only two floors, aware of Céline's little legs and flagging interest. But at every turn, one of us was able to point out something marvelous for the others to see.

"I'm sorry you didn't see it all," Philippe said as we left the rare air of the museum and exited into the late blue afternoon light.

"I'll come back another time."

"Yes, you'll live here a long time. You'll be able to see this and more," he said.

A long time. I looked at the Parisians reposing on the sides of the Seine, and it brought to mind my favorite painting of the day, *A Sunday Afternoon on the Island of LaGrande Jatte* by Seurat.

"What are they doing?" Céline pointed to men and women lining the banks of the Seine with paintings by their side.

"Selling their original work," Philippe told her. "Watercolors, mostly."

Both Céline and I looked longingly at the paintings as we walked by on our way back to the car park. I nearly pinched myself. I could hardly believe I was here, strolling along the Seine, looking at artists hawking their wares. In Paris.

We drove back from Paris in the early evening, via the Champs-Elysées, and talked comfortably all the way home. When we got back to the village, Céline and Philippe walked me to my door.

"Thank you for a lovely day," I said. "It was much more enjoyable to have someone to share my thoughts and feelings with."

"It was our pleasure," Philippe said.

"It was our pleasure," Céline copied, appearing very grown-up and very small at the same time. I laughed and ruffled her hair as she stood between us.

They walked back to the car, and I waved as they drove away. Before I closed my door, I saw the lace in Maman's sitting room window jiggle. I walked back into my house, looked at the chalkboard, and set out my Bible so I wouldn't forget to read Jean chapter three sometime soon.

First, I called Tanya. She didn't pick up, so I left a message.

"I went to the Musée d'Orsay today," I said. "It was great. I think I may have found one kid in all the world that I like." I mentioned nothing about Céline's dad, but I knew Tanya would ask.

Then I e-mailed Dan back and hesitatingly told him I'd like to see him in November and that he should send more details when he got them. I signed it, *Yours, Lexi.*

The next week at school, bread week, was *fantastique*! We rolled up our sleeves and kneaded dough until our hands ached.

I was stationed next to Désirée and across the huge work table from Anne and Juju. Anne's breads, in particular, were lovely.

"Your breads are so nice," I said once when we were alone, cleaning up our station. "The dough is always pinchably plump. And why are your raisins so moist?"

"Haven't you seen me soak them?" she asked. "I put them in a cup of warm orange juice instead of water for about twenty minutes before I add them. It softens them and plumps them, and the orange flavor makes the bread even tastier."

"No," I said. "I hadn't seen you do it."

She put her last mixing bowl into the sink and pulled down the industrial overhead faucet to rinse it out. "Désirée saw. She did it to her loaves yesterday." I heard an edge in her voice.

We went back to our table and began rolling loaves for baguettes. I'd helped Luc with bread in Seattle, but here it was Philippe and his guys in Rambouillet or Kamil's crew in the village who did the breads. I didn't expect to specialize in breads, but I knew I had to be better than proficient in order to get and keep a job. So I rolled dough, watched the others, and learned from their strengths and mistakes.

One day last week Juju's loaves came out nearly flat. I thought she was going to cry.

"Did the yeast bubble before you added it?" Désirée had asked, trying to help.

"I think so," Juju said.

Désirée shook her head. "Maybe not. If it didn't bubble after three or four minutes, maybe your batch was bad."

I'd said nothing, but that didn't make sense. We all drew yeast from the same tins. If I'd had a death wish, I'd have asked Monsieur Desfreres, but I knew a report would be going out to my *patron* that week, and I didn't want to draw negative attention to myself.

We placed our baguettes in the oven. Today, both mine and Juju's came out perfectly plump and tanned. We ate lunch with the cooking school—they were providing *soupe* and salade, and we were providing the bread. All of the school instructors and administrators would take note.

We removed our chef's *toques blanche* and took our bread to the dining room, then sat at tables for eight. It was fun for the baking students to mingle with the cooking school students.

"The bread smells delicious!" one of the cooking students said. "Nicely done!"

We bakers smiled. I looked at the table. "Is there butter?" I asked.

The rest of them looked at me quizzically.

"You baked it," a cooking student pointed out. "You know there is no butter in bread."

"Of course!" I commented, remembering the French didn't put butter on their bread. I wanted butter on my fresh bread. And a Coke.

But the soupe and salade—to-die-for. The French definitely won there.

After school, I asked Anne if she wanted to have coffee. We walked to a café and sat down.

"No work today?" she asked.

"No," I said. "I have to work on Sunday this week, so I have the afternoon off." I ordered café crème and she ordered an Orangina. No ice.

"Did you go to your Anglican church last Sunday?" Anne asked, tilting her face to the autumn sun. The people at the table next to us were engaged in a heavy argument complete with finger wagging, shrugging, and unprovable accusations. I smiled. They must like each other. It was the French way.

"I did go," I answered, moving forward like a woman walking on freshly frozen ice. "I liked it. And I saw someone I knew there."

"Non!" Anne said. "Another American?"

I smiled and took a sip of my café crème. "A Frenchman."

"At an English church?" she asked incredulously.

I nodded. "He's the baker at the Rambouillet bakery," I said. "Philippe Delacroix."

"Ah," she said. "One of the owners. What was he doing there?"

I explained about his late wife being English and her desire for their daughter to learn the language. I sipped my coffee slowly. In France, there are no coffee refills, so if you want to stay and chat at a café, you have to draw the drink out.

"I wish I spoke better English," Anne said. "It would make it easier to get a job. I could go to other places in the EU and work. As it is, if I don't find a job after school, I will have to go back to Normandy and live with my parents again, and be cooped up. My father and mother both smoke. If I stay in that household, I will lose the sense of smell I need to be a good baker."

I sensed there was more than that going on, since most of the French bakers I knew smoked, but I said nothing more about it. "You could come to the English class with me at church," I said.

"Non." She shook her head. "Church is not for me."

"But that's not true," I said. "I'm reading the book of Jean right now, and it's all about bakers."

She scoffed. "It can't be!"

"Yes, it is," I said. "I was just reading it last night. Jesus said, *'C'est moi qui suis le pain qui donne la vie. Celui qui vient à moi n'aura plus jamais faim, celui qui croit en moi n'aura plus jamais soif.'"*

I am the bread of life. He who comes to me will never go hungry, and he who believes in me will never be thirsty.

"Bah," Anne said. "That's not for bakers."

I grinned, and she grinned back.

"How about we practice English at the café one day a week," she said, "when you're not working. And I'll help you with French. So you can avoid the *faux amis.*"

I'd told her I'd made a few *faux amis* mistakes, but hadn't told her exactly which ones.

"Bon," I agreed.

Désirée walked over to the table, having spied us, I suppose, as she left school.

"My two friends!" she said. "Can I join you?"

It would be nice to have two friends, I thought. *Wouldn't it?* But the thought of Désirée as a friend unsettled me somehow.

Friday was our bread test. We spent the first few hours on the written test, covering everything from what happens when we overmix to what happens when we underproof. We filled in the blanks for missing recipes, including approximate weights of ingredients. Then we made them. Each of us was assigned one recipe from a selection of what we'd learned that week. Juju got *pain à la bière,* and the men across the table were assigned sweetbreads. Anne was assigned a *couronne,* and I was assigned *brioche.* Désirée got croissant.

"I'm going to the restroom," Anne said to me as we gathered ingredients. "Do you need anything from the prep room? I've forgotten the salt."

"Non, merci." I shook my head.

The bread room hummed quietly; no one talked. While breads were not the most difficult thing we would learn, it's hard to imagine anything else more central to French baking. I liked brioche—it was eggy, my specialty! I grinned. I knew I'd do okay.

I gathered everything at my work station, weighed it out, and then, when it was all in front of me, weighed it out again. I combined the ingredients in just the right measure and let the dough rise. I didn't leave while it rose, as I wanted to watch it the entire time. We'd be serving these for lunch, and I wanted the brioche to be perfect.

I finally put my dough into my number seven pan and delivered it to Monsieur Desfreres's assistant, who gave me a benign smile and put it into the oven.

I went back to our table. Désirée had delivered her croissant dough to the proofer and was now pulling it out and taking it to the ovens. Juju grinned over her creation, and indeed, it smelled great.

Anne, however, was close to tears.

"What's happened?" I asked, coming alongside her.

She shook her head. "I don't know. It never rose." I looked at the flabby, flat lump of dough slumping in the bottom of her mixing bowl. "I kept thinking maybe it needed more time, but it never rose."

Juju joined us. "Maybe it was the yeast, like my problem the other day."

Anne shook her head again. "I used the same yeast as the rest of you." She pinched the dough and put some in her mouth. "Try this."

Désirée appeared and pinched off a piece of dough. "Too much salt," she said authoritatively after tasting it. Then she walked over to talk with the men finishing up their sweetbreads.

Juju took her bread to the oven. Anne's eyes followed Désirée as she walked away. "I measured the salt exactly," she said quietly.

"And that wouldn't cause it not to rise, anyway," I said.

"Unless someone added salt while my yeast was proofing," she said. "Then it would kill the yeast."

My eyes widened. She was right. And she wouldn't have noticed, as long as it had happened after the bubbling began.

"Did you see anything happen when I went to the restroom?" Anne asked.

"*Non,*" I said. "But I was concentrating on my own bread, so that may not mean much."

"Perhaps we'd better keep an eye on everything from now on," she said, watching Juju and Désirée.

Monsieur Desfreres arrived. He looked at Anne's bowl and sniffed. "This, Mademoiselle, is not a crown," he said, referring to the shape couronne bread was supposed to be. "It is, instead, a flat tire."

He marked some notes in his book and kept walking.

Thankfully, my bread turned out perfectly, and I whistled "God Bless America" all the way to the bakery. Then I whistled "La Marseillaise." I was a true Franco-American.

Simone was tidying up the pastry cases and using her hand broom to brush bread crumbs from the bread cases before they were loaded for the evening bread rush.

"Can I help?" I asked, watching the chair she stood on wobble a bit too much for comfort.

"Merci!" she said. I held it steady, and she completed her job.

"Perhaps you should get a stepladder?" I suggested. "In case I am late tomorrow."

She smiled kindly. "I guess this chair is a little shaky. I just haven't wanted to make a fuss."

How different from Odious. Unfortunately, I had to spend the day with Odious on both Saturday and Sunday. Fortunately, Maman was letting me help with the bread since I'd had my bread course this week. I planned to bake up a little surprise for Odious. I grinned at the thought of it.

"Lexi, come here!" Patricia barked from the back. I stood, stunned, for a minute. Simone caught it too.

Patricia had called me by the familiar, friendly form of the verb, not the formal form she'd always used before.

"Get going!" Simone shooed me through the door.

Once in the back room, though, things were all business. "I heard you whistling up the street five minutes ago," Patricia said. "What took you so long?" I saw the softness of her face. She was truly pretty when she let her guard down.

"I was helping Simone," I explained.

"Well, I'm leaving in one hour for the train to Provence, and I need to give you instructions for the rest of the day. Too bad you'll be at the village bakery this weekend." She looked at me intently. "Philippe will be here all weekend, and he could use the help. But you'll see him at church on Sunday, I suppose. He'll have someone come in early so he doesn't miss." By her sniff, I could tell she did not approve of his choice.

"What about Céline after school?"

Patricia nodded. "That is the *problème,* isn't it? She'll be at my *tante's* house. Simone will be here to watch her today, as Philippe and my papa are looking at the building in Versailles to see if it's suitable for the next shop." She paused. "How was your schooling this week?"

"*Bon!*" I said, glad to be able to share the truth. "I made brioche—eggy, and just so." I grinned. "Everyone at the lunch table said it was tender and delicious."

"*Bon.* Today you will make brioche. Place the dough in the cooler overnight, and I will leave a note for Philippe to bake it in the morning. Make enough for ten loaves, as many people buy brioche on Saturday mornings."

What if I made a mistake? The bakery would have no brioche at all. I got the recipe card out and studied it, and began to measure bit by bit. I stationed myself at one of the huge dough mixers. "Can I use this?" I asked one of the bread crew.

"But of course!" he said.

I turned on my iPod and began the Paris Combo playlist. The jazzy, sensual music filled my ears as I began the yeast sponge, making very certain that no salt got in at this point.

I noticed, now that I was alone so much, that I talked with God more often, especially in the past couple weeks. In the morning, because there was no one else to converse with. To ask His opinion later in the day. To share my personal thoughts. Never before had it only been me and Him. I'd always had other people to turn to first.

Lord, please help Anne, I prayed as I mixed. *She looked so dejected after the failure with her bread today. And help me too. I don't want to let anyone down with the brioche.*

I envisioned Philippe coming in the next morning, taking out my dough, kissing his fingers into the air at the glossy, perfect sight of it, and baking it up brown and beautiful. Many customers would comment on the perfect, eggy texture. I grinned.

I supposed it was equally possible that Philippe would come in, shout, *"Quelle problème!"* at the greasy, flat tire of dough in the walk-in, and have to profusely apologize to his regular customers, who demanded a nonexistent loaf of their Saturday brioche.

I tried to keep that thought at bay.

Céline came in a few hours later and grinned at our two mascots, the shrunken apple heads, perched on the shelf above the dry goods. I turned off my iPod so I could hear her better.

"Goûter?" she asked hopefully.

"Ask Simone," I told her. "I'm busy baking."

"Baking, *beurk,*" she said. *Yuck.* She walked forward to get her treat, and I finished up my dough.

At school, I had let the dough warm-rise in a few hours. Today I'd let it slow-rise in the cooler so it would be ready tomorrow morning. I beat the butter into submission, slapped the dough, wrapped it, and put it in the walk-in. Then I went to the office to talk with Patricia.

"I'm just leaving," she said, looking vibrant. "I'm going to get my hair done before I catch the train."

"So you're very pretty for Xavier," Céline teased.

My eyebrows raised, but I said nothing. I knew who was the low employee around here.

"Xavier is my…friend," Patricia explained.

"Her *boyfriend,*" Céline said in a singsong voice.

"Back to work for you," Patricia told her. "If you are not getting the highest marks in all areas, you are not studying enough. I will be looking at your progress reports very soon." She tried to be stern but fooled no one, I think.

She closed the office door behind us and handed me a list of things to prep before I took the train home that night.

"Have a good time," I said.

"I will," she said. "I'm best in Provence."

I wondered if that had to do with it being her family home or with Xavier. I simply nodded.

"I have known Xavier a long time," she offered without my having to ask. "He was so happy when I came back from Seattle to stay. He is ready for someone other than his maman to cook for him," she said a little wistfully. "But he will not leave Provence."

Because she'd opened the door a crack, I tentatively offered a question. "And you do not want to move back to Provence?"

"I'd love to," she said, but nodded her head toward Céline, busy practicing her printing on the other side of the office window. "But who would take care of her…and Philippe?"

She looked at me and held my gaze just a little longer than she needed to.

Six

Sharing food with another human being is an intimate
act that should not be indulged in lightly.
M.F.K. Fisher

I didn't have school on Saturday, of course, so I worked the earliest shift at the bakery in the village. I was supposed to make petits fours. Cake! My favorite. And I had a little something else in mind too.

The village bakery didn't have the varied baking rooms of the bakery in Rambouillet, so I found a cool counter space near the walk-in and began to cut and frost tiny squares of cake. I looked at the clock and discovered that I had some time to play with, so I got out the marzipan and adorned the cakelettes creatively. If Maman didn't like the decorations on top, I could scrape them off and redo them.

I gazed out the window at the approaching autumn. Monsieur Desfreres told us to take our inspiration from everything around us, that we were not merely artisans, we were artists. I allowed myself to dream.

I thought of Céline and her missing tooth, and created tiny mice out of marzipan. I thought of autumn flowers and fashioned some blood red mums. I sliced thin squares of pound cake and sandwiched them with strawberry preserves, a last good-bye to summer flavors. I cut almond cake and sandwiched it with raspberry crème, delicate and refined. Chocolate cake was dribbled with Grand Marnier, the orange liqueur that originated hundreds of years ago in this very village. I enrobed them in dark chocolate fondant and piped tiny orange pumpkins on top.

After arranging them neatly on long, silver trays, I found Maman. "The petits fours are finished," I said. "Should you come and look at them before I put them out?"

Maman shrugged, annoyed at being bothered, I think, but knowing she had to check my work. *"Un moment,"* she said, and I went back to the kitchen to prepare tartes.

I thought again of the season and made baby tarte tatins blushing with cinnamon sugar. Then, daringly, I made faux-pumpkin pies out of some tinned squash I'd found in the market. *Très Americaine,* I guessed. But they tasted good and looked pretty, and I hoped they would sell.

An hour or two later Maman came to look at my work. She stared at the pan of petits fours for a minute before talking.

"I know they're a little different," I explained. "Monsieur Desfreres told us to take our inspiration from nature and life around us."

Better if I could pin it on a Frenchman. "The mice are for Céline and her missing teeth." I knew Céline would visit later in the day with Maman's husband, whom everyone called Papa.

Maman took one of the chocolate petits fours with an orange marzipan pumpkin. "Grand Marnier, from the village," she said as she ate it.

I nodded and said nothing.

She took one of the fake pumpkin pies. "Squash." I watched her eat it and then brush a crumb from her lips. "Bon, Lexi. These will do fine. Except," she pointed to the petits fours with mums on them, "not these. In France, mums are only for decorating graves on November first, All Saints Day, the day we remember those who have passed on."

She wiped her hands on her apron, but she took an extra petits fours and popped it into her mouth, then grinned. Her highest praise, unspoken but eaten. Maman hardly ever ate pastries. "Now on to the chouquettes, *ça va?*"

"*Ça va,*" I agreed, happy she was satisfied.

I got out the ingredients for chouquettes and whipped up a hundred of the typical recipe, then another hundred substituting dark cocoa for some of the flour. I'd already asked Maman if I could try it.

"Okay, all right." She'd waved me away with her hand. I heard her grumbling that they probably wouldn't sell as the villagers knew exactly what they liked and chocolate chouquettes were not it, and there was a lot of work to be done around here for *real* food.

I noticed she ate two or three as they cooled. I hid my smile.

Halfway through the day, Odette came in, just as I was putting out the sweets for the afternoon rush. She looked at the petits fours and sniffed, but said nothing. Then she pointed at the dark chouquettes.

"What are those?" she asked. "Too long in the oven?"

"Mais non," I said. "Not at all. In fact, I made them with you in mind."

She set her purse in the back and put on her uniform—embroidered, of course. Then she went to the case and took out one of the chocolate chouquettes. "Hmm." She ate it and then put one of the plain ones in her mouth. "Not bad."

"Not bad for a chouquette, you mean?" I asked with an innocent smile.

She looked at me numbly, with no comeback. She knew I meant myself, and not the cookies. *Airhead indeed,* I thought. Then I went into the back and cleaned up my dishes and Maman's.

My shift was over just before lunchtime. I took off my apron, wiggled my dead, tired toes inside my shoes, and began the long walk home. Maman had told me I'd need to be in by five the next morning to help with the bread.

That meant no church. I'd been reading through John, though. The gospel of love in the language of love, French.

I walked through the village, but no one waved at me. The grocer smiled when I bought a can of Orangina for the walk home, but carried on a long conversation with the woman who came after me. *I should really buy some food,* I thought, but I wasn't up for it.

I had no one to be with, to talk with, except God. *Not that I discount You,* I said in my head.

I made my way into the cottage and saw the light blinking double-time on the phone. Two messages. I listened to the first. It was Anne!

"I am going to the market this afternoon," she said. "I'm leaving about noon. Later is when the bargains can be found. If you want to come along, meet me at the entrance to the Rambouillet market about one o'clock. I'll wait for fifteen minutes, or you can call me on my cell phone."

I looked at my watch. If I ran, I'd make it to the train on time. I looked at the blinking light, wondering who the second message was from and if it required immediate attention.

I decided to skip it for now. The weekend stretched out long and lonely without company. Anne and the market it was. Jeans and sweater would have to do.

"You came!" Anne said as I reached the market entrance.

"I barely made it," I admitted. "I'd just gotten home from work." I checked my watch. It was 1:30, and the market would close soon.

"Have I made you late?" I asked, knowing that much of the best produce may already be gone.

"I kept hoping you'd show up," she said. "And you did!"

She showed me her woven market basket, a standard for every French woman. Hers had a design on it unique to Normandy, where she was from. "Do you have a basket?" she asked.

I shook my head.

She led me to a vendor at the market entrance and encouraged me to barter for a basket, using up more of her precious time. I bought one of thick, woven straw that looked and smelled like dry wheat and reminded me of the ripe, golden fields of the gorgeous countryside I now called home.

We wandered the market, running our fingers over the taut skin of happy pumpkins, shiny with flesh about to burst. One vendor selected a melon for me, invited me to sniff it, and I did, the sweet honeyed scent of it reminding me of summer breakfasts in Seattle. Knobs of earthy mushrooms sprouted everywhere, and Anne selected a few.

"I have a very small kitchen," she said, "but I am going to make a pot of mushroom soup tonight."

"Where do you live?" I asked, realizing I had no idea.

"A small rental studio in Rambouillet," she said. "I saved money working in the bakery in my small town so I could come to school. No *patron* is paying my way," she said, looking at me with gentle envy.

No one had provided a little stone cottage for her, either. I felt ashamed, for a moment, that I had felt such low worth about being "free" labor. Odette had planted that bitter seed, but I'd let it grow.

"Are you lonely?" I asked, and then realized how personal that sounded. "I mean, living by yourself. Like I do."

She nodded. "But there is an old French proverb, 'hunger savors every dish.' I think having to work so hard will make getting a job that much more rewarding. Assuming I get a job when I'm done."

We walked to the next market, and I chose some pickled green beans from a woman who had obviously canned the slender jade strands at her home. I bought some tiny potatoes, earth still clinging to them, having only birthed them hours before. Anne bought a head of spinach. Some of the vendors were closing down.

On a whim, I walked over to the fish market. "Let's go over here; it'll make both of us feel like home," I said. Seattle and Normandy were both coastal locales, and Anne had told me once, longingly, that she missed the well-salted air of her home.

We examined the large-eyed bass, who stared back at us. I saw, out of the corner of my eye, something that reminded me of home. Salmon! Smoked salmon.

I dug into my purse and bought a pound, expensive but worth it. I loved French food, but longed for a taste of Washington too.

After we shopped, we went to a nearby café and sat down. We each had a glass of white wine, and the waiter brought us a small plate of *gougères,* cheese puffs. We nibbled and talked.

"Do you think you can get a job here afterward?" I asked. "Do you know where to start?"

Anne nodded. "I'm hopeful, because I have a letter of recommendation from my boss at the bakery I worked at in Normandy. But a lot of the students at the school are already working in a bakery, like you," she said. "So I don't know how many places will be open. Some smaller shops, I suppose. But I want a future."

I nodded. "I understand. I'm hoping there will be a place for me with the Delacroix when I'm done, but I don't even know if I'll pass the exhibition well enough to please Monsieur Delacroix. Nor do I know if there will be a place for me if Dominique comes back."

"What about the bakery in Versailles?" Anne asked. "Surely if they open that, there will be a need for more pastry workers."

"It's my only hope," I said. "But even then, if Dominique is back...I don't know. And I don't have a job in Seattle anymore."

Anne sipped the last of her wine. "All I know is that the small inheritance I got from my grandmother and my savings will run out by January. But I can't return to Normandy."

"Why not?"

She hesitated. "My boyfriend was *abusif.* You understand? And my father too."

"Yes," I said. "I'm sorry." I wondered if I should say more, but decided to keep quiet, knowing this to be a very personal revelation for a French woman. I didn't want to press.

"Yes. I am sorry as well," she said, closing the conversation. She stood. "I'd better go and find the cream for my mushroom soup, eh?"

"And I'd better catch the train," I said. "I work early tomorrow."

"Oui," she said. "At the bakery." There was longing, but no resentment, in her voice.

We kissed cheeks as good French women did, and said *au revoir* until Monday morning.

I caught the train home, just beating an autumn rain. As I ran up the driveway to my cottage, I saw Céline's little face pressed against a windowpane in the big house. I waved at her, and she waved back, grinning.

I let myself in and set down my woven market bag, then caught sight of the blinking telephone light out of the corner of my eye. Oh yes! The other message.

"Lexi, it's Dad." I shook my head as I listened, clearing it from surprise, and also taking a second to go from the "French" track to the "English" track in my mind. "Call me back right away if you can."

I looked at my watch. Five o'clock in the evening here, so it was eight in the morning in Seattle. He must have left the message late the night before. I hadn't talked to him since Paris. What could he want?

My hands shook a little as I dialed, and it only rang twice before Mom picked up.

"Mom!" I said, and became a little girl again at heart as I heard her voice. "How are you?"

"The better question, young lady, is how are *you*?" Mom said, teasingly. "So busy you can't call more often?"

"Oh, Mom, I'm sorry," I said. "I've been really busy at work and school. And it's expensive!"

"I know," she said. "I'm glad you're having a good time. I miss you."

"I miss you too, Mom," I said. "I got a call from Dad."

"Yes." She lowered her voice, which sounded muffled, as if she was cupping the phone in her hand. "He's got an idea. He's very excited. I hope you can make it work, Lexi."

An idea?

"Oh, here he is now!" Mom said rather loudly and cheerfully. "I'll talk with you soon, honey."

I heard her fumble the phone over to Dad.

"Lexi? How are ya, honey?" Dad said.

"I'm good, Dad, how are you?"

"Fine, fine. All settled into the new house, and now the rains have started, you know?"

"I do, Dad."

"I'll bet you're wondering why I called."

"I'm always glad to hear from you, Dad," I answered, hoping he'd get to the point soon.

"Well, here's the thing. Do you remember Bob? From the recruiting station in Seattle?"

"Your friend from the navy? Yes, I do."

"Well, he put me onto this last minute travel Web site, where you buy available seats on planes that are flying soon. You know, remainders."

"I've heard of that," I said, putting the salmon into the fridge while we talked.

"So I was thinking, maybe I could get on a plane next Thursday and be there by Friday. We could spend the weekend together, and I could go back next Sunday afternoon. You know, just to check on my girl. Make sure they're treating you right."

"Next Friday?" I squeaked. "As in six days from now?"

"Well, yes. They are last minute deals," he said, sounding hurt.

"And next month it'll be Thanksgiving, and then Christmas. But I don't have to come."

I didn't think he really understood that I had school and a job here, and not a job with weekends off. I wanted to see him; it would be great to have a guest. But I didn't want to look sporadic at school or irresponsible at work.

"Um, I can try to work it out." I tried to sound hopeful and enthusiastic. "I don't get out of school until noon on Friday."

"I was in the military for years, honey. I can take a train from the airport and meet you. Or rent a car."

"Sure, Dad. You know, I live in a pretty small village. There's not a lot to do."

"I'm not coming to do. I'm coming to visit and make sure you're okay," he said.

Still, I felt there was something else behind his sudden desire to visit me.

"Do you want to sightsee in Paris?" I asked.

"Nah, Paris isn't for me," he said. "But I was wondering…well, you said you had a friend from Normandy and that it wasn't too far away. I thought, you know, maybe if you had the time, we could visit the beaches where the troops landed on D-Day."

He tried hard to not betray it, but I could hear the boyish eagerness in his voice. He was a lifelong marine and a military history buff. He'd made my dream come true by buying my plane ticket to France. Somehow I had to help make his dream come true too.

"Sure, Dad. E-mail the details to me, and we'll figure it out." Would Maman even let me take some days off? Well, why not? I hadn't done so since I'd been here. It *had* to be okay.

"Dad," I said. "There's one thing I'd like you to bring me. Mom can help you find it."

I told him, though I know he was confused by the request. That was okay. I knew what I was doing.

I woke up early the next morning and got dressed. Then I sat at my kitchen table and opened my Bible.

Alone, I sang praise songs—quietly, so as not to freak out Maman if she happened to hear through the open windows. I could imagine her eyebrows waggling over the American singing to herself, unaccompanied.

I prayed and read John 7 and 8. I grinned. Another food analogy. *"If anyone is thirsty, let him come to me and drink."*

I prayed out loud, conversationally, as I got ready for work. "So, Lord, is it because I've never really let myself get parched, always able to satisfy myself with the good gifts You'd given me, that I haven't had a thirst for *You*?"

It occurred to me that, in that way, I was much more French than I thought. I included God when it was convenient or cultural.

I heard nothing back as I put on my uniform and slipped on my shoes, but I didn't mind. On the way out, I wrote the proverb Anne had shared with me on my chalkboard.

Hunger savors
every dish.

I got to work just on time, and Maman was already there.

"I got a phone call this morning. One of the bread bakers has quit—*pouf!*—just like that. So I will take over the bread, and you will make the sables and the mousse au chocolat for me in the pastry area. Philippe will send someone over from Rambouillet if we need them, but he's short-staffed since Patricia has gone off like some crazy teenager chasing a boy."

I grinned at the description, but inside, I was worried. If everyone was short-staffed, how could I leave for three days? And yet, I had to ask for the time off today so Maman would have warning.

I made the mousse au chocolat and shook cocoa powder over each one. No one asked me to help with the bread, which was fine. I was inexperienced and, honestly, not truly gifted in that area. I hoped my brioche turned out all right at Rambouillet. I wondered if Philippe would say anything about it.

I wondered if I'd see him today.

I spent the day on my own, keeping everything clean and taking care of a small cookie order. Near noon, the end of my shift since the bakery closed early on Sundays, I approached Maman. She seemed to have everything under control, so maybe this would be a good time.

"May I speak to you?" I asked.

"*Bien*," Maman said. "What is it, Lexi?"

"Well, I had a surprising phone call yesterday," I started. "My father called to tell me that he would be visiting. Next week. He arrives on Friday. I wondered if I may have a few days off."

Maman motioned for me to follow her to the break table outside. She sat down and lit a cigarette. "*Normalement,*" she said, "this would be fine. Everyone should have a few days off now and then. But this week…" She inhaled her cigarette and shrugged her shoulders. "It will be difficult. Someone has quit. We will try to hire someone very quickly, but I may have to move someone to mornings from afternoons till we get a permanent morning bread baker hired. Which leaves me needing you in the afternoons."

"My dad was a marine," I said, hoping to appeal to her patriotic side. "He wants to visit Normandy." As soon as I mentioned Normandy, a thought occurred to me. "I do have one small idea," I offered, although a little discomfort popped into my mind as soon as the sentence had fled.

"What would that be?"

Too late to take it back now.

"I have a friend at the school. She is an excellent baker and worked at a bakery in Normandy for many years." I felt a little like I was offering my own head on a platter. "She has a letter of recommendation from her *patron* at that bakery. Perhaps she could fill in for me for a few days?"

Maman finished her cigarette. "She's experienced, you say?"

I nodded.

"Bon," Maman agreed. "Have her come with you on Thursday so she can fill out the paperwork for a temporary employee. And you can return to Rambouillet on Monday next week. Enjoy your papa."

I thanked her, took off my apron, and walked home. Anne's breads were better than mine. She made a perfect chouquette—not too eggy. Her tartes were delicious. My petits fours were better, but there was little call for them at the bakery. We had yet to compare cake baking, but Patricia did all the cakes at Rambouillet.

Inside, I felt sick. Anne was French. Anne was experienced. Anne would do better than I, and they'd see her skill up close and personal.

As I walked up the driveway of Maman's house, I saw Céline running toward me. Philippe was heading toward his car.

"Lexi!" she called. "Why weren't you at church?"

"I had to work, *jeune fille,*" I said, teasing her.

"I missed you. *We* missed you," she said, looking at her papa. "Gabby didn't." She giggled, and so did I.

"Can I stay with you instead of there?" she asked, motioning toward the big house.

Philippe joined us. "Céline, that is impolite. You don't invite yourself to someone else's house."

"Non, non," I said. "It's fine. I get lonely sometimes. I plan to make a salade for my dinner. A kind of salade niçoise, only Seattle style."

"I *love* salade niçoise," Céline said.

"You do not," her father teased. "Every time we're in Provence and it's served, you pick at it."

"I'd like Lexi's."

I flushed with unexpected pleasure, something akin to maternal pride, but not quite. Perhaps its next-door neighbor.

"Would you like to come to dinner?" I asked, emboldened by Céline's insistence and weary of dining alone. "Both of you?"

"*Oui,* we gladly accept. Thank you," Céline answered demurely.

"Normally, we eat the family meal on Sunday with my aunt and uncle and my sister. Today, I guess I have no choice. *La Patronne,* the boss, has spoken." Philippe winked. "I will bring some wine, some mint water for Céline, and a dessert from the bakery. I must go in for a few hours and make sure everything is okay there."

"Of course, we'll be fine, Papa," Céline said, tugging me toward my door. "See you soon!" She turned to me. "Now, let's do girl things."

I looked down at her small head. Her hair, while pretty, needed a woman's touch. On the way in the door, I noticed the phrase on my board, *Hunger savors every dish.*

Céline was hungry for girl things because she had no maman. I was hungry for company because I had few friends and no family nearby.

"First, we will cook," I said. She made a face. "But while I make the dinner, you will make the vase for the flowers."

She clapped her hands. I got out some tins of beans, peas, and lentils and let her layer them in a glass vase. When she was done, we'd add water and flowers.

I set about preparing the meal, wondering if Philippe would be comparing my offering to others he'd had.

Seattle Niçoise

Ingredients:

¾ pounds chunked (not thin-sliced), Alaska-style smoked salmon
1 ½ pounds new potatoes, red or yellow, scrubbed
1 cup bottled champagne salad dressing
Sea salt and freshly ground black pepper, to taste
4 ounces pickled green beans, cut in thirds
3 medium tomatoes, stemmed and quartered
5 eggs, hard-cooked and peeled, then quartered
½ cup niçoise, or other small, black, pitted olives

Directions:

Break the salmon into large but still bite-sized chunks and set aside.

Boil the new potatoes for about 15 minutes in salted water, till they are just cooked through (you can run a sharp knife through one) but not falling apart. Drain completely, cut into quarters or bite-sized chunks. Place in a bowl and pour half the dressing over them. Add the egg wedges, beans, olives, tomato quarters, and salmon chunks. Drizzle vinaigrette to taste, and then sea salt and pepper to taste. Gently stir together; garnish with parsley and serve warm.

After Céline and I had prepared dinner and played with makeup for a while, Philippe returned. I dragged another chair over to my small table. We laughed and drank wine—and mint water—and Céline imitated the man who honked his nose next to me at church. Apparently, his allergies were still in force.

"The salade was *fantastique*," Philippe said, and Céline nodded her enthusiastic approval.

I'd been so lonely for company that I was reluctant to call the night to a close. We sat at the table chatting for another hour, and then Philippe announced it was time to get Céline home. "School tomorrow for you," he said, and then looked at me. "You too!"

I laughed. "Both school *and* work for me," I said. I'd be at the village bakery for most of the week. "Will Patricia be back tomorrow? I know she's enjoying her time with Xavier. Maybe she'll stay in Provence." I smiled.

"She'll never leave Rambouillet," Philippe said. "She likes running the pastry room too much."

I looked at him, and he seemed genuine. He really didn't know why Patricia stayed in Rambouillet even though she longed to move back—to care for him and for Céline.

Seven

I will not eat oysters. I want my food dead.

Not sick. Not wounded. Dead.

Woody Allen

I wasn't scheduled at the bakery in Rambouillet for the whole week, so it made it easier to put thoughts about Céline and Philippe aside for now. Plus, my dad arrived in three days and I needed to get ready for that.

At school, Anne, Désirée, Juju, and I chatted easily, but we did more independent baking work as the days went by. There was so much to focus on and little time to talk. Juju was truly independent after school hours. I think she had a lot of friends to hang out with already. Désirée was harder to read. Anne and I grew closer, neither of us having anyone else.

Hunger savors friendship too.

"So why do you think Monsieur Desfreres doesn't like me?" I asked her on Tuesday.

She looked at me, wide-eyed like the bass we'd seen at the market. I turned around and saw Chef directly behind me.

I said nothing, operating on my mother's famous principle that the less said, the sooner something is mended. After a minute or two observing my granita—a slightly grainy, sweet coffee slush—Chef Desfreres moved on.

"Ooh la la," Anne said. "He heard."

I nodded. "But now that he's gone, what do you think? I think we have a personality conflict. I have a personality, and he has a conflict."

Anne laughed. "You are closer than you guess, I think. I had heard from one of the security guards that Monsieur Desfreres's wife left him for a Canadian and his milk has been curdled ever since."

"Oh, I'm sorry for him," I said, "but I'm not Canadian."

"No, worse," Anne teased. "You're American."

I grinned back at her. "And since when are you on close terms with the school security guards?"

"One of them lives in my apartment complex. He is working here part-time until his school permit comes through. He's from Germany, and will start graduate school in January."

I grinned at the nonchalant way she talked about him and winked at her. She blushed and turned back to making ice cream.

The entire week was dedicated to ice cream, sorbet, and granitas. Pastry chefs must be not only proficient but creative at ice creams. It's a staple on every menu.

To make ice cream, first you made a perfectly divine custard base, because that's what ice cream really is. It's thick with butterfat, which gives it that silky feel on your tongue. There was a sign on the wall in the baking school that read, "If your arteries are good, eat

more ice cream. If they are bad, drink more red wine. Proceed thusly."
I think that summed up French food philosophy.

Monsieur Desfreres allowed us to play with flavors. Now that
the first month of the course was behind us, he let us have more
autonomy in choosing what to create. With my new freedom, I really
experimented. We all did, and for a few days we had a sense of cama-
raderie instead of competition.

First, I brainstormed, what have other people done? What can I
do different? What flavors will work together? What colors? I ate
nothing but ice cream all week, excited to find something that made
me nearly as happy as cake. I laughed at myself. What an American I
was—the cake and ice cream girl. But how French I was becoming.
Monsieur Desfreres had been correct. The French train the palate.

I spent the week tasting, smelling, feeling, and judging the
responses of my classmates, along with the cooking students at
lunch. I made a tart but lush strawberry *crème fraîche,* gingerbread
with candy Red Hots swirled in, white chocolate-ginger, chocolate-
orange with candied peels, and almond sour cream.

Then I experimented with cool, sophisticated sorbets. Green
apple horseradish, cucumber melon, strawberry basil, pink grapefruit rosemary.

Monsieur Desfreres came around with a spoon and sampled our
works all week. His eyebrows raised at the pink grapefruit rosemary.
"Different, Mademoiselle," he said before marking it down and
moving on. But he didn't frown, and I took it as a compliment.

Anne was good at ice creams too, but stuck to typical French flavors. Crème brûlée ice cream, Grand Marnier granita. Juju brought
in flavors of the island like coconut-cream cheese and rum-raisin.

Désirée also stuck with more traditional flavors, but her mini sorbet *bombes* were not bombs at all. Layered in champagne glasses, they looked absolutely elegant. She had a touch. But as much as we complimented her, I noticed, she had very little complimentary to say in return. Or maybe she was just too busy flirting with one of the guys in class and buttering up the chefs.

On Wednesday, as I was leaving school to head toward the bakery, Chef Desfreres called me into his office. "Mademoiselle?"

"Yes, Chef?" I hurried into his office.

"Are you working at the Delacroix bakery this afternoon?"

"*Oui,*" I answered.

He handed me an envelope. "Can you bring this to Madame?"

"*Bien sûr,*" I answered. "Of course." I turned to go.

"Mademoiselle, I have not dismissed you," he said.

My face flushed. "I'm sorry."

He indicated for me to take a seat. "You realize you are the only American in our program, *non*?"

"Yes," I said.

"I have had other Americans come through the program. One or two were satisfactory. Do you know that I am not anti-American, Mademoiselle Stuart?"

"You've been most professional toward me," I said, giving a standard nonanswer.

"Of course." He shrugged. "I *am* a professional. France, Mademoiselle, is a small country compared to your own. However, we have a long and noble history. Unfortunately, French ways are being nibbled away, bit by bit, to where we are in danger of becoming typical. Indistinct. My job, Mademoiselle, is to be a soldier guarding the French way of life from being eaten alive by America and homogenized into the European Union. So you understand, there is nothing personal in my dislike."

"I am here because I admire France, sir," I answered. "I hope to become not just proficient, but to excel at French pastry making. I hope to contribute to the field and remain working here for quite some time."

"If you can secure a permanent position with the Delacroix, that will be something. Monsieur Delacroix has contacted me about finding an experienced graduate to work at the new *pâtisserie* in Versailles. In a few years, that may be you."

I guessed that to be a compliment. He dismissed me, politely but professionally, and I left, envelope in hand for Maman.

Someone experienced was already being hired for Versailles. How would I fit into the flagship bakery? What was I thinking? Things looked bleak on the employment front, and I had fewer than three months left.

On Thursday morning Anne and I were jotting notes in our recipe books when she leaned across the table toward me. "Are you sure you want me to come to the bakery with you?"

I wasn't sure. I had a feeling deep down in the pit of my stomach that this would lead to something I couldn't anticipate. But she was a good baker and a good friend.

"Yes," I said. "You'll enjoy it."

I swallowed the little nub of insecurity and got back to work.

At the end of the day, Monsieur Desfreres called for our attention. He handed out small, soft leather notebooks, one to each student.

"As you know," he said, "at the end of our course there will be an exhibition. This exhibition is where you will showcase the things you have learned in this course. Achieving your *diplôme* will consist of two parts. First, you will continue to take written examinations throughout the course, and at the end of the course, there will be a week of written finals. You will also perform and prepare recipes as I or my staff request that week. You must pass these examinations with ninety percent or better in order to earn your *diplôme*."

I recalled the test anxiety I'd had in junior high. And high school. Oh yeah, and college. Here, I hadn't felt it because I was in my element—not academic, but baking. However, I knew I was being tested by an instructor just as happy to let me fail as to see me pass.

Chef cleared his throat and continued. "Second, during the last week of class, all students will prepare for their exhibition. You must prepare several items: a bread, a tarte, a cake, ice cream, plated desserts, etcetera, that will be placed on your table as a final offering of your work. Your fellow students will comment aloud on your work, and you may invite your *patron* and any other pastry or baking colleagues to attend. Many of them will choose to do so and listen to the others' comments. This notebook is for you to jot down ideas for your final exhibition. Keep it private, please. Individuality, in addition to taste and presentation, will count."

I fingered my notebook and looked around the room. A soft hush had fallen, like sifted flour.

After school, Anne and I took the train to my little cottage.

"Très belle!" she exclaimed. "This is such a cute little place. How lucky you are to live here!"

"Yes, I am," I agreed. "It's mine until Dominique comes home."

"When will that be?" Anne asked, sitting in one of the mustard yellow chairs.

"I overheard Maman talking with Dominique on the phone yesterday," I admitted. "Dominique said she is bored in Seattle and wants to come home. I don't know how she could be bored!"

"Maybe it's something else," Anne said, looking around the kitchen. "Maybe she wants to come back to her little cottage and her maman and papa."

I nodded. "Maybe. But more likely she wants to come home to her boyfriend. I heard Maman say, 'Of course he will wait a few more months.' I think she's encouraging Dominique to come home anyway, because she wants her nearby."

"Can't blame her," Anne said as she took the glass of lemonade I offered.

"No," I admitted. "But that means I'll have an eviction notice in three months."

"Where will you live, then?" Anne asked. "Will you go back to the United States?"

I shrugged. "I don't know. No job there now. Nowhere to live there, either. And I like France."

Anne nodded. "I'm in the same position. Once I find a good job, I'll be settled." She looked at her watch. "Should we go? I don't want to be late."

I agreed and went to change into my uniform. When I came back, Anne was looking at my chalkboard. "What is this?" She pointed to the listing for Jean 9.

"My Bible reading."

"On the menu board?"

"I told you the Bible is for bakers and cooks," I teased. She grinned and we left, walking rapidly toward the village bakery.

We arrived just when I'd told Maman yesterday. I'd handed her the letter from Monsieur Desfreres, then too. I'd been dying of curiosity to know what it said, but of course, she shared nothing.

"*Bonjour,* Madame," Anne said upon introduction. "I am glad to be of help." She took a neat piece of paper out of an envelope and handed it to Maman. As Maman stood next to me, she held it out so I could read it too.

Dear Monsieur/Madame,

As the proprietor and chief baker of the Boulangerie du Belle Vue, I commend to you Anne Beaufort. Mlle Beaufort has worked at my bakery since the age of seventeen, starting as a *commis* but learning the trade in the ensuing years. I do understand her desire to live and work closer to Paris, but our loss is your gain, certainement.

Mlle Beaufort is trained in all forms of bread baking, specializing, of course, in those of Norman origin. She is also a growing pâtissière.

For further information, do not hesitate to contact me at the phone number below.

M. D'Aubigne,
Proprietor

"Bon!" A large smile crossed Maman's face. "You bake bread!"

"Yes," Anne agreed.

"And brioche?"

"Oui, I am fine at the brioche," Anne agreed. In fact, she was competent with all breads, which is why she knew it was not simply her technique or bad yeast that had been a problem at school some weeks back. But why did Maman bring up the brioche, specifically? Come to think of it, no one had said anything at all to me about the brioche dough I'd left for Philippe last weekend.

"Then you can come in the afternoons all weekend while Mademoiselle Lexi is with her papa," Maman said, interrupting my thoughts. "We're very glad to have you."

I smiled wanly. Had I replaced myself simply for the weekend or replaced myself altogether?

On Friday, I finished up my ice cream projects and then hopped on the train and came right home. I wanted to finish tidying up before Dad arrived and make him something special too.

I hadn't spent any time just with my dad for years. Usually Mom was there too. Since she'd just gone to Italy, I think she wanted Dad to have his special trip as well.

As I cleaned, I thought about my conflicting feelings for my father. I wanted to tidy up the place and make him proud—but I wanted him to be proud of me when I wasn't tidy too. I wanted him to be pleased with my new job, but also not care what the job was.

When I'd finished cleaning, I opened my laptop to check if his flight had been delayed, or if he'd be here on time.

No delays, in fact he'd landed a bit early. Allowing for time to rent a car, he'd be here in about two hours. I scanned the cottage. It was ready.

I checked my e-mail. A chatty one from Tanya, a forward from my brother. At the bottom of the list, one from Dan. With attachments.

I caught my breath and opened it.

Hi Lexi,

How are you? How goes the baking? Just checking to see if we're still on for my visit. If so, I'll be there in about a month. I'm looking forward to it. Any chance you can take a day off? I'd like to do a little sightseeing together. Not sure what your schedule looks like, or if you have time for an old friend.

Friend. My chest dropped a little.

Let me know either way, and if I need to make any arrangements. Otherwise, I'll plan to stay at the Sofitel in the Sixteenth Arrondissement, so it's closer to your village for drop-off, etc. I'll rent a car.

You asked about the softball season, and I'm sorry to be so long in replying. Things have been really busy around here. We came out nearly on top of the league, which was great. I attached a picture of us in case you want to see.

Talk with you soon,

Dan

Not "Yours, Dan," but "Talk with you soon, Dan."

Why did it matter that he was not "mine" anymore, anyway? I was the one who said we should leave things with no ties. I wanted to be fair to him. And, if I was honest, to myself, it was because I didn't know what job—or guy—might be waiting for me in France. I'd heard both that distance made the heart grow fonder and that distance made the fond heart wander. Maybe, in my case, it was the former and not the latter.

I clicked on the picture and downloaded it. When it opened, I saw a group of dusty, happy, young professionals with a sunny Seattle skyline in the background. My heart skipped a beat when I saw Dan. I hadn't forgotten what he looked like, but the picture brought it all back into my mind's focus. His boyish grin, the rumpled, attractive way he looked in the softball uniform. His strawberry blond hair slightly slicked back.

Right next to him, leaning on him, was the only other person I recognized. An attractive brunette with a sprinkle of freckles in a catcher's uniform, which made her look sporty and fun rather than bulky.

Nancy. The woman who had been coming on to him in his office last spring.

At the time, Dan hadn't been interested. But that was before I moved.

Yeah, Lexi, you moved. You picked your life, he's picked his.

I deleted the picture.

After shutting down the computer, I turned on the oven. Dan was coming in a month—as a friend. And as a friend, I'd show him around. I'd do it for anybody. But he'd moved on, and so must I.

I pulled out my dad's favorite cupcake recipe and began to mix, focusing on Dad again. This simple recipe was more special to me than almost any other, since it had been my very first. As I baked the cupcakes, though, I was thinking more about *mille-feuille*, someone else's favorite dessert.

A couple hours later a small Renault pulled into the driveway. I saw a curtain move in the big house. Papa had been peeking through the window. I didn't care. I ran out to meet my *own* papa.

"Dad!" I flew out the door and to the car. My dad, who had never been exceptionally affectionate, greeted me with a bear hug. Then he grabbed his small carry-on case from the passenger seat and walked toward the cottage with me.

"So here we are in France," he said.

"Yes," I grinned. "Here we are." Paris, my dream. Normandy, his. "Let me show you my home."

I ushered him into the cottage. "Ta da!" I showed him around the small kitchen, the living room, my bedroom. "You can set your stuff down in here," I said. "I'll sleep on one of the chairs in the living room tonight."

"Bah," Dad said. "What kind of gentleman allows a lady to sleep on a chair while he's in a bed? I'll sleep on the floor with a pillow and some blankets. And you made us a reservation for tomorrow night in Normandy, right?"

"Right," I said. "In Caen, near the beaches you want to see."

The tips of his ears went pink with anticipation.

After he'd settled in, we walked through the village.

"Wow, this is unusual—old and interesting," he said as we took my typical path past the rough rock walls, the stucco houses with age cracks lining their dignified faces, the wooden shutters keeping out both weather and change. He seemed surprised at the pleasant way people exchanged *"Bonjour!"* with one another on the streets. We sat down at the café in the village square to have a coffee, and then I took him to the bakery.

Odette was at the front counter. Her back was turned to me, and I saw her making pleasant—pleasant!—conversation with Anne. Anne looked in her element—confident, side-by-side with the baker Kamil. I sighed. If I hadn't known better, I'd have expected to see her name embroidered on her uniform.

"Is Maman here?" I asked Odious.

"But of course. Maman only takes a vacation in August," she said. I bit back the response that if she had a life, she might need time off too.

I introduced Dad to Anne, who tried out her shiny, new English on him. He took to her. I could tell by the way he leaned toward her before answering. I was glad.

Then Maman came forward.

"I'd like you to meet my father," I said, introducing them.

"Enchantée," my father said, taking off his cap and making a slight bow.

Maman giggled and responded, *"Enchantée,* Monsieur."

For a minute I was bemused, as she looked slightly flirtatious. Then I remembered she was flirting with my very married father.

"I hope our city is being as kind to your daughter as you have been to mine," Dad said. I translated for him.

"Your daughter is *très gentil,"* she responded. "I hope her stay with us will be memorable."

It was a nice thing to say, but it emphasized the impermanence of my visit. Dad glanced at me out of the corner of his eye. He'd caught it too.

We strolled back through the village, and two of the villagers said hello to me. One bakery regular stopped to converse, and I was so grateful she'd said hello when my father was along.

Dad bought a bottle of Grand Marnier to take back for Nonna. We stopped at another store, and he bought a beautiful silk scarf with a silver pin for Mom. Then we went back to my cottage for dinner.

I'd whipped up a little veal dish, knowing he preferred meat. And afterward, I presented the dessert.

He sat back at the table with his toothpick, which made me extremely glad we were alone, and a big grin broke out over his face. "White cupcakes with sprinkles," he said. "Just like you made me in your Easy-Bake Oven when you were a little girl."

I smiled. "They're the Dad Special." I put one on a plate for him.

"Speaking of little girls, I brought that trinket you asked for," he said. "I'll get it after dinner."

"Thanks, Dad," I responded. I know he wanted an explanation, but I didn't offer one. I wasn't ready to have a conversation about it yet.

We chatted for a while and then jet lag got the best of him.

"Well, hon, I'm heading to bed. Big day tomorrow, and I'm pretty beat."

I stood on my tiptoes to kiss him goodnight and he headed to the living room to sleep. I hoped Normandy would be more rewarding for him than Versailles had been for me. But I'd been alone.

I opened my e-mail before bed, just to check. Nothing new. Then I lay in bed for a long time, and when I fell asleep, I dreamed I was on the losing team in a softball match.

The next morning we got up early and packed the car. Dad stopped in the kitchen and looked at my blackboard.

"What's this?" he asked.

I explained to him about French café and bakery menus, and how I was using my blackboards for my own menus.

"Who's Jean?"

"It's French for John. I'm reading the book of John in the Bible. When I can get to church."

"You're going to church here?" He seemed surprised.

"Yeah, I am. I...I actually feel the need even more here than at home," I admitted.

"I'm going to church too," he said gruffly, almost under his breath.

Now it was my turn to be surprised. "Really?" My dad hadn't voluntarily gone to church for as long as I could remember.

"Well, since we moved, you know, your mother doesn't have her friends at church, so I said I'd go with her until she made some."

I nodded. Inside, I tingled. Here's hoping Mom didn't find friends at church any time soon.

It was four hours to the Norman beaches, but I loved the drive. Without a car, I was limited in my ability to sightsee, and with few days off and a heavy school load, my time was even more diminished.

"This is the old road Louis XIV used," I told Dad. We grinned at the pleasure of being somewhere old and established.

We traveled through folds of land, roads tucked into rolling hills, and lush green valleys dotted with little farmsteads hidden away and completely unspoiled, seemingly untouched by the march of time. The farms were family operations, with maybe two cows looking wonderingly our way, a couple sheep bleating, and weed-whacking goats. Bossy hens dominated many fields. Sometimes a tired old man on a tired old tractor ambled by, face grizzled by the sun.

"There are apple trees everywhere," Dad commented as we drove by yet another sign advertising tastings and visits to cider farms.

"Normandy is famous for apples," I said, glad to be able to share my knowledge with him for a change.

We drove up the narrow gravel road through an old apple orchard, finally pulling over at a crumbling Tudor building. It looked like Henry VIII could have hefted the beams himself during the meeting at the Field of Cloth of Gold. I liked being inside the musty building of stone and timber. We tasted both fermented and unfermented homemade cider.

"I like this one," Dad said after tasting the pommeau. I agreed with him—it tasted like a caramel apple to me. He bought a bottle from a wizened woman with skin like a walnut shell, and then we were back in the car and on our way.

Soon we arrived at Caen, where we would catch a tour bus to the beaches of Normandy. Dad was not an army guy—he was marine all the way—but all military men knew and honored the meaning of D-Day, the day the Norman beaches were invaded at great cost to American, Canadian, and English soldiers. It was the beginning of the end of World War II and the beginning of the end of the misery for the French of the time, who'd suffered starvation, humiliation, and hopelessness under Nazi occupation.

We toured the Caen War Memorial and ate lunch in the Memorial cafeteria. Then we boarded the tour bus. Dad pointed for me to sit near the window, but I insisted. "No, Dad. You."

The bus stopped at the artificial harbor at Arromanches and then at the German gun battery at Longues-sur-Mer.

"I can almost imagine the enemy entrenched here," Dad said quietly.

Lastly, we walked Omaha Beach. The sand was smooth and clean, white and peaceful, and dotted with carefree kids, as beaches should be. But thinking back to the war reel I'd watched with Dad as a kid, it didn't take much to imagine the bodies of the men who had died here, churning in the gunmetal gray surf. They'd died for me, for Dad, and for Anne and Maman too. I was profoundly thankful to them. In spite of the large number of people standing on the sand, it was silent.

"We'll save the American Military Cemetery for tomorrow," Dad said as we reboarded the bus, "if it's all right with you. I still have a little jet lag, and I don't want to be sleepy for that."

I nodded my agreement.

We got back to the car, drove to the hotel, and had a quick dinner. I ordered oyster shooters. Dad, predictably, refused them.

"I'll take a steak," he said. "American style." I refused to roll my eyes.

The next morning was Sunday, and as I got dressed, I was very aware of missing church. I wondered if Buki would be there. I wondered if Gabby was sitting next to Philippe. I wondered if Mom was okay sitting alone in her church on Whidbey Island. Tanya and Steve went to church together every week now, and I expected her to tell me any day that he'd asked her to marry him. I wondered if Dan was still teaching Sunday school. I wondered if Nancy was a Christian.

"Ready?" Dad knocked on my door and I picked up my travel case and followed him out. After a quick breakfast of yogurt, fruit, and a croissant, we headed to the American Military Cemetery at Colleville-sur-Mer.

Dad led the way. At the last minute, I took my Bible with me. We found a bench to sit on and looked at the miles of bleached crosses stretching out before us. We sat there for a long time, me reading ahead in John so I wouldn't disturb Dad or make him feel rushed. He remained quiet for a long time.

After half an hour, I came to John 15. I grinned. Another food analogy—the vine. I'd have to remember to tell Anne. I tucked it away to come back to later, as I felt the pressure on my heart to keep reading. When I came to John 15:13, I stopped.

Tell him, a voice whispered in my heart.

"Dad?" I said. "I came across something I want to share with you."

He turned away from the sea of graves and I saw a tear in the corner of his eye, clinging without dropping, like the last raindrop on a leaf. "Yes?"

I read John 15:13 aloud in French, then translated it for him. "Greater love has no one than this, that he lay down his life for his friends." I let my eyes rise to the field thick with crosses. "I no longer call you servants, because a servant does not know his master's business. Instead, I have called you friends."

It was a holy moment for both of us, but especially Dad. I felt God was working in his life in a way I couldn't understand, in a way that would not have happened anywhere other than the American Military Cemetery in Normandy, France.

We drove home and Dad dropped me off at the cottage before heading to the airport for his overnight flight back to Seattle. As we arrived at the cottage, Céline ran out of the house.

"Lexi!" She gave me a big hug and then saw my dad. *"Bonjour,"* she said.

"Anglais," I told her, indicating she should speak to my dad in English.

"Very pleased to meet you," she said in sweetly accented English. "Papa and I missed you at church today," she said to me. I saw Philippe out of the corner of my eye, heading toward us.

My stomach felt suddenly unsettled as he arrived. He smiled warmly at us, and I saw that his genuine kindness emanated even toward my dad.

"Dad, this is Philippe. He works at one of the bakeries. He's Luc's cousin."

"Pleased to meet you, sir," Philippe said.

"You too," Dad said. "So you're a baker?"

"He's the best baker. And the owner," Céline bragged. I smiled at her, remembering how I'd bragged on my daddy's rank when I was a little girl.

I saw my father's eyebrow raise. Philippe as the owner was much more interesting to him than Philippe as a simple baker. Dad cleared his throat. His bald patch turned red, and I realized he might have understood there was more to my relationship with Philippe than simply employer and employee. But Dad's manners were, as always, intact. "Thank you for giving my Lexi a job here."

"It's our pleasure," Philippe said. "Alexandra is a wonderful baker and her cheerfulness is a pleasant addition to any of our bakeries. We hope she'll be with us for a long time."

My dad nodded thoughtfully, not answering. I rushed in with some small talk, and then Céline and Philippe went back to the big house.

"Are you happy, Lexi?" Dad asked as he put his travel case in the passenger side of the car.

"I am, Dad," I said. "I don't know what lies ahead, but I know I'm very glad to be here. I'm starting to belong."

Dad smiled and looked at Céline as she entered the door to Maman's. "Is that who I brought the gift for?"

I nodded.

"She seems like a nice little girl. Like you were." He kissed my cheek and hugged me and then got into his car. As he started the engine, he rolled down his window. "Oh, one more thing," he said.

"Yes?" I said, fighting homesickness at his departure, something I'd successful pushed away with the business of the past few days.

"I'm not sure I'm ready for a grandson named Napoléon."

He grinned and I laughed. Then I watched his car drive away until I could see it no longer.

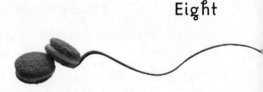

Eight

Nothing would be more tiresome
than eating and drinking
if God had not made them a pleasure
as well as a necessity.

Voltaire

T he next week I worked in Rambouillet, my homesickness seep-
ing away as the days went by. Because I worked afternoons and
Philippe was in early baking bread, our paths didn't cross until
Wednesday.

I put my apron on and went to the back.

Patricia caught my arm. "Maman passed this along to me," she
said. It was the envelope Monsieur Desfreres had given me the week
before.

"What is it?" I asked. She gave it to me to open.

L'École du Pâtisserie

cordially invites you to the Grand Exhibition, to be held 20 and 21 December at 7:00 pm. Alexandra Stuart will exhibit on 20 December. A light champagne buffet will be held afterward.

·*Chef Robert Desfreres*
·*Chef Denis St. John*
·*Chef Michel Aubussey*

I looked at Patricia. "Will you come?"

"Mais oui!" she said. "We will *all* come. My papa, Céline and Philippe, Maman, Kamil. I think Luc and Marianne will be back for Christmas, and they will come too. After all, the company sponsored you." She pulled me aside. "There are forty people in your class. The top ten will graduate with honors. My papa requires people to graduate with honors to continue at the Boulangeries Delacroix."

"Oh," I said. This was the first I'd heard of his expectations, though I knew from comments he was a tough cookie.

I laughed to myself at the incongruity of the cliché, and saw Patricia looking at me curiously. "It's nothing," I said, missing my own father even more.

She let go of my arm and headed back toward the bakery. "We have flan to make this afternoon, as soon as you're done with the dishes. And someone has to make brioche."

"I can do that too," I offered.

"Non, merci," Patricia answered.

I said nothing, but sensed something was wrong. I thought maybe she was covering for me, wanting me to succeed almost as much as I did.

I spied Céline playing with her dolls in Philippe's office. She hadn't been here other afternoons that week, probably because her dad had been working mornings.

"Hey, I have something for you," I said. I opened my purse and pulled out a small box.

"What is it?" she asked, setting her dolls aside.

"Open it and see!" I said.

A smile covered her whole face and her dimples deepened. She fumbled with the wrapping and took out a small pink satin box with a tiny Tinker Bell fairy embroidered on the lid.

"A fairy!" she breathed out.

"For your teeth," I said. I showed her how the box opened, like a hinged jewelry box. "When your teeth fall out, you put them in here, and then put the box by your bedside. During the night, when you're asleep, the tooth fairy will come and leave a treat or a euro or something in there."

"Where did this come from? California?" She could barely contain her excitement.

"Yes," I said. "California by way of Washington." *Disney was in California, wasn't it?*

"Oooh," she said gleefully. "I'm going to show everyone. I'm going to—going to keep a *fève* in here until I have a tooth. Just so they can see how it works."

"A *fève*?" I asked. *Fève* meant bean.

Céline looked at me, wide-eyed. "You don't know what a *fève* is?"

I shook my head.

She reached up to the shelf near Philippe's desk and took down a tiny porcelain figure. "These are *fève*. They're little dolls you bake into the cake for *l'Epiphanie*. Whoever gets the piece with the *fève* in it is the king or queen for a day." She looked at me with disgust. "I never get the *fève*. Maman always makes sure Dominique gets it even though she's not a kid."

She jumped off her chair and went to show Patricia the tooth fairy box.

I went back to the kitchen and washed some dirty bowls, wanting to get that over with so I could get to the flan. While I washed, I thought about flan and custards, crème brûlée in particular. What if I added lemon zest to it? And then…what could I brown over the top instead of sugar?

"Lexi!" Philippe's voice got my attention, and I shut off the water.

"I'm sorry!" I said. "I was thinking about crème brûlée!"

Philippe laughed. "A true pastry chef. However, I need you to come to the bread room while I make the brioche. I want to show you a few things."

I dried my hands. "Was there a problem with mine?"

He nodded. "Yes, but I think I can help you solve it."

We walked into the bread room, and I got down all of the ingredients and measured them. Philippe watched and offered tips along the way. I noticed he had a shadow of whiskers, which I found attractive in a rugged sort of way. He also had a shadow under his eyes. Normally, he'd be getting ready to leave and pick up Céline at this point. But he'd stayed to show me what to do.

We kneaded the dough, and then he reached into the big bowl where my hands were and took out some of the dough. Our hands touched, and he didn't move away. Nor did I, for a moment.

When I pulled my hand away, I looked up at his eyes. They were as kind as ever, but a little more knowing. He'd felt something too.

"I don't think you kneaded in the butter completely last time," he said. He showed me his technique, and then we slapped the dough, put it in another bowl, and set it in the walk-in.

"Thank you," I said. "Breads aren't my specialty."

"Not yet," Philippe answered encouragingly. He hesitated for a minute. "Thank you for the tooth box for Céline."

"Not at all," I said. "I'm glad she liked it, and it was easy to do. My father brought it last week when he came."

Philippe nodded. "Céline says you do not own any *fèves*."

I shook my head. "Nope, never heard of them."

"This will not do at all," Patricia said as she came into the kitchen. "You should take her with you next time you go to the flea market to buy some. Aren't you going on Saturday?"

Philippe laughed. "Would you like to go to the flea market?" he asked me.

"I haven't checked to see if I'm working Saturday," I admitted. School had been overwhelmingly busy that week.

"*Voilà*! You have the day off," Patricia said. "I just looked. Have a good time!" And with that, she bustled out of the kitchen.

I went back to the kitchen to start the flan, feeling excited about my outing but also slightly...managed. I wondered how Philippe felt. Would he have invited me of his own volition?

After the flans, I made the cookies for the dinner rush and put them in the oven. Then I thought about the crème brûlée again. What would go on top?

Still thinking about it, I absent-mindedly reached into the huge oven and pulled out the cookies. I bumped my arm against the side of the oven, and searing heat scorched my flesh. I smelled it before I felt it. Then I felt it.

"Ouch!" I cried out in English. Not again! I had burned my other arm the very same way in Seattle. I set the pan down and looked at my arm.

One of the bakers ran back to me. "Everything all right?" he asked.

"Burn," I said, indicating my arm.

"There's ointment in Philippe's office," he told me. Then he flexed both of his biceps my direction so I could see the burn scars all over them. "Baker's tattoos," he said.

"Yes," I grinned. "I've heard that. I'm gathering a nice collection on my own."

When I went to Philippe's office, Céline was already there, doing her homework. Philippe was just leaving.

"I've burned myself," I said. "Do you have ointment?"

"*Mais oui,*" he said, pulling some out of the drawer.

I sat in the chair across from the desk.

"Is that it?" Céline asked, pointing at the old mark on my other arm.

"No, that's a scar from another burn," I said. "Different arm, different oven, same mistake." I laughed and held out my other arm. "Here is my battle wound."

Philippe gently applied the ointment to the burn. It felt wonderful, caring and gentle. "If you rub this in, you won't scar as badly," he said.

I remembered something I'd recently read. "You know what the difference is between a wound and a scar?" I asked no one in particular.

"What?" Philippe answered, capping the ointment and getting out some gauze and a bandage.

"A wound is still tender, still hurts, is not recovered. A scar is a wound that has healed. I read that in a Bible study."

Philippe stopped what he was doing and looked at me for a long minute, then turned away, saying nothing.

Why did I bring that up? They're going to think I'm an idiot.

I turned to Céline, desperate to cover my *faux pas.* "Here's something for your studies. In French, the word *blessure* means 'to wound' or 'a wound,' like mine right here!" I pointed at my burn. "But in English, the word bless means the same as the French *benir.*"

"How can something that hurts also bless!" She laughed. "Bless is to do something good, like God does."

"It's funny how such different words can sound the same in French and English," I said.

"Yes," Philippe said, standing at the door, ready to get back to the baking floor. "I think they are called *faux amis,* correct? False friends?"

I looked at the evil grin on his face and knew he'd heard about my *préservatif* mistake. Simone? No, she would be too embarrassed to tell. Patricia?

I said nothing but blushed furiously.

"See you Saturday," Philippe said, still grinning, as he headed back to work.

Tanya called me early Saturday morning, as I was getting ready for the *marché aux puces,* the flea market.

"Hey, what are you up to?" I asked. "It's like, midnight at your house, isn't it?"

"Yeah," she said. "I just got back from a date, and we haven't talked in weeks. You're up, right?"

"Oh, yeah," I said. "I'm getting ready to go out. Where were you?"

"Birthday party," she said, "for one of our friends at church."

"That 'our' sounds awfully possessive and chummy," I teased. "What kind of cake was there?"

"Oh, Lexi. You would ask about the cake! I think it was from Safeway."

"Safeway? Please tell me you didn't bring it." A birthday cake from Safeway!

"If it makes you feel better," she said, "I didn't bring it. But I'm not saying I would never buy a cake from Safeway."

"Ooh la la," I said. "This is why I am here. So, tell me about the possessive and chummy deal." I looked through my armoire for something cute and warm to wear. I hadn't put this much effort into an outfit since...well, since I didn't go to Luc's wedding.

"It's getting serious," she admitted. "We've started to talk about the what ifs..."

"What if...you get married?" I stopped looking through my clothes and sat on my bed.

"Yeah," Tanya admitted. "We were also kind of looking at little houses by Fremont."

"Wow, this is going fast," I said. "Nothing definite yet?"

"No. I'll let you know. First, of course!"

"I know you will," I said swallowing down the bitterness of jealousy along with the sweetness of excitement for her. Tanya had a great job. Tanya was going to get married. Tanya was looking at houses.

"What are you doing today?" she asked.

"Going to a flea market."

"Alone? With Anne?"

"With Céline and Philippe," I said.

"Wow, you're doing quite a few things with them," she said. "I know you like the daughter. Do you like the dad?"

I thought about it for a minute. "Yes. I suppose I do."

"I don't hear great gushes of emotion," Tanya said.

"Maybe I've grown up a little," I answered, thinking aloud but not sure I'd put my finger on it, exactly.

"French bread?" Tanya offered helpfully. The year before, I'd been attracted to Luc before I knew he was engaged to be married.

I'd told my friend I'd always been looking for the exciting guy, the cake. But that now, maybe I was ready for something long term— bread. French bread, she'd teased, knowing I was going to France.

I wasn't exactly sure how I felt, or how the French Bread coming to pick me up in an hour felt.

"I'm having a good time," I said softly. "Maybe that's enough for today?"

"You're right, Lex," Tanya said. "You're changing. I miss seeing that change in you. Maybe we'll come to France for our honeymoon!" she teased.

"Oh yeah." I laughed. "Just what every guy wants. His wife's best friend along for the honeymoon!"

She laughed and we talked a while longer before hanging up. When Céline and Philippe arrived an hour later, I was ready for them—woven shopping basket and all. We set out in his little car, and he carefully drove down the road.

"Luc said all Frenchmen were crazy drivers," I said, trying to make pleasant conversation. "You certainly are an exception to that rule!"

There was a silence from both front and backseat. Finally, Philippe answered.

"My wife and my mother were killed in the same auto accident some years back. So, *naturellement,* I am more careful than some."

Great, Lexi! Way to start off the outing. "I'm sorry," I said.

"Not at all." Philippe looked at me and smiled. "You didn't know."

I said nothing, but I wondered about his first wife and why no one talked about her.

We drove out of the village and onto the autoway to Paris. I looked at the leaves changing from green to gold to cabernet outside my window. The day was gray but not wet, cool but not cold. I was glad I'd brought my sweater. Philippe had on a pair of jeans and a jean jacket and looked rather suave. He wore a watch with a black band.

"Brioche come out all right?" I asked, wondering about the dough we'd made some days past.

"Yes," he said. "Just fine."

But no one had asked me to bake bread since then. Perhaps the bread crew was fine. Then again, Patricia did fine with the pastries, and I always worked on those.

We parked at the flea market and Céline said, "See why we like it so much?"

I looked around and laughed with her, holding her hand. "Yes, indeed. It's like a treasure hunt." The market stretched for several city blocks before us. Haphazard booths squatted cheek to jowl with upscale tables, some tented to keep off the mist, some open to catch any ray of light to sparkle their wares. Women sat on low stools, gossiping, while their husbands wheedled.

"A treasure hunt, Papa," Céline said. Philippe took her other hand and she walked between us.

Philippe explained that flea markets—like everything else of import, he teased—started in France. The nobility sold their castoff clothing, some filthy and containing fleas, to tinkers and other traders who then resold them in the streets of Paris—a market of fleas. In the hundreds of years since, several flea markets had developed around Paris, selling all sorts of secondhand goods.

A swirl of chatter and bargaining surrounded us, punctuated by a laugh here and there or a call to old friends and new customers. We moved from booth to booth.

"Look here!" Céline said, and she and I picked through a table of old perfume bottles—rose cut glass, light blue crystal, hand-blown opal and amber. Some still had the little hand-held poufer, which, when squeezed, emitted a faint breath of floral air. I puffed one on Céline and then bought one for my Nonna at home.

We dug through a table of old military medals. "Fakes, I'm sure," Philippe said, but I picked one up for my dad, anyway. It was engraved with the words, "Napoléon, Emperor, King," and would make a funny gift.

Céline's eyes lit when she saw the next table. *"Les fèves!"* she said.

We walked over to the booth crammed with baking and cooking paraphernalia. I browsed through some old cookbooks and magazines, then looked at some tin Madeleine pans.

"Good quality," Philippe agreed as I tucked one under my arm to pay for later. At the table in the back were hundreds, maybe thousands, of hand-painted figurines. Some had professions on them—baker, fishmonger, cheesemonger, journalist. Many were in the figure of the Baby Jesus, Joseph, and Mary.

"Madame sees some she likes?" the proprietor asked me.

"Mademoiselle," I corrected gently. He looked at Céline and Philippe and shrugged.

"Mademoiselle," he said. "I have the best *fèves* in the market. Each and every one is hand-painted, and all have been lovingly baked into the best *galette des rois* in France."

I examined several and started setting some aside, appreciating them more now. After Céline had mentioned them, I'd done some research. The cakes, galette des rois, or kings' cakes, were baked on January 6, which is Epiphany. To celebrate the wise men coming to worship Jesus, French families baked the kings' cake with a bean inside it. Whoever got the bean in his or her piece would be the king or queen for a day, and have all their wishes granted. Later, porcelain figures replaced the beans, although they were still called *fèves*.

Philippe stood next to me, sorting through the pile for the best formed and painted ones.

"Is it strange to you that so many French customs and holidays revolve around Christianity, and yet so few French people have any desire for Christ Himself?" I asked.

He set a few *fèves* aside before answering. "In France, religion is very private. It is personal. People have their lives, their vacations, their food and wine."

"No need for religion," I said.

"Religion is okay," he corrected me. "As long as it stays a…condiment. Not a main course."

I nodded.

"When Andrea died," he said, "I realized I could fill myself with good things—with baking, with my career, with Céline, with anything I wanted—but the only thing that took away my pain was my faith. Until she died, I didn't realize that."

I smiled, thinking of my lonely weekend in Paris and the lesson I'd learned. "Until you were hungry, you had not developed the need."

"Oui," Philippe agreed. *"Exactement."* He handed me a tiny porcelain figure. "This, mademoiselle, is for you."

The figurine was a woman in a white apron holding up a beautiful cake. The title at the bottom was *pâtissière,* a cake maker.

I bought handfuls of *fèves,* taken with them. I didn't know why I wanted so many, but they were cheap and would make good gifts. They were just for bakers, and I was a baker.

We stopped at one last booth that sold marble cheese platters, as Philippe said he needed a new one. To the side hung a sign.

BACHELOR'S FARE
BREAD AND CHEESE
AND KISSES

"What is a bachelor?" Céline asked me.

I looked at the sign that had caught her attention.

"A man who is not married," I answered.

"Is my papa a bachelor, then? Even though he used to be married?"

I nodded. *"Oui."*

"Oh," she said.

Afterward, the three of us went to a café and had a drink. "Table for three?" the waiter asked, and Philippe nodded.

Céline ordered a *menthe à l'eau,* water with mint syrup. Philippe and I each had a glass of Burgundy, as the new wines had just been released. We nibbled on bread and a variety of cheeses.

We drove home together in companionable chatter. Céline stayed in the car as Philippe walked me to my door.

"Thanks for today," I said.

"Thank you," he replied. "I have not enjoyed the flea market like that in quite some time." He smiled and it lit up his face. I noticed the five o' clock shadow again along his jaw line.

"I'll see you at church tomorrow?"

"No." He shook his head. "I'll be working. I took today off instead."

Patricia had said he never missed church. Except this week. He'd taken a rare day off to be with me. Out of obligation? In the greater interests of warmer Franco-American relations?

When I looked up and caught his little smile, I knew it was something more. Maybe only a *bit* more, but more.

Instead of shaking my hand, he leaned in to me, near enough that I could smell his aftershave. He kissed each of my cheeks, French style, rough cheeks brushing against my smooth ones.

"Bread and cheese and kisses," he said, and left.

The next morning I went to church. I walked slowly from the train station to the church, half a mile. I had time, since the train schedules were a bit inconvenient on Sunday. Anne was going to meet me at a café in Versailles afterward, and we were going to shop for a while.

"Hello!" The vicar's lovely wife greeted me when I reached the church. "We've missed you."

"Even though I've just started coming, I missed being here," I said, honestly. "I had to work, and then my father visited from the US."

"Lovely," she said, handing me a bulletin for the day. "I'm glad you're back."

I walked toward the front, and recognized Gabby. "Hello," I said politely.

"Hello," she responded coolly. She looked behind me—checking for Philippe, I assumed—and saw no one. She allowed herself a small smile in my direction at that point.

As for me, I'd spotted the ever-rocking Buki. I slid into the pew beside her, and she greeted me with a hug and a grin.

The praise and worship service began, and I closed my eyes and let myself get into the song. I let both my hands rise in praise and drifted away in the Spirit toward the Lord. Somehow, here, in the midst of strangers, I was best able to be myself in worship.

I missed being here. I longed for worship with others. I yearned to hear someone talk about God, a closed subject in this very open land.

After the worship we greeted one another, some with hand-shakes, Buki with a hug.

"Staying for coffee?" the pastor asked as I prepared to leave.

"No, I'm meeting a friend in town," I said.

"Ah." He nodded. "Been reading Jean?"

I smiled. "Yes. In fact, I've read the entire book since I was last here!" As soon as the words left my mouth, I felt foolish, like I hoped he'd put a gold star on my bulletin or something.

"A quick, cursory read is a great way to start a study," he said. "What part will you focus your in-depth study on?"

Quick, cursory read? In-depth study? "John 15," I blurted without thinking. That was the chapter I'd read with my dad last weekend.

"Great chapter," he said. "See you next week?"

"See you next week," I affirmed, and then made my way out the door before Gabby could grab my arm and ask about Philippe.

I walked down the road, the October air slipping through my thick, cabled sweater. I'd need to start wearing my coat soon. I knew Versailles was a great shopping town, and I had a secret purchase in mind today. A parasol! Nothing too frou-frou. I could get an umbrella anywhere, but I wanted one that looked very French and perhaps just a little Marie Antoinette—in her town, of course.

It still awed me to walk casually down the streets of Versailles. The bakers for Marie Antoinette may have lived very close. Rose Bertin, her dressmaker, had driven her carriage of trunks of extravagant fabrics through these very lanes. The *château* in the distance dominated the town now as it did then. Louis the XIV's conquests may have retreated in shame or vainglory down the road I trod upon.

I came to the corner of the café and spied Anne, who waved at me. I smiled and waved back. *Thank you for this friend, Lord,* I said in my heart.

I had the distinct impression He wanted her as a friend too. The thought stopped me in my tracks for a moment. *I no longer call you servants, because a servant does not know his master's business. Instead, I have called you friends.* John 15. Yes, I would read that again in-depth.

We sat inside the café, drizzle starting to fall from the sky just as we arrived.

Anne popped shut an umbrella. "How was your morning?"

We passed the menu board, and I glanced at it, trying to choose one of the specials for lunch. Onion soupe sounded great. I'd made some from a recipe from *Gourmet* magazine at home last week, but I never grew tired of it.

French Onion Soup

Ingredients:

3 lbs onions, sliced into thin rings
2 bay leaves
1 tsp dried thyme
¾ tsp salt
½ stick (¼ cup) unsalted butter, cut in half
¼ cup all-purpose flour
¼ cup dry white wine
6 cups beef stock
½ day-old baguette
3 tsp butter
Onion salt or powder
1 cup grated Gruyère cheese

Directions:

Cook onions, bay leaves, thyme, salt, and half the butter in a large, heavy pot over moderate heat, uncovered, stirring frequently until onions are very soft and deep golden brown, about 45 minutes. It's okay if the bottom of the pan browns, as long as it doesn't burn. The brown "stuff" on the bottom of the pan is the fond, and having lots of it will make your soup taste richer. If it seems as though it may start to burn, turn down the heat.

Once the onions are browned and you have lots of fond, add flour and cook for 1 minute, stirring constantly. Add wine and cook 2 minutes, stirring constantly. Add stock and simmer, uncovered and stirring occasionally, for 30 minutes.

While soup simmers, put oven rack in middle position and preheat oven to 350°F.

Cut the baguette into large cubes and toss with the remaining butter and onion salt to taste. Arrange bread in a single layer on a large baking sheet and toast, turning once, until golden brown, about 15 minutes. They'll be like large, slightly soft croutons. Remove from oven.

Preheat broiler. Put 4 ovenproof soup crocks on a cookie sheet.

Discard bay leaves from soup and divide soup among crocks, then top each crock with croutons. Sprinkle Gruyère to cover tops of crocks. Broil 4–5 inches from heat until cheese is melted and bubbly, 1–2 minutes.

Anne ordered some soup too, and we chatted about the past week in school and started brainstorming about our projects.

The waiter arrived with the soup. *"Bon appétit!"* he said as we hungrily dug in.

"What did you do yesterday?" I asked.

"Read," she said. "Baked bread."

"Baked bread! On your day off?"

"Yeah," she grinned. "Keeping in practice."

"You're so good," I said, putting another spoonful of soup into my mouth. No wonder Maman couldn't stop singing her praises. I hadn't passed that on to Anne, though.

"What did you do?" she asked.

"Went to the flea market," I said. "Then I went to church this morning." I decided to ask again, though I didn't expect her to give up her sleep. "Sure you don't want to come with me someday? It'd be good for your career to speak English with more than one person!"

"Hmm…" she said. "I suppose so. It's kind of…quiet around my apartment. And I do need a job. I'll do almost anything to help my chances." She sat silently for a moment.

Almost anything? I wondered, doubt blooming in my mind.

"Maybe I will come with you," she said. "Why not?"

Nine

There are three possible parts to a date, of which at
least two must be offered: entertainment, food, and
affection. It is customary to begin a series of dates with
a great deal of entertainment, a moderate amount
of food, and the merest suggestion of affection. As
the amount of affection increases, the entertainment
can be reduced proportionately. When the affection
IS the entertainment, we no longer call it dating.
Under no circumstances can the food be omitted.
Miss Manners' Guide to Excruciatingly Correct Behavior

The next week we worked on breakfast pastries in class. If I had
to do bread, I'd want to do these. First we did filled croissants.
They're a staple, so it's important to get them right.

Jean-Yves, one of the French guys at our table, partnered up with
me that week, scooting Anne aside. I'd noticed he'd been avoiding

Désirée for the past week or two, and she'd been chasing him again that morning.

"Go ahead," Anne said. "It'll be good for us to work with new people." It was almost the end of October, halfway through our program. I agreed with her. She offered to work with another man at a nearby table, but he looked down his nose at her and declined. He found another guy to work with, and Anne worked with Désirée.

Jean-Yves and I rolled out our croissants on long tables. After cutting the dough into triangles, we stuffed some with chocolate nibs, some with tender almond paste, and the rest with pistachio paste—my idea, like I'd done at home last year.

We rolled them up, took them to the oven, and as soon as they were cool, ate one.

"Look!" Jean-Yves opened a jar of strawberry jam and a pot of *crème fraîche* and set them aside. We daubed it on the hot croissants. "My maman used to serve them like this."

"Delicious!" I said in English, and he laughed.

"Délicieux!" he agreed in French. I sat next to him that day at lunch, and he shared stories of growing up on a farm in Bresse, and how their chickens were the best.

Désirée joined us for the croissant desserts. "I'd like to try one of the strawberry croissants," she said, looking around the buffet, "but none were left. Perhaps you'd make one for me?"

"Perhaps," Jean-Yves said pleasantly. Then he turned to ask me questions about the US, and if everyone was really like the people on CNN or MTV.

"Do I look like I'm from CNN or MTV?" I asked.

"Non." He smiled flirtatiously. "You are much, much prettier."

Ooh la la, he reminded me of Luc and of the flirtatious French men who dropped their sunglasses and looked appreciatively and appraisingly at every woman on the block.

Désirée left the table in a snit.

Tuesday we made *kugelhopf.*

"Why are we making German pastries?" I asked as we whipped up the dough.

"European Union," Jean-Yves said as he helped me measure out my ingredients. "Look at Monsieur Desfreres. He looks like he needs smelling salts."

I laughed out loud. I gathered this was a part of the homogenization that got under his skin. Still, since I'd heard about his wife leaving him, I felt a little softer toward him.

Wednesday we made Danish pastries, but French style, with lots of butter and panache. The cooking school was working on breakfast dishes too, so each day at lunch we really ate "brunch." Désirée didn't try to sit with Jean-Yves, Anne, and I that day.

Anne and Jean-Yves each tried one of the Danish I'd made, with poached apricots, amaretto, and toasted almond slices.

"Not bad," Jean-Yves teased. "If I woke up next to you, I'd be glad to eat one of these in the morning."

"In your dreams," I said, but I knew he was teasing. He'd said something similar to Anne a few days ago, and I knew he had a serious girlfriend in Bresse. They planned to live together when he moved back.

So many people lived together, so few got married. Not me.

What would have happened if I'd slept with Greg, my ex-boyfriend. He had wanted me to. And, to be honest, I'd wanted to. I could understand Jean-Yves and his girlfriend's desires. But now Greg was on his third girlfriend since our breakup.

Nah. I'd wait.

Wednesday, after school I went to the bakery in the village. I'd been there all week because Maman had thrown her back out. Patricia came once in a while to do the pastries, but they let me do the cakes, petits fours, and mille-feuille. I was in heaven!

I headed toward the kitchen, excited to start baking. As far as I knew, the customers hadn't noticed any difference. I would have been sure to hear about it otherwise. Odette would have let me know.

Monsieur Delacroix stood in the doorway between the shop front and the kitchen.

"*Bonjour,* Monsieur Delacroix," I said as I passed.

"*Bonjour,* Mademoiselle Stuart," he said, retaining less of his original formality but still with a modicum of professional pleasantry.

He turned toward the hooks that held the aprons and chef jackets. He searched through a few, looking at the embroidered names. "*Je regrette,* I am unable to find yours. I was going to hand it to you," he said.

I blushed and reached for the apron on the far peg. "This is it."

He looked confused.

"No name on it," I reminded him gently. I was the only temporary employee, and he didn't spend a lot of time in the bakery proper.

"I hear you spent the day with my granddaughter searching for *fèves.*"

"Oh yes!" I said, face lighting up with delight. "She taught me all about them."

He cracked an actual smile at that. *"Naturellement,"* he said. "She's a Delacroix!" As his face softened, I could see Philippe in him. It endeared him to me in a fatherlike way.

Odette came into the back with a cup of coffee. *"Café,* monsieur?"

"Non, merci. We do not have the machine for *express,* here, which I prefer. But thank you."

"Of course," Odette said cloyingly.

Ick. I turned to go back to my work.

"Mademoiselle Stuart," Monsieur Delacroix called.

"Oui, Monsieur?"

"I have received the invitation to your exhibition in two months. I always invite the entire staff to professional exhibitions. We are all looking forward to seeing the culmination of your studies."

"Thank you, sir," I said.

"Can't wait," Odette said quietly as she left.

A few minutes later, she came back, this time urgently.

"Monsieur?" she said, seeking out Monsieur Delacroix. "It's the telephone for you. It's Luc."

Luc? I checked my watch. It was two o'clock in the afternoon here, five o'clock in the morning in Seattle. The start of his baking day.

Monsieur Delacroix's face hardened as he took the phone. "Not again," he grumbled to himself. "Another *problème?*"

Thursday morning I arrived at school extra early. Chef Desfreres had told us the school had a special order for four thousand macaron cookies for an industrial client—Airbus, I think. French industries often placed large orders with the school—the price was cheaper, and they got a government write-off for supporting other institutions.

French macarons are not like American macaroons. American macaroons are made of coconut held together by egg white and sugar—tasty but sweet, and honestly, a little unsophisticated.

French macarons, on the other hand, are two light cookies, airy almost, with a thin, smooth shell that crumbles at the slightest touch. The inside of the cookie is chewy and sticky, and the bottom, called the foot, is firm. Between the two cookies is sandwiched a flavored buttercream. French chefs, in their individual *laboratoires,* or pastry kitchens, compete to come up with novel-flavored macarons.

Today, each student was to prepare one hundred perfect macarons in traditional flavors—vanilla, chocolate, coffee, and raspberry—and box them up for Monsieur Desfreres.

Because we couldn't all be at the oven at the same time, we worked in shifts. As soon as my macarons were done, I carefully made my way back to the table where my butter cream pots waited. I worked next to Anne that day, but Jean-Yves called me over.

"Come see what I've made!" he said. Anne and I walked over to the oven where he was taking out a batch.

"I've snuck in some ingredients," he said. "My hundred are done, and I wanted to try something new."

We tried his jet black anise, or licorice, flavored macarons. *"Fantastique!"* Anne said.

I tried one with rose water. "Different! Artistic!" Like so many other French artists, he'd started with the traditional and spun off into strange but wonderful directions.

It made me think about what kinds of macarons I could come up with.

When I got back to my station, though, I had a nasty surprise. Nearly half of my cookies were crumbled into bits and pieces. I looked at the clock. I didn't have enough time to mix and bake four dozen more. I had made ten extra as a margin for error. That still left me needing about thirty.

"What happened?" Anne asked.

"I don't know. When we came back, and this was what I found."

I would definitely be marked down if I didn't turn in one hundred macarons in the box marked number seven to Monsieur Desfreres.

"I have twelve extra," Anne said.

"Thank you," I said gratefully.

Désirée walked up. "What's going on?" she asked.

Anne and I looked at each other. The fact that we both thought the same thing without saying anything lent credence to our suspicions. "Some of my cookies were damaged," I said.

"Don't worry, they are tricky to handle. But…so many?" Désirée said. "I could give you some extra, if you like."

This was no time for pride. I swallowed hard. "Thank you."

She brought four over. I noticed she'd already bagged up some other extras—to take home, I presumed.

Jean-Yves came over and she drew near to him. "Lexi's have crumbled," she announced.

Jean-Yves flicked her off like a fly. "Here, I'll help."

He brought over a dozen extra, slipping in some of the rose ones, which looked like the raspberry. Unless Monsieur Desfreres tasted them, he'd never know.

Juju barely had enough on her own, but another man from the next table over gave me enough to round up to a hundred. I turned in Box 7 and received a neat smile from Monsieur Desfreres.

Afterward, I had time to come up with a few clever flavor concoctions of my own. I made a batch of macarons from ground peanuts and sandwiched chocolate ganache between them. Then I made some chocolate cookies and whipped a little fluff for the filling. I presented them to Anne and Jean-Yves at lunch.

"*Très Americaine,*" Anne said, helping herself to a second.

"*Très délicieux,*" Jean-Yves agreed. "What would you call these?"

I grinned. "Nutter Butters and Oreos. Gone uptown."

Monsieur Desfreres stopped by our table to talk with Jean-Yves, and looked at the macarons. "May I?" he asked.

I nodded. I could tell the others held their breath. He chose a chocolate and fluff one, for which I was glad, knowing peanut butter was not a French taste.

"Bon," he said, wiping crumbs from his mouth. He said nothing more but took a second as he left. Jean-Yves and Anne grinned with me. No one spoke. No one needed to. Victory!

Jean-Yves went to make a phone call, and Anne and I talked over the earlier situation regarding my destroyed macarons.

"So, is it Désirée who's been sabotaging us?" I asked. "She seemed so nice. And in the movies, you know, it's never the person you think it is."

"Life is not like a movie, my American friend," Anne said. "It's more like math. One plus one equals two."

I nodded. She was right.

"Plus, she was mad because Jean-Yves is paying attention to you this week."

"He's got a girlfriend!" I protested.

"It doesn't matter. Some people can't have attention on anyone but themselves. From now on, we'll be more diligent about watching the other's work. You have met your first living *faux amie*. There's no telling what else she may try."

Sunday morning I met Anne at the train station. She looked nervous.

"Have you ever been to church?" I asked her.

"When I was baptized as a baby. But my family does not go by religion too much," she admitted. "And I've never been to a church that spoke only English."

"Good!" I said switching to English. "You've reminded me of our purpose. Use English, please, mademoiselle!"

We walked in the cool air toward the church. I'd worn gloves for the first time. The air was crisp and fresh as an apple, sweet as pie. After a few blocks I pushed open the large wooden gates to the churchyard and ushered Anne inside.

We walked through the gardens, nearly dormant already, a few branches dangling here or there, waiting to be trimmed for the winter. I entered the church first and held the door open for my friend.

"Good morning, Lexi!" the vicar's wife said. "And your friend is…?"

"Anne," I said.

"Good morning," Anne said in English.

The pastor's wife smiled at me before answering my friend. "Good morning. I'm glad you could join us. You are visiting France?"

"No," Anne admitted. "I'm a Frenchwoman. I'm here with Lexi."

"To enjoy the service—and practice her English," I said, putting more emphasis on the latter.

"Oh!" A woman handing out bulletins on the other side of the door understood my intention. "We have a wonderful English conversation club. I'll find a flier for you."

"Thank you," Anne said.

We walked down the aisle looking for a seat. I saw Philippe already seated, with Gabby next to him. I bit back a grin.

"How good of you to join us again," Gabby said. "We'll miss you when you go back to the United States!"

I saw Philippe hide a smile too. I introduced Anne to them

both, and then we made our way down a few more rows toward the pew where the faithful Buki usually sat.

A few minutes later, the woman who had greeted us earlier brought a brochure for Anne. "I hope to see you there—I am one of the coordinators!" she said. "I will look for you."

As she turned away, she winked at me. I knew she'd be praying for Anne.

The service went great, especially the worship, and I enjoyed learning more about John. I leaned over during the sermon.

"Are you following this?" I asked Anne.

"Mostly!" she said. She looked triumphant. I knew being proficient in English would help her find a job in the EU if she couldn't get one in France. I wanted her to get a job as much as I wanted to get a job myself.

Almost.

The vicar began the Communion service, but I didn't go forward. It would be awkward to leave Anne alone. I knew she wasn't comfortable going forward, and she shouldn't, not being a Christian.

I looked at the quiet line of people waiting for the elements, the memory of the body and the blood of Christ. Sustenance for the long week that lay ahead for most of us.

For the first time, I yearned for Communion and was denied.

I think I understood the meaning of "communion" for the first time. In French, the word had a feeling of intimate communication, sharing thoughts and emotions. I supposed it did in English too, but the word had become so everyday to me that I'd forgotten the depth of its meaning.

Alone here, in many ways, I realized how much I yearned for intimate communication, for sharing my thoughts and emotions. Looking at the elements of sacrifice in front of me, I understood the sacrifice He made in order to achieve that intimate communication.

I bowed my head and prayed instead.

After the service, Buki talked Anne's ear off, her silver hoops wiggling in her dark brown earlobes as her enthusiasm level rose. Anne's face lit up. I knew she had been lonely too.

Gabby was on call to serve coffee, and I saw her reluctantly leave Philippe's side. He made his way forward to me.

"How was school?" he asked. "You've been at the village, I hear. Pastry chef for the week."

"Yes." I grinned. "Not that I wish ill health on Maman, but it was nice to be in charge of my own *laboratoire*."

"Oh yes, like all women, you want to be in charge," he teased.

"We did macarons at the school," I continued. "I ate the most fantastic kinds. Rose. Anise."

It was fun to talk with him in English, something we never did at work. Somehow, being able to converse in two languages bonded us in a way I didn't feel with anyone else. Not even Anne, perhaps because her English wasn't as fluent or nuanced.

"Have you been to Ladurée?" Philippe asked, naming a famous *pâtisserie* in Paris. "Or Gérard Mulot?"

I shook my head.

"Ah, then, I would be remiss as a member of the House of Delacroix if I did not show them to you. Perhaps one day this week, we may go? I'll pick you up at school, and we can go from there. I will put it on the work calendar. How do you Americans say? A field trip!"

I don't know why, but I asked, "Will Céline be coming?"

He shook his head. "*Non.* I will leave her with Patricia."

A corner of some kind was being turned, and I knew it.

"*Bon,*" I said. I did want to see the *pâtisseries,* and it was only one…date. "I would love to go," I finished in English.

He laughed, "Good! I will call and let you know what day I can arrange for us to play hooky."

I laughed too. "All right. Now you're taking this English slang thing too far."

Anne and Buki came alongside us. "Coffee?" Buki asked, pointing upstairs. We headed that direction. Philippe gathered Céline from her classroom, and she joined us as well.

She sat next to Anne. "You are a baker too?" She sighed dramatically. "Can't I ever get away from bakers?"

We burst out laughing. Buki, a doctor, reminded Céline that she was not a baker.

"I'm glad!" Céline said. I marveled at how easily she moved between English and French, a compliment to her father…and her mother.

After coffee, Anne leaned over. "Do you have plans for the rest of the day?" she asked.

I shook my head.

"I have something I want to show you," she said. "Let's walk in Versailles for a while. I'll show you my surprise, and then we'll have a bowl of soupe before returning home."

I nodded my agreement. "We're going to go," I said to everyone else.

"That's fine," said Gabby who had just rejoined the group. "Philippe is driving me home today. Nice to see you again."

I grinned. *I bet.*

Anne and I walked to the shopping area in Versailles, stopping at our café for lunch. I ordered French onion soup and a small quiche. Anne ordered a *croque-monsieur* with duck. I loved those!

"What'd you think of church?" I asked between bites.

"Nice people," she said. "It seems very English."

I laughed. "It *is* English."

"Religion doesn't seem very French to me anymore." She took a bite. "This sandwich is fantastic! I think the cheese is smoked. Try some."

I forked a bite into my mouth.

"Delicious?" she asked.

"Yummy!" I answered in English.

"Yummy!" she imitated and I laughed.

"I disagree with you about the French and religion," I said, bringing the topic back around. "I think in your hearts, you French are very religious. Look at your national slogan—liberty, equality, brotherhood. Those are all Christian ideals, really. Liberty—freedom from self and sin. Equality—God counts a person's value according to his faith, not according to his deeds. Brotherhood—I have sisters and brothers all over the world due only to the fact that we believe in Christ."

She nodded slowly, though maybe unwillingly. "I'll think about it. Church was better than I thought."

We finished our lunch and discussed our exhibition projects.

Anne was already clicking through her ideas. I hadn't had my inspiration yet. I didn't know if anyone else would do so, but I wanted a theme.

"Let's go see the surprise I was telling you about," she said. We asked for *l'addition,* the bill, and left.

"It's just a few blocks away," Anne said, turning toward the *château* and into the more exclusive streets. We passed a jeweler and an upscale clothing store, and then she stopped.

The long, deep storefront before us was empty, but gorgeous. The long windows were broken up into sections, the trim painted a brilliant blue. Some of the windows were broken into smaller panels, which had been painted with aristocracy in the Louis XV style. I peeked through them at the gorgeous marble floor inside, then peered up at the ceiling, where cherubs and angels holding shafts of wheat were painted on a cerulean background. Brass fixtures were propped up against one wall, though it was clearly under construction.

"What is it?" I asked. "It's drop-dead gorgeous."

Anne tugged me toward the door, which was cut crystal and had a border of small flowers painted along etched vines. A small sign hung in the center.

Permit request posted.
Future site of Boulangerie Delacroix.

I exhaled slowly. The village bakery was quaint, cozy, and fit the homey village. The bakery at Rambouillet was busy, friendly, and sweet in its own right. Simone kept it decorated seasonally, and it always looked and smelled warm and inviting.

But this—this was the flagship for sure.

"I would love to work here," I said. I wondered if I could graduate in the top ten of my class. Not if my macarons kept crumbling.

"Who wouldn't?" Anne agreed, still peering in the door.

I was shocked when he pulled up. In fact, I didn't realize it was him at first.

I looked out my window, and as I did, I saw Papa drop the lace back into the window at the big house.

Maybe he couldn't believe it either. Philippe was driving a motorcycle!

I flung open the door in surprise and stood there. He took off his helmet, unsnapped one from the back and walked toward the door.

I ushered him in. "I didn't know you drove a motorcycle!" I exclaimed.

"I haven't for a long time," he admitted. "But it feels really good. And it's much easier to park and get around Paris. Are you up for riding?" He held the helmet toward me.

"Yes!" I'd never ridden on the back of a motorcycle. Another exciting experience to chalk up to *La Belle France*.

I put on my leather jacket, and he helped me onto the back of the bike. I held on to him for stability, but I couldn't help drawing nearer to him, and he did not pull away. It'd been a long time since I'd been this close to a guy. It felt good. It made me realize how much I craved touch and intimacy, and brought up conflicting feelings about Philippe. And Dan.

I pushed the thoughts away for the moment and turned my head toward the wind to breathe in a less personal—and less enticing—scent than Philippe's cologne.

We took off down the road, to the autoway, and then to the Périphérique, the road that circled Paris. First stop, Ladurée on the Champs-Elysées. I loved the feeling of nothing between me and the city as the wind caressed my skin.

Philippe parked the bike, and we walked into the bakery. He nodded to the young Japanese girl behind the counter, who recognized him. The Bakery Fraternity in action, I imagined.

We looked at the long row of pastries, including shimmery delicacies with piped light cream, covered with fresh raspberries, and sprinkled with gold. He pointed out the macarons.

"Different flavors, see?" Philippe ordered a lemon grass one, and then one of peppermint. The macarons were so light, they were the essence of the flavor and melted on your tongue.

"Pastry should be light," I said. "Not heavy, sitting in your stomach afterward. They should be whipped and formed to be as airy as possible, silky as possible. A punctuation to the meal."

Philippe smiled at me. "*Exactement!* You get it now."

I looked over the cases, the lighting perfect, like jewelers' cases. The glass was polished and buffed until it almost disappeared. There was a beautiful *mousse au caramel,* with an odd pattern on top—cross then dot, cross then dot.

"How did they make that?" I asked.

"They sifted cocoa through a rattan screen," Philippe explained. "You can sift through almost anything to make a pattern."

We hopped on the bike and went to the next Ladurée, on the Madeline, the "Ooh La La" district of Paris. Walking in felt more like entering the elegant salon of an aristocrat than a restaurant and pastry shop. The walls were walnut panels and gleaming cases tempted passersby, promising a momentary distraction to the harried day.

I drank it in. The minutes-old Madeleines, crisp and hot with a tender crumb inside. The *palmiers,* handprints made of puff pastry and dusted with sugar. Mousses and flans and cakes more elaborate than any I had ever seen—all for daily consumption.

"Truly incredible," I whispered. "We have nothing like this in the US. At least not in Seattle."

"So I understand," Philippe said. "Though Luc has tried." A troubled look crossed his face, and I remembered the urgent phone call from Luc to Monsieur Delacroix the other day.

"He is trying," I agreed, hoping I hadn't slighted his cousin and my friend.

We went to a few more shops and then stopped at a restaurant for dinner. It felt exciting to pull the motorcycle helmet off my head and stroll into a café to ward off the cooling Parisian night.

"Two?" The waiter held up his thumb and forefinger.

"Table for two," Philippe confirmed. This was definitely a change from our usual table for three.

We sat down, and he ordered a carafe of water and one of wine.

"Is it okay if I order for us?" he asked.

"Please, do," I said.

The waiter brought some freshly cleaned radishes, a plate of softened butter, and a small, scooped gourd which held sea salt. I watched as Philippe spread a little butter over his radish, sprinkled salt on it, and bit in.

I did likewise, and the explosion of taste and texture was amazing. Sweet, hot, peppery, crisp, velvet. I took a drink of wine and tried another.

"Why did you decide to take your motorcycle today?" I asked, unable to quell my curiosity any longer.

Philippe laughed, and like his sister, the years dropped away from him as he did. I could imagine him as a teenager. "Always curious, you Americans, aren't you?"

I grinned. "But of course, it's one of our best qualities."

"And one I enjoy," Philippe said, smiling in return. "I have had my head down, as you say, into my work for so long, that I have forgotten, I think, how to have fun. I have taken care of Céline, of course, but mostly my life has consisted of working and duties. Going to the museum with you was fun. Riding my motorcycle, I have put it away for quite some time…out of fear."

He stopped there, and I waited for him. The waiter brought out our first course and I bit into my fish.

"Is it good?" Philippe asked before continuing.

"Divine," I said. He looked pleased.

He took a bit of his *sole meunière.* "I've been a cautious driver—and I will continue to be so. But perhaps I've been a bit too cautious. I'm aware that I'm the only parent Céline has, but I also want to teach her to live and to take risks. And laugh, Lexi, like you do so often."

I blushed at the frank compliment, but he was right. Lately, I'd begun to laugh a lot more. Take a few risks. Maybe it was French *joie de vivre.* Maybe I was simply letting go.

We chatted about his childhood and mine, and I thanked him for taking me to visit the *pâtisseries.*

"I saw the new Boulangerie Delacroix in Versailles," I said. His face cooled. I proceeded slowly. "It looks…lovely."

"Oui," he said. "I picked out the site. Me and…my father." He bent to take a bite of his salade, the next course.

"Does it bother you, working with your father?" I asked. I hoped I wasn't treading on ground of too personal a nature.

"Oh, I like my father well enough," he said, "but every man wants to have a place of his own from time to time. Not have his parent looking over his shoulder every day."

"I understand," I said. "I've experienced real freedom, in a fresh, adult way, since I came to France. Without my parents."

"Oui. If he'd stay in Provence, we'd be fine," he continued. "That was the plan. Now with the new bakery and *pâtisserie,* I don't know if he will. But I must talk to him about it, even if it forces a confrontation."

"Do you plan to bake at Versailles?" I asked.

"Bread at Versailles, that is the plan. Kamil will take over for me at Rambouillet, a step up for him." He sighed. "But I doubt my father will return to Provence until things are running to his satisfaction." He shrugged. "Whenever that is."

I wondered if the *laboratoire,* the pastry kitchen, was big enough to justify an assistant to the person Monsieur Desfreres recommended. Some kitchens had more than one pastry chef. I'd have to find out.

Or maybe there'd be another opening, somehow. Perhaps Rambouillet?

Ten

I have long believed that good food, good eating is all
about risk. Whether we're talking about unpasteurized
Stilton, raw oysters, or working for organized crime
"associates," food, for me, has always been an adventure.

Anthony Bourdain

The next week was odd. Monsieur Desfreres was home sick the first few days while we worked on pastry doughs. I wanted to point out that Désirée was particularly good at manipulating pliable dough, but no one but me would get the connection. And besides, my mother taught me that if you can't say anything nice, don't say anything at all. The fact that I was tempted to slip into cattiness meant that I had better amp up my prayer life. I'd noticed I was only super critical in areas I was insecure.

On Tuesday, I saw Jean-Yves and Désirée working on *pain au raisin*—raisin pastries—and of course, she used Anne's raisin plumping method. Jean-Yves left his *tartes aux fraise*, strawberry tarts, on the long cool table they shared. When Jean-Yves came back, Désirée was hovering over them with a spray bottle.

"What are you doing?" he asked.

She backed away, flustered. "Nothing! Just looking. They look so beautiful."

He calmed down and said nothing more. I looked to my side and saw Anne glance up at me and nod.

Monsieur Desfreres was still not there the next day, but the other two chefs helped us along. We were coming to the final six weeks of the course and had much more freedom. We were supposed to do plated desserts that week, but were waiting for Monsieur Desfreres. I didn't mind. It gave us some time to specialize.

That afternoon, Désirée gave a little cry of surprise. We all looked over to her work station. "My *gâteau au fromage blanc,* it is completely runny!" she said. "I know I measured everything just so."

Her small brood of hangers-on ran over, clucking in a superficial display of sympathy. Jean-Yves, because he was so kind, went over to see if he could help her figure it out, as did Juju, though I could sense her reluctance. The rest of us went back to work.

I spent the rest of the day forming my brioche—some I made with almonds, some with emmenthale cheese—to be served for lunch tomorrow. One I made into the shape of a teddy bear for Céline to take with her when she went to Provence on Thursday.

After the brioche was set to rise, I took out some puff pastry and experimented.

"What are you making?" Anne asked, coming alongside.

"Les religieuse." I piped cream into the puffs and then swirled them in chocolate. Afterward, I piped tiny dots all the way around

each one. I dipped some in coffee-flavored glaze and striped them with tiny lines.

Anne laughed. "They are beautiful—treasures. But it's taken you as long to make a half dozen of them as it's taken me to make an entire pan of mille-feuille."

I agreed with her, chagrined. I had more fun being the artiste than artisan.

Anne and I sat at lunch that day with a couple of women from the cooking school. The four of us had become an informal critique group of one another's work. It was much more pleasant, in any case, than sitting at the table where Désirée held court with her hangers-on. I think most of the people buttering her up—literally— hoped she could get them a job in one of the many pastry shops her family owned around France. Today, of course, everyone commiserated about her runny cheesecake.

"Have you ever felt tempted to befriend her?" I asked Anne as we changed into our street clothes before leaving for the day. "She does have a lot of connections." Deep in my heart, I knew I was asking about myself as well as Désirée.

Anne shrugged. "I have to admit, the thought crossed my mind at first, but only for a second. Don't worry, Lexi. I would never befriend anyone for a job. I've been applying at bakeries all over Paris. I'll find something on my own." She smiled her honest smile, and I felt bad I had wondered, and that she'd known I was referring to myself too.

"Sabotage makes you question everyone, doesn't it?"

"*Oui,*" she said.

"I don't question you," I reassured her.

"Nor I, you."

We said our good-byes, and I walked to the bakery at Rambouillet. Patricia was allowing me to do more in the pastry kitchen as long as she looked over my shoulder. However, I was doing less and less in the bread bakery, which was fine by me. I'd understood it was going to be part of my training, though.

When I walked in, I could see Philippe and his father in the office with door closed. No Frenchman was known for a quiet arguing voice, and I couldn't help overhearing as I slipped my chef's jacket off the wall.

"Are you going to come and pay your respects?" Monsieur Delacroix asked. "We leave tomorrow."

"Yes, Papa, I am coming," Philippe said. I could hear the exasperation in his voice. "And so is Céline."

"Bon," his father said. "Sometimes I wonder."

"Wonder what?"

"If this religious attitude of yours makes it easy for you to overlook those who have passed on."

"No, Papa," Philippe said. "Of course I miss Maman, and Andrea too. But life moves forward."

"So why do you think this great God of yours felt it necessary to take your mother—and Céline's?" Bitterness galled Monsieur Delacroix's words.

Why were they arguing about this today? Their wives had been gone for several years.

"He gives and takes away," Philippe said quietly. "I think He's giving me good things, even now."

"I give you good things," his father said. "Like a job."

"I'm very aware of that," Philippe said, bitterness poisoning his voice too.

I slipped back toward the pastry kitchen, wanting to escape before they saw me. As I entered, I looked at Patricia, who looked tired.

"Everything okay?" I asked quietly.

"Oui," she said. She curled her finger to indicate I should come closer. "Lexi, I have a favor to ask of you. Friday is November first, All Saints Day. In France, we visit the graves of our family who have departed and pay our best wishes, and those who want to, pray. My brother and I are going with our father to Provence tomorrow night so we will be there on Friday. I would like to ask Monsieur Desfreres if you could miss school on Friday and come in to work all weekend. I will arrange for there to be help, but you will have to take over some of my duties entirely for three days."

I grinned. "Of course! I am glad to help." She trusted me with the entire *laboratoire* at Rambouillet—the big kitchen—for three days!

"Bon," she said. "We will go over the lists together, everything that needs to be made and when. I will divide the work, of course, and leave your list with you. I need to call someone else to come in as well. Would it be okay if we contacted your friend, Anne? The one who worked at the village bakery? Maman said she did a fine job."

"Of…course," I said. "She is a fine baker."

We sat down and went over the weekend orders. There was a special order for petits fours.

"I know you do these beautifully," Patricia said. "Madame

Gasçon is having company for November first, and she will pick them up early tomorrow. Make sure they look beautiful. Saturday morning, Monsieur Étienne will be by for *tarte aux nougat-pommes.* Can you make one?"

"Oui," I said. I would come in extra early to make sure it was perfectly crafted. I'd leave myself plenty of time—and no room for error.

"Bon," she said.

"Will you see Xavier in Provence?" I dared to ask.

"Oui," she said, features softening. "I may stay at his house. I am not sure. He wants to talk."

She showed me what I needed to prep for that day, and then turned back. "I hear you and Philippe went to Paris last week."

I nodded. No secrets when you work in a family business.

"Did you enjoy yourself?"

"Very much."

She gave me a satisfied smile and started humming. I, on the other hand, felt slightly claustrophobic.

I turned back to my prep work and had been chopping and measuring for half an hour when I felt, more than saw, someone come up behind me.

I turned around. "Hi," I said in English.

"Hi," Philippe said, smiling. "You may have hit upon a good idea."

I looked at him questioningly.

"If we speak in English, few other than Patricia will understand the whole conversation."

I laughed. Even Patricia's English was iffy. Somehow, speaking together in English, in France, seemed even more intimate. I wasn't sure if I was ready for that.

I switched back to French. "Patricia asked me to come in while you are gone."

He nodded. "Yes, and it was her idea, so that's a big step. She told me she was impressed with your petits fours. Otherwise, she'd have made them before we left. I think she wants you to feel at home in the *laboratoire*. Someday you'll have your own."

I grinned. "I hope so. I *know* so." My tone sobered. "Will you and Céline be okay with the…situation in Provence?"

He reached for my arm and tugged the sleeve of my chef's jacket up until he came to the well-healed burn. "Oh yes," he said. "It's a scar, now, Lexi. Not a wound."

His hand felt cool and soft on my arm, friendly and familiar and welcome. He pulled the sleeve back down.

Thursday morning I arrived at school a little late, but with enough time to change and quickly run into the classroom. Anne desperately tried to catch my eye, but there was no time to talk. Monsieur Desfreres was back, the picture of health and running the classroom like a ship.

"I want to make sure each of you is working on your exhibition ideas. If you need to consult with me, please feel free. Or consult with some of your colleagues," he said, waving his hand over the classroom. "But remember that when you graduate, your classmates will be both colleagues and competitors."

On that cheerful note, he began the day's lecture on rolling *tuiles,* tile-shaped cookies. My mind was far away, dreaming of my exhibition. I had one thought, one item I planned to make especially for Monsieur Delacroix. As my hopefully future employer, I wanted to impress him. But I wanted to thank him too, with something special just for him.

The rest of my theme was beginning to take shape in a far-off way. Despite Monsieur Desfreres's insistence that we must do things the French way, I had decided to be risky—not to rely solely on traditional French recipes and presentation, but to meld the best of American Lexi and French Lexi. He had told us to take all that was in us, and all that was around us, and let that influence our work, *n'est-ce pas?*

I had no idea how it would go over, but I was ready to take risks.

After class, Monsieur Desfreres motioned for me to come to his office. "Mademoiselle Anne too," he said.

I glanced at Anne, who seemed to know what he was up to. We followed him down the hallway.

"Mesdamoiselles." He ushered us into his office. "My good friend Monsieur Delacroix has asked me if it would be all right for the two of you to miss school tomorrow so you can help in the bakery while they are in Provence for All Saints Day. I, of course, gave my permission. Working in a real bakery is an important part of your learning here. I assume that each of you was already asked if this would be okay."

Anne looked at me—for an okay to move forward, I gathered, which I appreciated. I nodded and smiled, glad for her desire to make sure things were good with me first. Patricia must have already asked her to work at the bakery.

Monsieur Desfreres dismissed us, and we went to change for the day.

"Is everything okay with this?" Anne asked.

"Oh, sure," I said.

She was a good friend, and I completely trusted her honesty. It was just that she was so…competent.

I got up early on Friday morning in order to make it to Rambouillet on the first train. I checked my e-mail before leaving, as I always did. There was a message from Sophie.

> Hey Lexi! How ya doin'? Things are going well here. Kind of.
> Sorry about Dominique coming back to France, but with
> everything that is going on for Luc, I think he's kind of glad to
> get her out of his hair. Margot will be extremely glad to have
> her out of the kitchen. Even more than Patricia, she likes to
> be in charge of her own stuff. Dominique is no help up front
> because she doesn't speak English, and she's kind of
> spoiled, so she's no help in the back, either. We'll all breathe
> a big sigh of relief when she's gone.
>
> Where will she live? Will you have to leave? I don't know
> the timing anyway.

In spite of all the bad news with the new shop here, we're picking up a lot of special orders. It's been the only growing part of the business.

Hey! Speaking of special orders, I saw your friend Dan the other day. He had been sending his assistant to pick up the special orders, but she was sick, I guess. He came in with another lawyer, a brown-haired woman. She seemed awfully clingy toward him, though he didn't seem to like it. I just couldn't be nice to her. Luckily, I'm the boss now. Bwah ha ha. So I can do what I please.

Anyway, not much else new. Got my hands full. E-mail soon. Miss you.

Soph

Dominique was coming back to France! No one had breathed a word of it. Where was I going to work? Even worse, where was I going to *live*?

And apparently Dan's lawyer friend was a better catcher than she let on, and I didn't mean softball.

I dashed off a quick e-mail to Sophie asking for details. When was Dominique coming back to France? What was wrong with the new store? What was wrong with Luc?

On that unhappy note, I looked at the next e-mail, which was, unbelievably, from Dan. I scanned it quickly, not wanting to miss the train. He wanted to know how to contact me. I quickly, efficiently, and nonemotionally jotted down my phone number.

It wasn't just out of rush. I was detaching from him out of self-protection, like I'd done in Seattle. But back then, I had been full of looking forward to the promise of Paris. Now, I realized I'd left an ache behind in Seattle.

I ran for the train.

I was delighted to note I'd arrived before Anne, then immediately chided myself for being petty. It wasn't a contest, in spite of what Monsieur Desfreres said. Somedays I thought his brain had been overproofed and his heart underbaked.

The bakers were just arriving, and I noticed Kamil had come from the village bakery to work here in Philippe's absence. Preparation for when Philippe moved to Versailles, I was sure.

"Hey, it's my favorite American," he said.

"I'm the only American you know," I teased back.

"Yes, but you're still my favorite!"

I grinned at him. He'd been kind to me since day one. I would enjoy working together this weekend.

Anne arrived shortly thereafter, and it was fun to have my friend baking with me. Anne worked on breakfast pastries. She worked quickly, quietly, and with intensity. Nearly everything came out as nicely as if Patricia had done it herself. I worked on the petits fours that were to be picked up in a few hours. I had to refrost several of them, as my mind was not on my work.

It was on Dan and Nancy, and if they stopped in L'Esperance together to eat breakfast pastries. I wondered if he was happier than Sophie made it seem, good friend that she was.

I needed a break and some food therapy. I picked an almond croissant from one of Anne's baking racks. "These look good enough to eat!"

"Thank you," she said, blushing. I grinned. I wasn't the only one who blushed easily!

At ten o'clock, Simone came back to the cool room. "Madame Gasçon is here for her petits fours," she said a bit timidly. I realized she truly wanted me to succeed. I motioned for her to come back.

"*C'est si bon?*" I asked her. "Are they good enough?"

She looked over the ones I had decorated like gifts, and some with tiny sprays of autumn flowers piped on them. I had made some dots of grapes nestled among tiny chocolate leaves, just turning colors. I'd made some with squash and pumpkins and *courgettes,* zucchini. All fall themes, but unusual décor for petits fours.

"*Très, très belle,*" Simone said as she exhaled. "Like nothing we've seen here before. With an American touch, perhaps?" She grinned at me, grabbed my shoulders, and kissed each of my cheeks. "*Allez!* Madame is waiting!"

I quickly boxed them up and delivered them to Madame Gasçon. I opened the box for her. "Will these do?" I asked.

She looked them over and smiled. "*Oui,*" she said. "The most beautiful! *Merci.*"

"*Bon,*" Simone said as Madame left. "She is a hard biscuit."

I wrinkled my brow. "A hard biscuit?"

Simone's face dropped. "I am trying my English. Hard biscuit is not right?"

I switched my brain back to English. "Ah!" I said, the light going on. "A tough cookie! Someone hard to please!"

"Yes!" Simone said. "That is what I mean. Jerry Lewis says that, *n'est-ce pas?*" We giggled together, and I knew our misunderstanding about *préservatifs* was now corrected.

I made myself a café express, thankful Monsieur Delacroix required espresso as much as any Seattleite I knew and had installed a machine in the back. Besides, a little coffee might help me catch up to Anne's productivity.

I set about making the apple galettes.

Simple Apple Galettes

Ingredients:

1 sheet frozen puff pastry (approximately 8 ounces)
2 Granny Smith apples
2 Tbs butter
2 Tbs brown sugar
¼ cup slivered almonds, toasted
⅓ cup whipping cream
½ tsp almond extract
3 Tbs sugar

Directions:

Preheat the oven to 400 degrees. Thaw and bake puff pastry sheet as indicated on box. Set aside to cool.

While puff pastry is baking and cooling, peel apples and then slice into about ½-inch thick wedges. In a small saucepan, melt 2 Tbs butter; stir in brown sugar, then stir in apple slices. Cook over medium heat till slices are softened but not mushy. Remove from heat.

Whip together cream, almond extract, and sugar. Beat until cream holds peaks when beater is removed.

Cut puff pastry into four squares, top with apple mix, then whipped cream, and sprinkle with toasted almonds. Serve.

Anne and I took a late lunch together at a café a few blocks from the bakery. "How are things going?" I asked.

"Good!" she said. "I love working there. What a nice bakery. Patricia and Philippe wrote out everything they needed done, and Kamil is a great help too."

"You're very fast," I said. "Normally, Patricia does both our jobs. Philippe is faster than Kamil, I know, but he's catching up."

"I've been talking to some other people in class, and I know being able to produce good stuff relatively quickly is important in employment. I'm trying to get faster."

I wasn't fast. Maybe it would come with time and practice. Unfortunately, I only had six weeks left to practice, whereas people like Anne and Kamil had worked in bakeries for years.

"Speaking of other students," Anne said, "what do you think of Désirée's gâteau au fromage blanc?"

"I was surprised," I said. "I truly thought she was sabotaging everyone else."

"And what do you think now?"

"I still think she is," I said. "Though I'm surprised she was willing to risk looking bad in order to draw attention away."

"Did you notice she did it on a day when Chef Desfreres was not there?"

"*Oui,*" I replied. "I'd noticed. She's smart...and maybe dangerous."

"I don't know that she's dangerous. Just perhaps, *dramatique*. We will have to watch out for her," Anne said. "We can watch out for one another. I think Jean-Yves and Juju know too."

"What's the worst she could do?" I asked, spooning up another mouthful of butternut squash soup. I loved squash.

"She could ruin the exhibition, somehow," Anne answered.

I set my spoon down. That *would* be bad.

"Speaking of the exhibition," Anne said. "My mother is going to come. And maybe my boss from the old bakery. It's a big deal."

I was so happy for her. I'd wondered if she'd have anyone there.

"Everyone I know in France and maybe my old boss from America is coming to see me," I said. "Patricia told me I have to be in the top ten in order to work for Monsieur Delacroix."

"You can do it!" Anne said. "I know you can. We'll help each other."

After lunch we went back to the bakery. Simone was in a dither.

"Lexi! Anne! A birthday cake order has come in for Sunday. A very large cake—four layers. White chocolate with raspberry filling, decorated *parfaitement.* I would normally have said *non,* since Patricia is not here, but the lady ordering the cake is the schoolteacher of Céline. I did not want to turn her away. Can one of you make it?"

"I can," I said before Anne could say anything. I looked at her. "If it's all right with you."

"Bien sûr," Anne said. "Of course. Your work is much prettier than mine." She sounded matter of fact, though I wondered if I had jumped in too quickly. But I wanted this chance.

I'd work on the cake Saturday night and Sunday morning after my other orders were done. I wanted it to be perfect.

Saturday I came in early and finished the strawberry tarts. Anne helped me brush glaze over them, and I made two extra—one for each of us to pop into our mouths with the midmorning express. Then I made the tarte aux nougat-pommes for Monsieur Étienne. As soon as I was ready to box it up—two hours early—it fell apart. The nut powder in the recipe made them notoriously crumbly, but I thought I had added enough butter to compensate and hold it together.

"Help!" I called to Anne. Kamil nodded that he had everything under control, and she helped me fashion another crust. I filled it with apple filling and caramelized another topping. Ten minutes before Monsieur Étienne was to arrive, we finished.

"Thank you," I said. "I'd have never been able to do it without you." How did Patricia do this on her own? Would I ever be able to do this on my own? Or was this destined to be yet another career that Lexi tried, couldn't master, and failed?

"No *problème*," Anne said, ending graciously with, "I wouldn't be here without you."

I brought it forward to Simone, who kept it set aside for Monsieur Étienne. She reported later that he had sniffed and said it would do, which was apparently high praise.

I was just settling in to prepare the large birthday cake when Simone came to get me.

"I'm leaving," she said, "but there is a phone call for you. An American man."

Anne was pulling on her coat, getting ready to go home for the night. "I think I'll stay for just a minute," she said, grinning. I grinned back. It was okay to be nosy if you were a good friend.

I picked up the phone. "Hello?" I said in English.

"Lexi? It's Dan. Is…is this the right number? It's the one you e-mailed me."

I was not prepared for the jolt I felt upon hearing his voice. You know the old cliché about knees going weak? It made my knees go weak.

"Hey, Dan. I'm sorry. I was in such a rush yesterday morning that I must have given you the bakery number. I'm—I'm glad you got me, though."

"I'm glad I got you too," he said. Did he intend that double entendre? He'd started out the conversation with a very businesslike tone of voice, but he'd softened. I wondered how his knees were doing. I wondered where Nancy was.

"I'm leaving tomorrow for my sister's wedding, and I just wanted to check in with you and make sure we're set for next weekend. I wondered if you'd be able to take any time off. I'll be in Paris for three days."

"I think so. I'll have to check," I said. "Will you be in touch through e-mail?"

"Yeah," he said. "Don't worry, the weekend is my treat. You show me the sights, I'll pay the way."

"Okay," I said. "See you soon."

"I'm looking forward to it," he said softly.

I hung up the phone, and stood there until Simone nudged me.

"Ça va?" she asked. "Is everything okay?"

"Oh, oh yes," I said. I went back to the kitchen.

"You look like you've been standing near the oven," Anne said. "What's going on?"

"A man I'd just started dating before I moved to France is coming to Paris next week. He wants me to show him the sights, and I told him I would. That's all."

"I'd be glad to fill in for you next week if you take time off," Anne said. "It'll be a nice break from job hunting!"

"Thank you," I said, with mixed emotions. "I don't know how I feel about it yet. Seeing him again."

"Ah," Anne said. "And here I thought there was something happening with Philippe."

I said nothing.

"Is there?" she asked. "You don't have to tell me, of course."

"No, no," I said, keeping my voice down so the others couldn't hear. "It's all right. When I left Seattle, Dan and I parted with no strings attached, you understand? Because I may live here forever and, well, who knows?"

"I understand," she said. "But you still have strong feelings for him?"

I nodded.

"And Philippe?" she continued.

"I don't know yet," I said. "I like Philippe, but I'm the girl who's had three boyfriends her entire life. We've been out a few times, nothing serious, but I like him. And Céline." I shrugged in confusion. "I don't have a recipe to follow for this."

"You bake by instinct, anyway," Anne said. "I've been watching you. I prepare. You create. Create what you want from this."

She kissed both of my cheeks and left me in the *laboratoire* by myself to create the cake.

The only difficulty was, I didn't know exactly what I wanted to create or how to go about making sure it turned out perfect.

I took the last train home that night, and before I flopped into bed,
I checked my e-mail. One from Sophie.

> Lex, not much more I can tell you. I have no idea when
> Dominique is going home. She and Luc have had several
> screaming sessions behind closed doors. Marianne tries to
> fix things, but we don't see much of her, especially now.
>
> Luc leased a new place in Fremont, thinking it would
> be a great new bakery. Remember, he was looking for one
> when you lived here? Well, after he signed a one-year lease,
> starting in January, he found out there is a license for food
> preparation but no service license—no one can eat there.
> That might work in France, but not here. People expect to
> be able to sit in the café and eat. Especially for a kitchen this
> size. I have no idea what he's going to do, and I suspect his
> uncle and mother do not know yet. Don't spill the beans. He's
> going to try to get out of the lease, and I'm betting he can.
> And then, with him and Marianne...well, I've probably said
> too much already. Don't want to gossip.
>
> Wish we could have lunch. How about I fly over tomor-
> row? Ha ha. Just kidding. I'm lucky if I get to Oregon.
>
> Soph

Wow. I didn't envy Luc having to tell Monsieur Delacroix the
bad news. I said a quick prayer that Luc would be able to get out of
the lease. I, like Sophie, bet he could.

The next morning I hopped on the early train to the bakery.
Kamil and his crew were already baking. Anne had arrived early too.

"Come here," I said, leading her to the walk-in. I opened the door and showed her the birthday cake I'd made last night.

"Oh, it's *fantastique*!" she said. "The raspberries, dusted with gold, look like jewels! The pink ribbon encircling each layer looks like the satin bow on a wedding dress!"

Something clicked inside. I made a mental note to come back to it later.

"Do you want to go to church today?" she asked. "It's a slow day, and I can handle it."

I wrestled with conflicting thoughts—on one hand, I didn't want to leave her working here while I did something else. On the other hand, things really were under control, and I had stayed really late last night.

Trust me, I heard in my heart.

"Yeah," I said. I looked at my watch. "If I go now, I'll make the service. Then I'll come straight back."

"No *problème*," Anne said. "It's under control."

I walked into church in the middle of the worship tunes. I noticed Gabby was absent, and wondered for a moment if she'd finagled herself a trip to Provence. Buki was there and scooted over to make room for me in her pew.

"Thank you," I said, and she took my hand and squeezed it. The simple display of Christlike friendship brought a tear to my eye. I told myself I was just tired.

After the sermon, the pastor invited us for *La Sainte Cene,* the holy late meal, which is how the French refer to the Lord's Supper.

I was so glad Anne had come to church with me last week, and yet so glad she wasn't here with me this week. I wanted to be intimate

with my Lord—to remember Him, yes, but also to enjoy the inde-
scribable mysticism that came from sharing His body and blood.

I waited in line with the others, eager for the sacrament.

It looks good now because you're hungry, I thought. I'd had to be
empty and alone before I realized my hunger for Him. I had to stop
stuffing myself with distractions in order to feel my need. It took me
leaving home to realize how hungry I was for God.

As I received the bread, I heard a still, small voice gently say, *Bon
appétit. Enjoy the meal for your soul. Food is life.*

I took the bread, remembered, and drank the wine, still a little
surprised at the taste of it. I'd never been in a church that served wine
rather than grape juice. But it felt and tasted right, rich and deep and
bittersweet, like that which it represented.

"Merci, Seigneur," I answered the Lord.

Back in my seat, I looked at my program for the day and read
again John 6:53–58, the passage the pastor had preached on.

Jesus said to them, "I tell you the truth, unless you eat the
flesh of the Son of Man and drink his blood, you have no
life in you. Whoever eats my flesh and drinks my blood has
eternal life, and I will raise him up at the last day. For my
flesh is real food and my blood is real drink. Whoever eats
my flesh and drinks my blood remains in me, and I in him.
Just as the living Father sent me and I live because of the
Father, so the one who feeds on me will live because of me.
This is the bread that came down from heaven. Your fore-
fathers ate manna and died, but he who feeds on this bread
will live forever."

I smiled, remembering the pastor had told me Jean was a great book for chefs. I understood more deeply than I had before. Food is life.

Eleven

There's nothing better than a good friend,

except a good friend with chocolate.

Linda Grayson

Monday afternoon I went to the village bakery. Odious was polite to me, so I instantly knew something was up.

"Lexi, would you like to make the chocolate nubs for this week's *pain au chocolat*?" Maman asked. She too seemed rather chipper. Maybe it was just that I'd been at Rambouillet the last week. "I understand you're working with chocolate at school."

"I am," I said. I went to the back of the prep kitchen and took down the thick bars of chocolate. I would have to temper the chocolate and form it into the long sticks we rolled croissant dough around.

"It's fun, isn't it? And I'm sure you do well." Maman bustled back to the dough she'd been stirring in the back.

I watched her walk away and shook my head to clear it. I wouldn't have to wait long to find out what was going on, though.

"How was Rambouillet?" Odious came back a few minutes later to ask.

"Very nice," I answered. "It was fun to be in charge of the *laboratoire* for a few days," I threw in, just in case she didn't know. She registered no surprise, so I gathered she did.

"I hear Philippe was kind enough to show you some of the famous pastry houses of Paris," she continued. "I'm sure you have nothing like that in America."

"Not that I know of," I cheerfully admitted. It's not like that was any great secret, and I wasn't going to let her get under my skin. I think she was more mad about my date than anything else.

She turned to go. "Dominique is coming back soon. That's why Maman is so happy. She misses her daughter, and I miss my friend. It will be nice to work with her again."

I felt like telling her that from what I heard, the two of them deserved each other. Instead, I kept my cool so the chocolate wouldn't seize.

Apparently it wasn't true there were no secrets in a family business. It's just that I wasn't in on them. I should have figured Maman would be happy about that. I wondered when they'd tell me officially.

Tuesday after school I went to Rambouillet to work for the rest of the week. I wondered why I was being scheduled to work at Rambouillet so much more often than the village. Not that I minded. It was bigger and busier, so that was probably why. I think Patricia did most of the scheduling.

After putting my apron on, I worked on the chocolate Patricia had left for me to temper. After cakes, I liked working with chocolate best. It allowed me to be creative. It wasn't quite as—dare I admit it—pedestrian as bread and typical pastries.

Plus, they were both made in the same cool room to keep the chocolate or icings from getting too warm. The room was painted a soft green, and I had turned the radio to classical music to keep my mind soothed and freed while I created truffles, bonbons, dipped delicacies of every kind. My new favorites were softly dried cherries with dark chocolate drizzles.

A little after three o'clock, Céline raced into the cool room, pigtails flying behind her.

"Lexi!" she said, her joy in seeing me obvious.

I broke out in a big grin. "Céline, *ma jeune fille,*" I said. "How are you? I've missed you!"

"I'm fine, *très bien,*" she said. "But I've brought someone to meet you. Come on!" She tugged on my apron.

I washed my hands and followed her to the front. There, chatting with Simone, was a middle-aged woman with a neat chignon.

"Madame, this is Lexi," Céline introduced us, sounding much older than her young years. I suppose not having a mother made her grow up faster than she should have had to. "Lexi, this is my teacher, Madame Poitevan."

"*Enchantée,* Mademoiselle." Madame Poitevan extended a thin, well-manicured hand toward me, and I shook it. I hoped I'd gotten all the ganache off. "I wanted to come by and thank you personally for the stunning cake you made for my husband's birthday on Sunday. It really was fantastic; we were most impressed. When I found out it wasn't Patricia who made it, why that made it even more remarkable."

"She told Papa it was the best cake they'd ever eaten," Céline said. She quickly lowered her voice. "But don't tell *Tante* Patricia."

From out of nowhere, Patricia materialized. "Don't tell *Tante* Patricia what, *ma puce?*"

"De rien," Céline answered, holding back a smile. "Nothing at all."

I turned back to Madame Poitevan. "Thank you very much. It makes me truly happy that I was able to assist your celebration in any way."

"I will ask for you again," Madame Poitevan reassured before turning to chat with Patricia for a moment, and then leaving with a bag of fresh chouquettes.

Céline chose some chouquettes for herself and Patricia led her back to the office to begin some homework. That left Simone and I alone in the front.

"How did she know I made the cake?" I asked Simone.

"After you went to church, Madame Poitevan came by to pick up her cake. I was busy, and your friend Anne helped carry the boxes to her car, to assemble at home. I heard Madame exclaim how lovely it was and try to thank Anne, but Anne would have none of it. She made sure Madame knew it was you who had dreamed it up."

I smiled. Dear Anne.

Simone saw me. "You have discovered a few *faux amis*," she said. "I think you have also found some wonderful *vrais amies,* true friends, in France too."

"You among them!" I said, giving her a quick hug, which seemed to both surprise and delight her. Then I went to the back.

I stopped in first to see what Céline was doing. "Homework?" I asked.

"Oui," she said. "Just a little, until my papa comes to get me. He's with my papi this afternoon in Versailles." She sipped her hot chocolate, a perfect drink on a chilly day when the sun was setting early.

"Did you have a good time in Provence?" I asked softly. I didn't know if I should approach the topic of her mother.

"Oui," she said. She lowered her voice. "Don't tell my papa this, because it would hurt him, but I don't remember my maman much. I was very little. I just have her picture."

I squatted down near her. "I understand," I said. "That's not bad. You can still love someone who's hard to remember."

She nodded, relieved at having admitted that to someone, anyone.

"I think next time I lose a tooth, I am going to ask for a maman." She stared at me intently.

"You can't simply wish for a maman." I rumpled her hair. "But you can talk with God about it. He listens and hears you. He says the angels of His children are very near to Him."

"I have an angel?" Céline nearly stood up out of her chair.

"The Bible says you do," I reassured her.

"You know the best things," Céline said.

I didn't know what else to say. Life was simple for her. For me, it was complex and getting more complicated every day.

I went back to the cool room, where Patricia was collecting ingredients. "Chocolate in school this week, *n'est-ce pas?"* she asked.

"Oui…" I had two questions I wanted to ask her.

"I heard that Madame Poitevan was especially happy with her cake. The petits fours were a big hit too. You must have a good boss teaching you all of these things." She beamed with something like maternal pride.

"Absolutely!" I grinned back. "Thank you so much." Now seemed like a good time to ask. "I wondered—would it be okay if I experimented a little with the chocolates this week? I've been thinking about the family being from Provence, and thought I might make some Mediterranean chocolates. With figs, maybe. Lavender, of course. Some orange peel, pistachio."

Patricia smiled. "*Bon!* I used to do some of that myself before I got too busy with the day-to-day things I need to do in the *laboratoire.* Yes, you may do that. I think our customers would be glad to see that. Philippe and Papa too," she said cheerfully.

I guessed by her demeanor that things had gone *fantastique* with Xavier last week.

And now, for the second question. "I have a friend coming from Seattle this weekend," I said. She didn't need to know my friend was male. "I'd like to do some sightseeing. Would it be okay if I took a little time off?"

Patricia cocked her head. She nodded, not pleased, really, but not angry. *Bless Xavier,* I thought.

"Would your friend Anne be able to come in?" she asked. "I hear she did really well last weekend, and that would keep us from being in a pinch."

I'd anticipated this. "She offered to do so," I said, feeling a little deflated.

"Bon!" Patricia said. "Have a good time with your friend. I will let Maman know that I have arranged this."

"Thank you," I said.

Patricia had met Dan in Seattle. He'd been in the bakery a couple of times, and I think she realized we'd dated. I wondered if she'd have been as eager to help if she knew who was coming.

Wednesday at school we intently worked on chocolates. We had little tempering pots and molds to make our fillings. I based mine on my new Mediterranean fillings. I chopped and molded figs, placed them on a little square of shortbread, then dipped the whole thing in the darkest chocolate we had. An upscale Fig Newton, if you will.

I poured little squares of chocolate and set a small curl of candied orange peel and a salty, roasted pistachio on each one. I made fillings of creamed lavender honey and drizzled them with milk chocolate.

Chef Desfreres came by and noted his approval. He tasted one and nodded. "Trying to impress someone from Provence, Mademoiselle?" he asked in his cool, professional voice. But I noted a softening in his gaze.

Juju made chocolates from the island, absolutely divine, with bananas and coconut and lemon grass.

"Making chicken-flavored chocolate?" I teased Jean-Yves.

"Cluck cluck," he said, and laughed.

Easy But Impressive Chocolate Truffles

Ingredients:

8 ounces good quality semisweet chocolate chips
½ cup heavy cream
2 Tbsp liqueur, such as Crème de Cassis or Crème de Framboise,
or vanilla or almond extract
½ cup sweetened cocoa, sifted
½ tsp Gold or Silver Luster Dust
(Can purchase at www.confectioneryhouse.com)

Directions:

Place chocolate chips in a bowl. Bring cream nearly to a boil in
a small, heavy saucepan. Stir frequently, until steaming but not
boiling. Be careful to scrape the bottom of the pan constantly
so the cream does not scald. When hot, pour cream over
chocolate chips. Let stand for 3 to 5 minutes; gently stir until
smooth. Add liqueur or extract and stir to combine. Cover
loosely with plastic wrap and refrigerate for several hours, until
firm.

Sift cocoa and luster dust into a bowl and gently blend with a
fork until dust is evenly distributed. Using a measuring
teaspoon or a small melon baller, scoop up chocolate chip
mixture and quickly roll between your palms until you have a
smooth ball. Roll each truffle in cocoa to coat. Chill until firm.
Store in an airtight container in the refrigerator for up to 2 weeks.

You may have to wash your hands and/or cool them off during
the process if the chocolate is melting too quickly. Truffles will
be firm once refrigerated. Let them come to room temperature
for about 10 minutes before serving.

I had to ask Chef Desfreres for some saffron, as it was so expensive, and went to find him in his office. At the door, I overheard his voice and another man's. Since Chef often had students in his office, I stood outside, listening to see if the conversation was casual and I could enter or if it was private and I should leave.

"I appreciate your giving her another chance." It was a hardened man's voice I did not recognize. "Her sister and brothers had no problem at all the first time around. I don't know why it's so different for her. Her mother has indulged her, I think."

Chef Desfreres answered in a reassuring, calm voice. Almost like a subordinate to a superior, I thought. I wondered if the other man was one of the school's owners. "Give her time," he said. "She's still very young."

"I have standards, and with everything she's been given, she should stand above the crowd," the man said. "I'm losing patience. If she doesn't do well this time, then as far as I am concerned, she can make crêpes at a stand outside Nôtre Dame." His voice had the edge of a man used to getting his way. There was no love, only insistence that she meet his expectations.

I scurried back to the classroom and found Désirée at my table. She was looking my chocolates over. I scanned them for signs of arsenic or damage, but saw nothing.

She looked up at me. "I've finished early. Do you need help?"

"No thanks," I said. "I'm almost done."

"*Bon,*" she said. "I won't be eating lunch with you guys today, so please let me know how my *caramel au chocolat* goes over with everyone else. My papa is here today, visiting with Chef. I'll be eating with them."

I felt a rush of pity toward her, almost like I felt with Céline. Her papa was here to do some finish-line damage control, I guessed.

"I'll let you know how they go over," I said softly.

She nodded and left.

At lunch, I sat with Anne. I pointed to Désirée and the two men at a distant table. "See who she's eating lunch with?" I asked.

Anne nodded. "*Oui,* there's a lot of gossip about favoritism. I believe that is her papa, the famous Monsieur LeBon, who owns three famous *pâtisseries.* Sitting apart won't make her any friends."

I leaned close to Anne and whispered what I'd overheard. "I still don't trust her, perhaps more than ever. But I understand now."

"Me too," Anne said. "I have an awful father as well."

For the first time since my dad had gone home, I felt heartsick for my family. Dad was so normal and nice, and my mom was usually supportive. Neither would ever talk about me behind my back, or gossip, or use words or anything else to abuse me.

Seattle seemed a long way away.

Because I had the afternoon off, Anne and I made plans to go to Paris after school. "Come shopping with me. I want your opinion," I told her, and she happily agreed.

"I'd like to stop in a few bakeries in Paris too," she told me. She hoped to find a job in Paris when we graduated in four weeks.

We hopped on the train and went to the secondhand boutique first.

"Ah, Mademoiselle!" the chic shop lady greeted me at the door. How many customers did she greet each week—each month, each year? And yet I'd only been here twice, and she remembered me. "The wedding, it is back on?"

Anne looked at me wonderingly, and I told her I'd explain later.

"*Non*, but I have a special dinner on Saturday night. Nothing too fancy, but I want a dress that will be remembered," I said.

She efficiently bustled about the shop and finally came back with two outfits. One was a camel-colored, light wool dress, and the other was a red dress, with elbow length sleeves and a fitted bodice, that hit just above the knee.

"La Véronique," the shop lady said, mentioning the designer. "Are you feeling subdued or bold?"

Anne and I looked at each other and both said at once, "Bold!"

Madame smiled. "*Bon*. You try this one, and I will find some accessories."

The dress fit perfectly, close enough to flatter, but not too tight to move freely. Madame came back with some black pumps and a gold necklace with a black onyx drop in the middle.

"Lexi!" Anne said. "You look perfect!"

I looked in the mirror, turning this way and that. It looked good. Even better than the navy blue polka dot one I'd had to bring back a few months ago.

"And you, Mademoiselle?" Madame turned her formidable talents toward Anne.

"Oh, no, not me," Anne said.

"Why not?"

Madame went back to her racks and brought back two outfits. One was a professional but completely fabulous navy blue suit. When Anne changed from her jeans and sweater into the suit, she looked *fantastique*.

"And now, this." Madame handed over a soft, midcalf-length

dress in a Moroccan print. The deep blue perfectly set off Anne's blond hair.

"Go on," I said. "They both look gorgeous."

"Well," she wavered, "I do have a date this weekend."

"You *do*?" I said. "You didn't tell me."

"With the security guard," she admitted sheepishly. She looked at herself in the mirror again. "I do think my *grand-mère* would have wanted me to have some fun with her money."

"Absolutely!" I agreed.

"May I wear the suit out?" she asked the saleswoman.

"Of course."

We paid and walked toward the first of three bakeries Anne planned to visit.

At the first one, the woman at the counter took Anne's name and number and promised to have Madame call her.

"But," Anne said dejectedly, "I turned around to get the name of the woman who would call, and as I did, I saw her throw my name and number into the *poubelle,* the wastebasket."

"I'm sorry," I said. "But, *bon courage.* Let's go to bakery number two!"

The second bakery was more promising, as Anne got to talk with the proprietor. He said he'd keep her in mind, and folded her name and phone number in half before putting it into his wallet.

"Final bakery, and then dinner and the train," she said, a little buoyed.

The last bakery was rather small but cute. I waited outside while Anne went inside. She stayed for a long time. I didn't want to peek, so I walked up and down the street and window shopped.

Finally, Anne came out, looking triumphant. "He's interested! He said to come back just before Christmas, when they need extra help. I can work a few hours, and we'll see how things work out."

"Extra!" I said, using my new favorite French word.

"But they're so small," she said. "I don't know how they'd be able to keep someone new after Christmas."

"Don't worry," I told her. "It's a step. Have faith."

"I don't need faith, I am not applying to be a *religieuse,* a nun," she teased. But she seemed chipper. She'd told me she'd gone to the English-speaking practice group at the church the week before.

"We both have something *super-bon* to wear on Saturday night," Anne said as she prepared to get off the train at Rambouillet. "Now may we both have a *super-bon* weekend."

Indeed.

Twelve

I recognize happiness
by the sound it makes when it leaves.
Jacques Prévert.

I had said I'd meet Dan in the lobby of his hotel.

It was a quick train ride from Rambouillet and then only a few minutes on the Métro. The hotel was midsized but luxurious, a Sofitel in the Sixteenth Arrondissement. It seemed like a good place to meet. The plan was to have dinner, and then I'd go home on the train before it was too late.

I asked the front desk to call him, then sat in the small, perfectly appointed lobby. I wore a slim jean skirt, a black sweater with three-quarter sleeves pushed back, a thin, long jean coat, and some silver bangle bracelets and earrings. I'd brought my feminine but not too frou-frou parasol, as it was a little drizzly out.

I tried to look casual, but as Dan turned the corner from the elevator to the lobby, I couldn't stop the rush of feelings. It was a huge *bouillabaisse* of *homesick*—*I still like you*—*this is an adventure*—*you look good*—*we've moved on*—*what's going on?*

He complicated my dreams and my plans.

"Hi, Lexi," he said, coming forward to hug me as I stood to greet him.

"*Bonjour*, Dan," I said more softly than I'd meant to. "Oh! I'm still speaking French. I'm sorry."

"It's pretty," he said, adding softly, "Like you." With him, it sounded earnest, honest, almost a bit embarrassed. Not like the typical French come-on. I got the feeling he wasn't expecting to still feel as strongly about me as he did, either.

"In any case, it's good to have a French-speaking tour guide." He grinned. "Should we go?" He offered me his arm, and we walked out onto the street. "What's the plan? You're in charge!"

We talked as we walked the streets, getting reacquainted and catching up, but it seemed as though we were instantly comfortable with each other again. I was thankful and, truthfully, blissful we experienced no awkwardness.

I took him on the Big Red Bus so he could get an overview of the city. "This way you get to see everything and decide what you want to visit," I said.

"I'll let you decide that—except for dinner tomorrow night," he said. "I have a special plan for that."

"Okay," I said. What could that be?

We climbed to the top level of the bus. "Don't plug in your earphones," I whispered. "I'll be your guide."

Now was my chance to redeem my first, lonely visit to Paris. I shared with him everything about the monuments and sites we passed, things I knew from my years of study and things I'd learned since I'd been here.

"There's the Louvre." I pointed out the glass triangle that stood before the main entrance. "The building that is now the museum used to be the royal palace. Louis the XIII lived there, as did Louis the XIV before he built Versailles. Then, in the Revolution, it was turned into a homeless shelter. Pigs even stayed there. It was reinstated as a museum to hold the treasures the French people returned to themselves from royalty.

"Fascinating!" he said. "If there's one museum I want to visit while I'm here, that's it."

I was glad he hadn't said the Musée d'Orsay. Better a fresh museum than one with recent, complicating memories. "Then let's go tomorrow," I said. "I'll come in early and we can go before lunch."

We rode up the Champs-Elysées. "Lots of shops here," I told him. "We can visit tomorrow and you can buy something for your mom or whatever souvenirs you want. The street is called the way of diamonds and rubies."

"Because of the jewelry shops?"

"No, because of the head and taillights of the crazy traffic," I said, laughing. Dan joined me.

We got off the bus and wandered around the neighborhoods for a while, chatting about architecture and music and the food stalls, which he seemed taken with. We stopped by my favorite old bookshop.

"You should like this bookstore," I teased. I pointed to the name over the door.

"Mille Feuille!" he said. "I thought that was the pastry you baked me."

I grinned. "Yes. But it means 'a thousand sheets,' like sheets of paper, so it works here too."

We browsed the racks together, delighted and surprised by the titles we liked in common. He didn't go for poetry, though I did. I thought about buying a leather bound collection of poetry by Jacques Prévert, whom I loved, but it was signed and just too costly.

Moving on, we stopped into Ladurée, where I'd been just a few weeks before with Philippe. I showed Dan all of the pastries.

"I've never seen anything like this. It's like a high-class salon," he said. "A jewelry store, almost."

I nodded thoughtfully. "Yes."

He looked at me. His hair was slightly slicked back by a little gel, a little mist, and the wind from the bus. The cold air had given his cheeks color, and he was getting an evening shadow along his jaw. I found him more attractive in Paris than I had at home.

I grinned to myself. Perhaps everyone was more attractive in Paris!

"What's so funny?" he asked.

"Oh, nothing," I said. "Can I tell you what any of these are?"

"I know the Napoléons," he teased, pointing at one in the case. I'd never let him get away with calling them that in Seattle. They were properly called mille feuille, a nod to their many thin layers of flaky pastry.

"Just try ordering a Napoléon here and see what they say," I challenged.

He grinned. "I'll leave the ordering to you."

We settled on a pastry and a coffee, not wanting to eat too much before dinner, and sat down at a table.

"How was your sister's wedding?" I asked.

"Very nice," he said. "I admit, I wasn't expecting to like the guy she married. I'd hoped she'd marry an American and live nearby. And, you know, it's hard to imagine what people from another country are like before you know them. But he's a decent guy, and he seems to really love her, so that's enough. She'll visit once a year, and I can come back from time to time and see her too."

"She's happy in Belgium?" I asked.

"Yes." He sipped his coffee. "Are you happy here?"

I bit into my pastry to buy some time. "Yes," I said. "I'm fitting in more and more. But there are things I miss from home too."

"Such as…" Dan finished his mille-feuille and looked me in the eye.

"Oh, fresh salmon," I said. "Lattes. Mostly people, though." I avoided meeting his gaze. "We'd better go. Paris is beautiful in the twilight. Let's walk for a while. And I'll point out the Sainte-Chapelle and we'll go by Nôtre Dame. Then, would you like to eat dinner on a riverboat restaurant cruising the Seine?"

I'd always wanted to do that. But not *alone,* of course. It was too romantic to waste.

"That sounds great," he said, offering me his arm again. It wasn't as intimate as holding hands, but it wasn't nothing, either. I had the feeling we were both holding back, not really sure where things may—or may not—lead.

We strolled down the streets lit by green street lamps, the air misty enough to bring atmosphere and romance but not enough to get us wet. We talked about his job and how it had been easing up lately. He shared funny stories about the fifth grade boys he taught in Sunday school.

"If they don't know their memory verses, I turn them upside down in the garbage can," he admitted.

"Head first?" I asked, horrified. "Is it empty?"

"Nope," he grinned. "Full of papers. They're boys, Lexi. They love it."

An hour later, we chose one of the several riverboat restaurants and boarded. Dan paid.

"I insist," he said.

We were shown to a table near a window. A candle glowed in its center, and the seats were upholstered in red velvet.

I smiled as Dan took off his coat. He'd worn his suspenders.

He caught me looking at them and turned pink. "I remembered you liked them," he said.

We talked about funny things from home, and the more he talked, the more homesick I felt. But I'd felt this way when my dad visited, and when he'd left, I felt fine and French again. It was all very complicated. I felt totally comfortable with Dan, like we'd never been apart. The kind of vibe where you know what someone is thinking, where conversation is easy and requires little thought and no second guessing. But there was also a feeling of expectation, things we both, I think, felt but weren't ready to say. The tension made things more poignant by denying them voice.

After dinner we took the Métro back to Dan's hotel, and he insisted on paying for a cab to take me all the way back to my cottage.

"I don't think it's good to ride the train this late," he said, although I insisted it was perfectly safe.

I finally acquiesced, and we agreed to meet in the hotel lobby the next morning.

"How do you say good-bye in French?" Dan asked.

"The French love nuance," I said. "*Adieu* means 'I won't see you again for a long time.' *Au revoir* means 'good-bye for now.' *À bientôt* means 'see you soon.' Take your pick!"

"Till tomorrow, then," he said, apparently not willing to risk mangling the French, I thought.

The long cab ride home gave me time to think and to smell the rose he'd swiped from the dinner table.

I hadn't expected to have that much fun. I hadn't expected to feel yearning.

The next morning, I dressed in nice but casual clothes, and I packed my new dress and shoes in a bag. I wasn't going to be able to come home between sightseeing and dinner.

I took the train in and met Dan in the hotel lobby.

"Here," he said, taking my bag from me. "Let me put this in my room for now."

He did it quickly and efficiently, so as not to make it seem like more than it was, but it still felt intimate to me. I was glad when we left the hotel and started walking toward the Louvre.

The day was chilly but gloriously clear and beautiful. We stopped at a Starbucks as a joke and had a coffee. Then we arrived at the Louvre and stood in line with half of Paris.

I talked about my work, school, and Anne. I told him I had a friend at work who had a daughter I adored. I didn't mention the friend was male and that we'd been on a date. I talked about my exhibition.

"What are you going to do for your theme?" he asked as we moved closer to the entrance.

"I'm not exactly certain," I said. "I have a few thoughts of what I'd like to make, but I don't see how they all work together yet. I'm waiting for it to just make sense."

"I hope it makes sense soon," he said. "You only have a few weeks left, right?"

"A month," I agreed. "Two weeks, really, until my exams start. So I need to start planning."

"And then what?" he asked. "Stay here? Come home?"

"It all depends on the job," I said. But even as I said it, I knew it wasn't entirely true.

"Speaking of jobs," he said, "I see your friend Luc once in a while, when I pick up special orders. We've been placing quite a few with them, as business has grown."

"Yes, I heard," I said. "I'm glad things are looking up for you."

"I'm helping him out with a business issue too," Dan said as we neared the entrance.

That got my attention. "What is that?"

"He signed a lease that turned out badly. He asked if I could get him out of it. I told him I didn't specialize in real estate law, but I had a friend who did."

"Will your friend be able to get him out of it?"

"Yes," said Dan, pulling out his wallet to pay for our tickets. "I'm pretty sure we can."

That was a relief. Luc wouldn't have to face Monsieur Delacroix after all.

"Thank you," I said to Dan. Somehow, I knew he was doing it more for me than for Luc, whom he knew only on a professional level.

"He helped you, didn't he?" Dan said. "Though I don't know if I should pay him back for that." His eyes twinkled.

We paid and walked into the huge gallery of the Louvre.

"We should do the top three—the Mona Lisa, the Venus de Milo, and Napoléon," I said. "Then you can pick what you want to see, because I can come back."

We stood in line for the gallery that housed the Mona Lisa and Venus de Milo. When we finally stood in front of the Mona Lisa, I have to admit, I was impressed.

I was prepared not to be, because generally speaking, I'm not into anything surrounded by a lot of hype. But her skin was so luminous, alive and vibrant, her coy smile reaching out from the poplar panel for five hundred years. Dan was taken by it too. He stood before her, silent, for five minutes.

"We don't have this at home, do we?" he asked. "Seattle Art Museum or no."

I shook my head. We walked in companionable silence to the Venus de Milo. "Where her missing parts lie keeps her shrouded in history," I said. "She's not easy to understand."

"Maybe that's part of her appeal," Dan said thoughtfully.

We wandered through the sculptures for a couple hours, and by then we were tired. We sat at a café and had a carafe of red wine and a hearty pasta dish before poking around in the high-class shops. I helped him select a bottle of perfume for his mom, and he chose a cigar guillotine for his dad.

"Chop chop," he said, moving the guillotine up and down. "Watch your head."

At the last minute, I bought one for my dad too. It was exactly the kind of corny thing he'd love.

"Do you want to visit the Eiffel Tower?" I asked. "You should do that before you go."

"I've made dinner reservations there," he said.

"How?" I asked, shocked. It could take months to get reservations at Jules Verne, the restaurant on top of the Tower.

"Connections. Planning. And a good administrative assistant," he admitted. "I was hoping to surprise you."

"Consider it a success," I said softly.

As we walked down the street, we passed a jewelry shop. "Wait!" I said. "Can we stop here?"

"Sure," Dan said, a little confused.

I looked at the various setups, the staging, the way the jewels were arranged by occasion or holiday. The tables were covered with velvet, jewelry pieces scattered appealingly across them. Some large displays, some small, all very much a fairy tale. Suddenly, I knew what my theme would be for the exhibition.

"Thank you!" I said, putting my arms around Dan and hugging him.

He laughed. "For stopping?"

"Yes," I said. "And for giving me the seed of an idea yesterday when you said the pastry displays at Ladurée looked like a jewelry store."

He held out his elbow again, and we linked arms, but I thought it was a bit closer than the night before. We were close enough to touch, to feel one another's warmth, but far enough apart for the uncommitted.

We talked all the way back to his hotel. I waited in the lobby while he changed, and when he was done, he handed me his room key, and I went upstairs to get ready.

Being in his room felt odd. Intimate. His shaving stuff was on the counter, along with his aftershave. The room, like all Parisian hotel rooms, was tiny. I set my purse on the desk and saw that his laptop was on and his e-mail was open.

There was an e-mail in his queue from Nancy.

I turned away and went to the bathroom to wash up and get dressed. After changing into the bold red dress, I packed my casual clothes into the bag and went downstairs.

"You look great," he said. He cleared his throat. "I guess I should have worn my red suspenders," he added, making the moment lighter.

I laughed with him.

As we had reservations at Jules Verne, we didn't have to wait in line. I'd always thought of the Tour Eiffel as black, but it wasn't—it was brown. A soft powder brown, and at night, like now, it twinkled with thousands of lights.

We reached the top of the tower and the restaurant, and sat by a window. It was definitely a table for two.

Paris—the city of lights, the city of romance—was at our feet.

Much to Dan's relief, the waiter spoke English. I think he was tired of relying on me to translate all day. I was glad to have the duty relieved too. And, truth be told, I liked the man in charge.

Tasting Menu, €142

~ *Foie Gras Terrine "a la Lucculus"*
　　toasted Parisian brioche
~ *Large Roasted Langoustine*
　　green beans and chanterelle mushrooms
~ *Baby Purple Artichokes*
　　barigoule sauce
~ *Turbot "cuit a plat"*
　　baby spinach
~ *Milk-fed veal*
　　simmered baby carrots, young potatoes and
　　spring onions, cooking sauce
~ *Tower Bolt*
　　dark chocolate praline, hazelnut ice cream

"This is a beautiful pleasure," I said quietly. "Thank you for bringing me."

"My pleasure," he said, grinning.

We talked casually through the early courses. Each plate was flawlessly presented, impeccably cooked, and perfectly enjoyable. I couldn't imagine a better date.

But did I mean the event or the man?

"Have you learned anything new about yourself or baking while you've been here?" Dan asked.

I nodded. "I learned I like creating beautiful things, that I enjoy cake and chocolate, that I don't work fast but I like detail work. My friend Anne, on the other hand, likes to make everything. She keeps things humming. She can do pretty things, but she doesn't have to. She can do the backbone baking, which kind of bores me."

"Sounds like you make a good team," Dan said. I was surprised by the thought.

"True," I said. "But I'll learn to enjoy the backbone baking too. My job will require it."

"My job's gotten a bit easier," Dan said. His tone changed, and I had the feeling the conversation wasn't casual anymore. "I've put in my grunt time, and now I'm getting projects that don't take so many billable hours. I'm doing some literary copyrights too. No more John Hong and the Ding Dong rap cases like I had as a grunt."

We laughed.

"I feel like I can settle down now," he said. "Seeing my little sister married before me, well, it reminded me that life goes by quickly. It's made me reevaluate my priorities."

I sipped my wine and nodded, not ready to ask him to elaborate because of what he might say. We talked and laughed through dinner, and then walked back to his hotel through a light rain which moistened my face enough to make it glisten but not enough to ruin my makeup. It felt delicious on my skin.

"I'll get your bag," he said, and went up to his room. I sat in a chair in a private corner of the lobby and waited. When he came down, he had a soft hand towel as well. "I noticed your face got a little wet in the rain. I know mine did," he said.

He wrapped the towel loosely around his hand and gently stroked my cheekbones, my eyebrows, my eyelids.

It was gentle, and sweet, and sensual all at the same time. I'd never felt like that before. I didn't want him to stop. He looked me in the eyes, and I allowed myself to fall into the intimacy of the moment and stay there, meeting his purposeful gaze and not wavering for ten long seconds.

Dan broke the spell, handing me my bag. "Thank you for everything, Lexi. I could think of no one I'd rather be with in Paris."

"You're welcome," I said. "I had a great time." *I've missed you,* I thought, but didn't say it, not yet knowing what my future held.

"Keep in touch. I'll pray for your exhibition. Let me know what you decide to do after that, career-wise. It's the point of no return for you, isn't it?" He spoke softly, and the rest of the room disappeared.

"Yes," I said.

He kissed each of my cheeks, French style. Then he lightly kissed my lips before pulling away.

"*À bientôt,* Lexi," he said. "I hope."

Thirteen

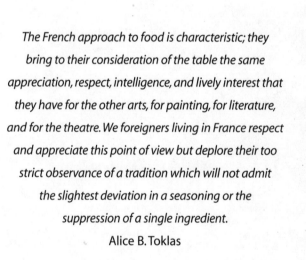

*The French approach to food is characteristic; they
bring to their consideration of the table the same
appreciation, respect, intelligence, and lively interest that
they have for the other arts, for painting, for literature,
and for the theatre. We foreigners living in France respect
and appreciate this point of view but deplore their too
strict observance of a tradition which will not admit
the slightest deviation in a seasoning or the
suppression of a single ingredient.*

Alice B. Toklas

F or two weeks after Dan left, I was incredibly busy preparing for
my final exam and the exhibition. Still, I noticed that Philippe
seemed a little…cool. We didn't run into each other at the bakery
too much, because he worked in the mornings while I was at school.
One week he missed church because he was in Provence with his

father and Céline, and the other week he was friendly, but we didn't make plans to do anything together.

The triumphant look in Gabby's eyes irritated me.

I knew I was prone to imagine things where romance was concerned, but I didn't believe I was imagining this. Had someone told Philippe about Dan? And even if they had, while Philippe and I definitely enjoyed each other's company, we weren't exclusive yet.

"The girl always thinks it's about her," my brother Nate had told me the year before. He was probably right.

Probably.

The last week of December, Chef Desfreres posted the topics for the written examination. Most of them were things we'd already been quizzed on, but this time we'd be expected to know everything from definitions to techniques to tastes and textures on dishes we may not have prepared for months.

L'École du Pâtisserie Examination Topics

Palate development	Baking chemistry
Measuring	Baking finance
Techniques and methods	Product identification
Génoise	Butter work
Flavored cakes	Fillings
Wedding cake assembly	Icing and glazing
Sugar work	Sugar decorations
Pulled sugar	Sugar blowing
Caramel cages	Petits fours
Puff pastry dough & Danish	Bombes using molds
Coupes with fancy decorations	Fancy ice creams
Charlottes	Custards
Bavarian creams	Mousses
Soufflés	Chocolate artistry
Chocolate tempering	Advanced chocolate decorations
Macarons	Breakfast pastries
Croissant mastery	Bread baking
Brioche	Tartes

During our English lessons, Anne and I studied together, mostly at the café, though we sat inside now that it was cold. The café had been strung with pretty white lights, and we ate *gougères,* hot cheese puffs, and drank *vin chaud,* warmed wine, while we studied.

"I want to know the names and terms in English too," Anne said. "I've sent a few inquiries to England and Germany, just in case the bakery in Paris doesn't work out."

"Still working for the Christmas season?" I asked.

"Oui," she said. "And hopefully beyond. I plan to pump out plenty of Christmas breads and *Bûche de Noël.* I start next week after the examinations."

"Oh, I hope to make a Bûche de Noël too," I said. But I didn't know who I'd make it for. The traditional Christmas cake was a filled chocolate layer cake rolled in the shape of a log. "I could decorate it with little mice and meringue mushrooms," I said.

Anne laughed. "Back to work!" She tapped her notes. "The examinations begin next week."

The next Monday I arrived at school to find the classroom both eerily quiet and buzzing with tension.

Désirée looked like her face had been made up with lead powder, the whiteness of her skin more dramatic against the darkness of her hair. Although Jean-Yves and Juju still kept clear of her, I tried to be more sympathetic now that I knew what was riding on her examination.

I still watched my back, though.

The first day of exams was the hardest, as I had to recall how much sugar and butter to remove if you substituted white chocolate, how much butter would be required for a certain sugar, how much flour to replace with cocoa in order to make a recipe chocolate. The chemistry was difficult, but Anne and I had studied hard, and I felt confident I passed.

Each day after the written examination, Chef Desfreres or one of his colleagues handed us a piece of paper with the name of a dish or dessert on it, and we had to create that dish under their watchful eye. After baking, chilling, or decorating, they would sniff, pinch, pull, break, look at our product from all angles, and finally taste it. No smiles, no affirmation, simply notes in the book next to my number.

I breathed a sigh of relief when I was assigned brioche. I'd have to thank Philippe for training me so well.

I pulled mille-feuille as my pastry assignment and I asked, a bit boldly, I thought, if I needed to make traditional mille-feuille or if I could do a variant. One of the younger chefs was grading me that day, and he agreed to let me make a raspberry mille-feuille. I reduced some sweet ice wine down to syrup and drizzled it across the top. Chef Desfreres may not have approved, but this chef did. He ate more than half of it—much more than the one bite required for judgment.

I also made croissants, and I thought I did them competently, though mine didn't shine like Anne's did. Anne's croissant had more layers than you could count; they tasted like soft sheets of butter. They were perfect. Even the formidable Chef Desfreres ate the entire croissant when she was tested.

Désirée was always a good baker, so I assumed she'd struggled with the math and food history before. This time, she seemed to do well on her written exam—she finished as soon as or sooner than most of us. Of course, she'd taken the exam before, and I am sure her father made certain the answers were drilled into her this time. Chef seemed to go a little easier on her. I wasn't sure if it was because her family funneled students his way or if he simply felt sorry for the fragile woman. She made her gâteau au fromage blanc, and it was not runny at all. She made a lovely butter cake and, when compared to Anne, serviceable breads. Unless her exhibition was a disaster, she would earn her *diplôme.*

Which reminded me I needed to ask Patricia for a couple afternoons off to assemble my props for the exhibition. I'd work late other days doing prep work to make up for it, if I had to. I knew the bakeries would be busy now, preparing for Christmas. Patricia had already asked if Anne could work part-time during the holiday season. With relief, I'd told her no. Anne had a job in Paris.

She'd looked disappointed. Who wouldn't? Anne was very good.

I worked in the village that day. After learning the reason behind Désirée's behavior, I looked in vain for some explanation for Odious. Did she have a pushy dad in the background? Not that I could see. He visited the bakery on occasion, and she seemed as rude to him as she was to me. I guess some people were just rude—no reason required.

After work I walked home slowly, savoring the village dressed in its Christmas best. Swags of greenery hung over each storefront, and I peeked in several. The *boucherie* had its finest wares for the season out—large hunks of beef and skinned rabbits hanging by their not so lucky rabbits' feet in the coolers, prime for the season.

The *charcuterie* had bean salads and prepared potato dishes on display under bright lights. Cheery children eagerly anticipated Father Christmas.

The church, however, stood empty.

I walked past the hotel in its pink stucco splendor, hung with lights and bulbs. I saw the chef through the window and stopped to watch him practice his art. He saw me and waved. I blushed, caught admiring his skill, and waved back.

When I arrived home, I kicked off my shoes and noticed the light blinking on my answering machine. I listened to the message.

"Hey Lex, it's me."

Tanya.

"I have something exciting to tell you. Call me back right away. Don't worry about the time."

I looked at my watch. Six o'clock here, eight in the morning for Tanya. She must have called before she'd gone to bed last night, while I was at school this morning.

I dialed her number and she picked up right away.

"Good morning," I greeted her.

"You don't sound like a good morning," she said. "You sound dead tired."

"I am," I said, remembering Chef's admonition that the most important skill a chef required was the ability to be on her feet all day. "I had exams today, and then I worked. I'll do both again the next few days, and then Saturday I have the day off. I'm going to go Christmas shopping in Paris. But enough about me. What's the great news?"

I knew what it was before I asked.

"Steve and I went ring shopping this week. He didn't officially ask me. Or my dad. But we did go and pick out what I liked. I'm expecting he'll formally ask me for Christmas. If you were here, I'd want you to know all the details. Actually, you're not here, and I *still* want you to know all the details."

"Tanya, I'm so happy for you!" I said. I knew what courage it took for her to overcome her inhibitions after being date raped. Now she was ready to get married.

"Scars, not wounds, right?" I said.

"Scars, not wounds," she said. "They're there to stay. But even Christ kept His scars."

"Yes," I said. "So when is the big day?"

"I don't know. Sometime next spring, I imagine. June maybe. Will you be able to come?"

"Absolutely," I said. "I'm not sure when I'll arrive, but it will definitely be in time to make sure you don't order a wedding cake from a grocery store!"

"So, speaking of romance," Tanya continued. "Any further contact with Dan? Or thaw from Philippe?"

I sighed and sat in one of the needlepoint chairs. "Nope. Dan's been pretty quiet lately. And Philippe is—I don't know. A couple weeks ago, I had two guys whose company I enjoyed, and they enjoyed mine. Now, the only affection I get is from Céline."

Tanya laughed. "Do you remember when we did that magazine quiz in high school where you had to pick whether you wanted kids or a husband, but not both?"

"Yes," I said with chagrin. "You picked kids. I picked a husband."

"Now I'm getting married, and you have a kid who loves you."

I laughed with her at the irony of it. "Céline isn't my kid, but I am growing to like her a lot. And hopefully you'll have kids."

"And you'll get married," Tanya said with finality.

"We'll see," I said. "Right now, I'm focused on finishing school. That reminds me—have you been browsing Web sites for your wedding preparations?"

"Of course!" Tanya was ultraorganized.

"Will you send me some links?" I asked.

"Sure," she said.

We finished our conversation, and I thought about my brother's wedding last June and now Tanya's this coming year.

Always a bridesmaid and never a bride?

Trust me, I heard as I fell asleep.

When I walked into the bakery at Rambouillet on Thursday, Simone grabbed my arm and pulled me aside.

"Lexi," she said. "Is it okay that I told Patricia about the American man who called a few weeks ago?"

I nodded slowly. "Yes. Why?"

Simone exhaled her relief. "I just wanted to make sure. I was telling her that I was practicing my English with you, but then when a man called speaking English, I could not understand him. She looked surprised, and asked who had called speaking English. So I told her."

Ah ha.

"Was that the friend you were in Paris with a couple weeks ago?"

I nodded. I had nothing to hide. "Yes."

Simone said, "Patricia thought so too."

I heard a slightly raised voice in the back. A man's voice.

"I'm glad it was okay," Simone said. "You wouldn't know it was almost Christmas with the *problèmes* going on around here."

A customer came in the door, and Simone went to help her. Before I went into the back, I noticed the beautiful, artistic touches Simone had made in the shop. Lovely garlands, swags of greenery, and ropes of cranberries decorated the display cases. She'd lined each case with forest green velvet and sprinkled gold dust throughout.

It was a wonderful place to work.

I went into the back and looked for my chef's coat on the hooks near the office. A muffled, rapid-fire French argument took place on the other side of the door. I couldn't hear the words, but I could tell it was Philippe and his father.

I went back to the cool room. On the way, I prayed for Philippe. When I got to the kitchen, Patricia was already there.

I turned on my emotional radar. Patricia smiled at me, genuine. I relaxed.

I knew she was used to getting her way and being in charge of the kitchen, but what she did for Céline and Philippe was truly selfless. She wouldn't hold it against me if it didn't go according to her plans, which made me want to help her even more.

"How were the examinations? Did you pass with one hundred percent?" she asked.

"I think I did well," I said. "Better on cakes and mille-feuille than bread. Thankfully, they tested me on brioche. Philippe helped me with that, so I was right on."

Patricia smiled. "Philippe, he is a good man."

"Yes," I agreed, "he is." I changed the subject. "You said it was okay for me to take a day to gather what I need for my exhibition. I'd like to go to Paris on Saturday, to the flea market. Would that be okay? I think I can get most of what I need there."

"Oui," Patricia said. "Can you stay late tomorrow night, then? I will too. We'll work together and I can show you a few new things."

I smiled at how far our relationship had come since Seattle. "I'd love that."

"I'm not good for the chocolate today," she said. "I'm going to prep the dough for tomorrow's kugelhopf."

She handed over the chocolate to me. We were dipping chocolates for the Christmas season. The good news was I'd purchased some red and white striped peppermint candies and crushed them in dark chocolate, and the bakery customers liked them. The bad news was I tried to make chocolate peppermint croissants, and they had to be thrown away.

An hour later I saw a special order for a local business—four dozen petits fours. I smiled, remembering the special orders I'd filled—and occasionally messed up—in Seattle. I decided to check with Patricia before filling this one.

I washed my hands and walked out of the cool room. I headed toward the oven room, where I could hear Patricia and Philippe talking.

"She needs to go to the flea market on Saturday," Patricia said in a low voice. "You could take her. I can take care of everything here."

I heard Philippe sigh. "I can't, Patricia. I told Papa I would bake here in the morning and meet him at Versailles right after. And then I have a program to go to at Céline's school."

"Ah," Patricia said. "I just think it's better, you know, *à deux*. And Andrea has been gone some time, now."

My heart clenched. What did I want him to say—to feel? What did I feel?

"Listen," Philippe said. "I like Lexi. Very much. But between you and Papa, you're trying to run my life. I am a grown man with a child. I will run my own life, now. *Ça va?* Please give me some space."

I slipped back to the cool room and decided to take some initiative and do the petits fours. I had a lot of time to think as I worked, cutting, filling, icing, and decorating with the smallest of tips, the littlest knives.

I didn't hold Philippe's lack of clarity against him, as I suffered from it myself. Somehow I knew things were getting sorted out for both of us, though perhaps slowly.

I wondered if Philippe had only been interested in me because of Patricia's pushing. I wondered if she was pushing harder now, because of Dan. Every day life became more complicated.

Friday I came into work and found Patricia making couronnes.

"What can I do?" I asked.

"Help me with the breads," she said. I rolled up my sleeves and helped her form the dough into the couronne's crown shape. We put them into the proofer, and she took me to the back to show me the growing list of orders for Bûche de Noël.

"I want them to be decorated nicely. Would you like to figure that out?"

I grinned. "Would I! I told Anne I'd love to do that, and now I can."

I sat down and sketched out some ideas before I got to work. The roll was chocolate cake with a smooth filling, rolled into a log shape. To my American eyes, it looked like a huge Hostess Ho Ho. I laughed.

After making the cake, which could be filled with coffee cream too, I frosted it with chocolate icing. Dragging a comblike tool through the icing gave it the texture of a tree trunk. I mixed white fondant for the ends, and dragged some brown icing through them so they'd look stumpy. Meringue mushrooms and twigs made out of chocolate-covered orange peels completed the look. Maybe I'd make some marzipan poinsettias to bring in some red.

As I iced, I felt someone come up behind me. I looked up. It was Philippe.

"Hi!" I said in English.

"Hi. That is beautiful." He pointed to my cake.

"Patricia asked me to make the designs for this year's Bûche de Noël. Most of it's pretty traditional, but I thought the chocolate-covered candied orange peels made a nice twist."

"*Exactement,*" he said. "You're right. Well done." He smiled more personally toward me than he had in a while and left the room.

I felt toasty with praise.

At the end of the evening, Patricia came into the room.

"I have been neglectful of your pastry education the past few weeks. We can finish up here and then would you like to see the bakery in Versailles? It's very close to being finished."

We got into her car and headed toward Versailles. She put the proverbial pedal to the metal and took off. So did her mouth.

"Which way will you turn? Pick one, any one, and get going!" she said to the driver in front of us, stabbing the air with her lit cigarette.

A car came through the roundabout and cut her off. She held up her hand as if she were going to flip him off, looked at me, and changed her mind.

My new nickname, I thought, smiling. *Pop-up blocker.*

"Christmas is coming, but the lights are always either red or green!" Patricia shouted. If I hadn't been worried for my life, I'd have been amused. Instead of focusing on her driving, I looked out the window.

There was a light snow falling, unusual for Paris, but beautiful. It softened the edges of an already soft city, spreading more light through the area around the City of Light. Once in Versailles, we drove down narrow cobblestone alleys.

"I'm taking you the back way," Patricia said. "The roads are narrow because they were built for horse and carriage."

If I closed my eyes, I could imagine the royals and their friends bustling down these streets, Marie Antoinette escaping the grandfather king to party and play.

A few minutes later we arrived at the bakery. I recognized it from my trip with Anne.

Patricia parked a block away and we got out and walked. We approached the window, and I could see work had been done since Anne and I had stopped by. The shop was twice as big as the one in Rambouillet, and at least twice as expensive. In luxury, it rivaled some of those I'd visited in Paris.

"We repainted," Patricia said, showing me the royal blue woodwork and molding that framed the windows.

"And the gold!" I exclaimed. "It's been dusted with gold!"

"Philippe's idea," she said, proudly. We looked at the windows, some of them freshly etched with sheaves of wheat and bars of chocolate. "Let's go inside."

Inside, the building was just as beautiful. The marble floors were polished and the display cases gleamed with polished brass.

"And now," she said, "the thing you've been waiting for. *La laboratoire.*"

The pastry room was fantastic—and huge! It had dozens of compartments on the wall for neat organization of tools and ingredients. It had a freezer simply for marble slabs, and its own ice cream maker.

"Wow!" I said, and then realized I was speaking English. *"Extra!"* I repeated in French.

"Oui," Patricia said. *"Extra.* Chef Blois agreed to work here only after my father told him he could design the pastry room for himself and his staff on his own."

"Who will the staff be?" I tried to sound nonchalant.

Patricia shrugged. "I don't know. He'll probably bring them with him."

After a few more minutes, we walked outside to the car. "I hope we have a white Christmas," I said, looking at the snow again. "We hardly ever have a white Christmas in Seattle."

"There's nowhere as beautiful as France for Christmas." She looked at me very pointedly. "Or any other time."

Saturday morning felt like a holiday in itself—no school and no work. I woke up early, made a cup of coffee, and checked my e-mail. I had a new one from Sophie.

> Hey, Lexi, how are you? We are doing well here. Have fun
> with Dominique next week. Good luck. Maybe she'll live with
> her Maman. Maybe you could room with Anne if you take a
> job there? I won't miss Dominique, but I will miss Marianne.

I stopped reading. Was Marianne coming back to France for good too? I felt sick. It had only been a few months ago that I'd wanted to go to their wedding. What had happened?

I kept reading.

> Anyway, things are going swimmingly at the shop. The new
> guy is working great, and Margot loves him. He does whatever
> she tells him to do. I've been taking art lessons; I've been
> meaning to tell you. And my dad gave me my old piano from
> childhood; I moved it into my apartment and started playing

again. Life is good! Oh, hey, do you have the maintenance
log for the Jetta?

I made myself a mental note to ask my dad.

But, really, what I wanted to tell you was that Dan stopped in
the other day and asked for your address. I was in a hurry, so
I just jotted it down on one of my business cards and handed
it over, but I wanted to say, "Hey! Why don't you ask her
yourself?" So...heads up. More later.
     Love, Soph.

Why did Dan need my address? He sent me a nice e-mail after
he returned to Seattle, but nothing too personal. I know he was giving me space to make my own decisions, and I appreciated that.
Maybe he was making some decisions of his own.

I suddenly wanted to hear his voice.

I gathered my notebook with my exhibition notes in it and set
out for the train.

First, I went to Paris. I visited the swankiest jewelry salons, and
once I told them what I was doing, they were eager to help even
though I wouldn't be buying anything expensive. Then I visited my
friend at the secondhand designer store.

"Mais oui!" she told me. "I will be glad to help." We paged
through some catalogs she had, and she asked, "But what will you
wear for this event?"

"My chef's uniform," I admitted. "Nothing fancy."

"We can fix that." She went to the accessory area and chose a crystal-encrusted hair clip for me to affix in my French twist. Then she chose some vintage earrings to match.

"Borrow them," she said when I inquired about the price. "When you return them, you can tell me all about your great triumph."

Unexpectedly, she too was a French *vrais amie.*

Lastly, I ended up at the flea market.

It felt sad, being there alone. I kind of wished Patricia had been able to convince Philippe to come with me, and Céline too. Last time it had been the three of us, and we'd had so much fun. It reminded me, in a way, of my first trip to Paris when I arrived in France.

"You're here with me, aren't You?" I said quietly to God. I felt the gentle reassurance of Him.

First I went to the porcelain booth and selected several small, fine cups and saucers. Then I went to a booth that sold old costume jewelry. I picked through it for quite a while before deciding what I wanted to buy. I found a booth that sold only fans, beautiful, old-fashioned ones. I bought one for Nonna for Christmas. Then I bought one for Céline. That gave me an idea.

I went back to the costume jewelry booth and bought some clip-on earrings and long ropes of beads. A few booths over, I bought some dress-up clothes, extra small, extra gaudy.

Finished picking through the booths for my exhibition, I started looking for gifts.

Not all of the booths sold used items. Some were brand new. One booth sold men's silk ties. Way in the back were several pairs of suspenders. One of them, a tasteful black, had gray Eiffel Towers scattered on them.

I bought them. How could I not?

On the way back to the train there was a *bouquiniste,* a bookseller, set up by a bridge over the Seine. I stopped to browse, and one book in particular caught my eye. It was a beautiful, out-of-print book on pointillism with Seurat, one of Philippe's favorites, on the cover.

After lugging my bags home on the train, I made myself a cup of *chocolat chaud* and sorted through my purchases, setting materials for my exhibit to one side and gifts to the other. I wondered what Anne's exhibition would be. She was keeping hers a secret too. Not to protect it from each other, but to surprise each other.

I'd have to remember to get her a Christmas gift too.

I looked out my window and saw the lights blazing in Maman's house. Dominique was coming home this weekend. I'd still never been invited inside.

I looked at the gifts I'd bought and suddenly had a most unwelcome thought.

Perhaps I'd spend Christmas alone.

Fourteen

She tells enough white lies to ice a wedding cake.

Margot Asquith

About sixty percent of us passed the written examinations, including everyone at my table—me, Anne, Désirée, Juju, and Jean-Yves. That left twenty-four people for the exhibition. Chef divided us into two groups as the exhibition room would not accommodate all of us and our guests at once. My table of eight was paired with four from another table. We were to exhibit first, on the Monday of the third week of December.

"Bon," Patricia said at work that day. "We will all be there." Like a benign stage mother or a big sister, I felt she was as nervous on my behalf as I was.

The week before, I'd been at the village bakery only once. Odious was in the corner chatting with a young woman I didn't recognize. Odette dragged her to meet me as soon as I arrived. I noticed her uniform and her name, Dominique, embroidered on it.

"Dominique! Meet Lexi—she's the person using your house for now," Odious said.

Dominique approached me and coolly held out her hand. She reminded me of Désirée. *"Enchantée,"* she said.

"Enchantée," I responded. "Thank you for letting me borrow your home. I hope I'm not inconveniencing you."

"I will stay with Maman and Papa until after the first of the year," she said, waving her hand as if she were shooing a mosquito. "It's fine."

I reached for my chef jacket, but Maman came running forward.

"Ooh la la," she said. "Lexi, I am so sorry, I forgot to tell you. Since Dominique is back, she will be at the village bakery until the end of the year. I know Patricia could use your help in Rambouillet during the holidays, so she's scheduled you there through…the end of the month." She wavered slightly before saying it. "You can have today off. Perhaps you can do some Christmas shopping or prepare for your exhibition. How is that?"

"That's fine," I said, hanging up my chef's jacket. Somehow, I didn't feel like I'd been given a day off. I felt dismissed.

Maman was certainly chipper. A result, I figured, of Dominique's return. Luc was back too. Philippe had told me that Luc had driven Marianne to her parents' house in Bretagne for Christmas, but that he'd come back for my exhibition. I took a deep breath. Everyone would be there.

Seeing Maman with Dominique, their heads close together as they talked, made me miss my own mother. We chatted on the phone once in a while and e-mailed each week, but it wasn't the same as being together in person. For months—years, even—I had wished Mom would minimize her mother hen hovering. Suddenly, I wanted less distance and more hovering.

I went to the back of the bakery to talk with Kamil. "I'll be there next Monday," he said. "You will do just fine."

"Thanks," I told him. "You've been a good friend."

"One outsider knows how another feels," he said. By that, I think he was talking about his Algerian ancestry, as he'd been born in France. Funny that he still felt like an outsider. I wondered if Buki from church did too.

"I hear you'll be baking at Rambouillet soon," I said.

"Yes!" His eyes lit up. He glanced over at Dominique basking in Maman's fuss. "I'm looking forward to it."

I grinned with him and left. I went home and put on Bing Crosby's Christmas music as well as my favorite, *C'est Noël.* Then I sketched out the final layout for my exhibition.

The following weekend, the school hummed as we prepared for Monday's exhibition. From time to time, I looked at what the others were preparing, but mostly I was so focused on getting mine right, that I didn't have time for more than the most casual glance. We each had screened-in sections in the walk-in, designated by number, where we stored the pastries, cakes, and chocolates we made. Breads, of course, would be made on Monday.

A few times, Désirée looked over my shoulder, trying to ascertain what I was doing, and what Anne was doing, as well. But mainly she focused on her own work.

Saturday I spent time at school making petits fours and decorating them just so. They would store well for two days. So would my lemon crème brûlée, which I made Saturday evening.

I put my materials into the walk-in cooler, in Box 7, and Anne and I went to a café together. Neither of us was working that weekend in order to be ready on Monday.

I noticed Désirée was still at the school, nearly by herself, when we left.

"Do you think that's okay, given our last conversation?" I asked.

She nodded. "Eric is there until they close the doors at ten," she said. Eric was the security guard she was dating.

"Okay." I picked at a croque-monsieur, but I was too tired to eat very much.

The next morning I went to church. Although I was tired and had a lot to do, I felt encouraged and strengthened by it. Buki was gone, which was a disappointment. But hope seeped in through my ears in praise music, my skin in hugs, and my spirit in communion.

Philippe came up to me afterward, even warmer than he'd been in the past few weeks. Maybe work was easing up. He looked happier, more relaxed than I'd seen him in months.

"Where's Buki?" I asked.

"Back to Nigeria for Christmas," he said. "To visit her family."

Dominique was with her family for Christmas, and Buki with hers. I knew where Céline and Philippe would be. I just didn't know where I'd be.

I slipped into my coat. "Can Céline and I drive you to school?" Philippe asked. "I know you're going to work on tomorrow night's exhibition, and I can save you a little time."

I smiled. "Sure."

Céline was beside herself with happiness when she saw we were going to be in the car together. "Are you coming to my house?" she asked.

"No," I answered. "I'm going to work on my exhibition."

"Oh," she said dejectedly. "More baking."

"Perhaps we can give Lexi something to look forward to afterward," Philippe said. "Father Christmas will visit the town next Friday. Would you like to come with us? And then Patricia will take Céline for the evening if you'd like to have dinner. To celebrate passing your exhibition, of course." He smiled.

I sensed a new joviality in him, but he wasn't divulging the reason, and I didn't know if it was too forward to ask.

He pulled up at the school and parked the car.

"I'd love to," I said. "I only hope I pass!"

"You will," Philippe said, then leaned over and slowly kissed each of my cheeks before I got out of the car. I liked his aftershave. It was masculine without being overpowering.

"*Au revoir,* Lexi!" Céline bounced in her seat as I got out. "See you tomorrow night!"

When I entered the school, Désirée was already there, as was Jean-Yves and a few others. Anne was not. But I had my entire cake to assemble, and I couldn't worry about anyone else.

I took the three large layers out of Box 7 and brought them back to my work station in the cool room. I cut some dowels and slipped them through the layers for stability, then piped a heart-shaped squiggle of royal icing, which would dry firm, to keep them in place. I took an hour to ice the layers, smoothing them with an offset spatula, then dotted pearls all over the cake with a special icing I found in Paris that had the opalescent sheen I was looking for.

Anne came in as I was piping the pearls. "Oh!" she said. "Where did you find that kind of icing?"

"I blended it," I told her, excited and anxious. "Need some?"

"*Oui,*" she said. "It'll be just the thing." When I was done with the pearls, she borrowed my piping tubes and took them to her own table.

A few hours later, my cake was done, and Jean-Yves helped me carry it back to Box 7. I got out some sugar and prepared to make my spun sugar creation, and near the end of the night it, and the macarons, were done.

I had almost everything I needed in my box. The props I'd bring tomorrow, and I'd make the bread and cookies then too. I looked over my list and checked the mille-feuille.

My heart squeezed a little at that thought. Dan loved mille-feuille.

Anne finished about the time I did, and we decided to have a quick dinner together again at the café, as neither of us was prepared to cook that night. The night was freezing, snow falling over the city, and we linked arms to keep from slipping on the sidewalk.

Anne pulled open the door to the café, and out rushed steam and warmth and chatter. I ordered *cassoulet,* my all-time favorite French dish. I chipped the edge of my cassoulet, savoring the warmth of the beans, the smoke of the sausage, the crumbly crispness of the bread crumbs framing the meal like fine artwork.

"Ready for tomorrow?" I asked.

Anne nodded, and bit into her noodle dish. "I think so. My

mother is coming in the morning, taking the train with my *patron* from my old bakery. I am thankful they are coming."

"So many people from the Delacroix bakeries are coming to see me," I said. "I only hope I don't let them down."

"Are you worried?" she asked.

Surprisingly, I wasn't. "I feel confident in my work, but it's maybe not the kind of thing they're used to seeing. It's the best of French traditions with American sensibilities. I think that's probably what I do."

Anne nodded. "I go back to the bakery in Paris on Tuesday."

"How is it?" I asked her. We'd been so busy preparing for the exhibition that I hadn't really asked.

"Okay," she said. *"Pas mal."* *Not bad.* But she said nothing more. I pushed away my doubt, unable to deal with it right then.

We paid and left the café to go our separate ways, and Anne gave a cry of surprise. "Oh!" she said. "My keys! I have left them at school."

I looked at my watch. The school would close soon. "Come on, let's go back and get them."

When we got to the school, the security guard was having a loud argument on his cell phone and didn't even glance our way as we rushed past him. Anne went to the bread room, where she thought she'd left her keys. I went to the walk-in for a last peek at my cakes.

When I opened the door to the cooler, someone was already in there.

"Désirée!" I said, and she nearly jumped off the floor as she heard my voice. "What are you doing here?" I had seen her leave hours earlier, before Anne and I had even left.

"Oh," she said. "Just checking on my stuff."

She stood in front of box number two, which was Jean-Yves's. Her box was number five, an odd number on the other side of the room, next to mine.

"That's Jean-Yves's box," I said.

She nodded. "He asked me to check on something for him. I was just about to do that."

I yanked open Jean-Yves's box and scanned its contents. Everything looked fine. Unsabotaged, from my practiced eye. "What did he want you to check?" I asked.

"To make sure his icing hadn't run," she said, her face red.

That was unlikely, in the cooler.

By that time, Anne had joined us.

"Hi, Anne!" Désirée said too brightly. "Nice to see you."

Anne nodded. "I found my keys," she said. "I'll meet you outside."

"We should just check everyone's," I said to Désirée. I pulled open all the boxes, including hers, and couldn't see any damage. I'd apparently caught her before she was able to wreak havoc.

"Ready to go?" I asked. I wasn't leaving the room without her.

"Um, yes," she said, wringing her hands.

"Would you like to have a glass of wine with us?" Anne asked her as we gathered outside and exchanged glances.

What was Anne doing? I didn't need another glass of wine. I needed to go to sleep.

"Sure!" Désirée said.

We stopped at a closer café for a quick glass of wine, and after half an hour, Anne looked at her watch. "Better get to bed. We'll see you tomorrow, *n'est-ce pas?*"

"*Oui,*" Désirée said, and turned to walk toward the luxury apartment complex where she was renting.

"I called Eric and asked him if, as a special favor to me, he'd come in and guard the walk-in for the rest of the night," Anne said. "The other guy was clearly not paying attention."

"Ah," I said. "Hence keeping her distracted for half an hour."

"*Voilà, c'est ça,*" Anne agreed. We hugged and kissed cheeks and parted ways for the night. It's not like we could turn her in. She hadn't actually done anything. And I'm not sure we would have, anyway.

As I walked up my driveway, I realized I'd been so overwhelmed with preparing for the exhibition that I hadn't picked up my mail in several days. I opened my mailbox and took out several letters, some Christmas cards, and one small box.

Oh! It had been mailed from Davis, Wilson, and Marks, Dan's firm. I grinned and went inside to open it.

Dan was so thoughtful. I wondered what it could be. Though he'd kept his promise to let me figure things out by myself, I knew this would be something special. After all, it was our first real contact since Paris.

I slit the box open with a knife and unwrapped the bubble wrap. Inside was a letter opener and a form letter thanking me for my business that year.

I set the letter opener down, and looked at the knife I'd just used to open the box.

Well, I guess I can use one, I thought, grumpily.

If I hadn't already sent the Eiffel Tower suspenders, I might not have sent them at all.

Fifteen

If you are not nervous about your passion,

you are not passionate about it.

Chef Bobby Flay

We were all extremely nervous on Monday.

I had to have bread for my exhibition, so I made brioche and some tiny couronnes. The exhibition was scheduled after the traditional dinner time, as we would have a champagne reception and eat the food we had prepared.

At five o'clock in the evening, we began to lay out our displays. The twelve tables were arranged in a semicircle around the main teaching classroom. Mine stood just to the right of the center of the formation. I was across the room from Anne, but only two tables down from Désirée. I had no idea if she'd tried to access the school again the night before. Eric was gone by the time I arrived that morning. I slept well, though, knowing he'd been there.

I took the long lengths of velvet and silk I'd bought at the flea market and laid them over my table. Anne covered her table in sand for her Normandy theme. She had made thin *tuile* cookies and rolled them around a pin, then piped in "pearls" using the opalescent icing I'd loaned her. They looked like open oysters. She'd made seashell chocolates swirled with dark, white, and milk chocolate. My favorite were her caramels made with sea salt. Her breads looked beautiful, of course, as did her tartes.

"Well done," I whispered to her as we set up. The room was hushed with expectancy and anxiety.

She smiled. "Thanks. Can I help you set up?"

I nodded. "Please!"

We went back to Box 7 and removed my pastries. In the center of my storage space, of course, sat the wedding cake, decorated with pearls and multitinted flowers. I'd found a technique to make the roses yellow with red-tipped ends by putting a bit of red icing in the edge of the tube. I brought out my little couronnes—they looked like wedding rings—and set them around the table. The petits fours, decorated to look like wedding gifts, went neatly to one side. I'd made my brioche in the shape of a large wedding braid with a breath-light veil modestly covering it. I scattered the wedding jewels from the flea market over the table, which I'd covered in deep brown velvet, smooth like a chocolate ganache.

"Ooh, look at this!" Anne said as she brought out my mille-feuille. It was a long rectangle of puff pastry with cream filling and a smooth icing on top. After the icing had set, I'd taken a very small tipped pipette and written it up to be a wedding invitation—for Tanya and Steve, of course.

The crème brûlée was smooth and creamy with a gold sprinkled filling. To the side of the cake were the beautiful tea cups I'd found. Into each one of them I'd baked a dark chocolate cake, and then frosted it with fluffy, swirled white frosting.

"Café express?" Jean-Yves asked, pointing at the little *tasses à thé.*

"Oui," I said. "Coffee with the wedding cake—and a nod to my employer."

The *pièce de résistance* was the spun sugar carriage with macarons for wheels. "To leave the wedding, like Cinderella," I explained. "And for Céline."

"Très belle," Anne said. Even Désirée nodded.

"Whose wedding?" Anne whispered, winking.

I blushed and turned away. Would it ever be my turn, as she implied?

I looked at Désirée's table. Her cakes looked pretty, and her breads were risen just right, baked crispy brown but not overdone. She had a Paris theme and had several different types of crêpes. She'd also constructed an Eiffel Tower out of chocolate twigs. The tower was quite clever, and I told her so.

"Merci," she said, nervously looking at the door. People were starting to file in.

Chef had some of the cooking students acting as roving waiters, bringing glasses of champagne to the guests. Anne's mother and former employer arrived, and she introduced me to them. Her mom looked like Anne, but tired and beaten down. I hoped Anne would be able to find a job here and not have to return to Normandy.

Then came three women I kind of recognized but didn't know from where.

"Oh!" said Anne. "Welcome!" It caught my attention because she spoke in English. "It's my English practice group from the church," she said, beaming.

Patricia arrived, Maman, Kamil, and Luc behind her.

"Alexandra!" Luc said, holding out his arms. He gave me a big bear hug and then three kisses on the cheek. "Here you are, a regular French woman, ready to conquer the world of pastry, eh?"

I grinned. "Hardly. I can't believe this is my last day at school. But it is. And," I said, "I owe it all to you."

"We'll talk later about what you owe me!" he teased. "Marianne says she is terribly sorry she can't be here. She's at her Maman's house, but will be back after the New Year. She sends her best."

I was puzzled. Apparently their marriage was okay, though I had assumed it wasn't and thought that's why Marianne had come home.

Luc waved as Céline and Philippe came into the room. One of the waiters handed Philippe a glass of champagne and a glass of fizzy apple juice to Céline. She carried it, very ladylike, over to my display table.

"Ooh, Lexi, is this yours?" she asked.

"Oui," I said. "Can you guess my theme?"

"Cinderella?" she asked.

I laughed. "Almost. Weddings!"

Patricia grinned broadly, which made me a bit nervous.

I introduced Luc to Anne, and then we all stood back as Chef Desfreres began to speak.

"This, of course, is the culmination of our course work. Each student will have the opportunity to explain what he or she chose to present, and then the students can ask questions of one another, as can those who have come to visit. Please, let us start with Monsieur."

He indicated the snotty man who was his favorite. I looked at Anne under my eyelashes and saw her grin.

A few students later, Monsieur Desfreres arrived at Désirée. I looked around. Her father was definitely not there, nor did there seem to be any member of her large, pastry-loving family.

I remembered the pencil she'd given me the first day of school and spoke up. "How do you get your pound cakes to remain so moist?"

She looked at me with thanks and answered. "Do not overmix. Combine only until the ingredients are blended, but whipping any further introduces air, which dries the cake out much more quickly."

Just as it was my turn, I noticed Monsieur Delacroix slip into the room. A few students asked me questions, only one of which I tripped up on. Then Monsieur Delacroix asked me a question.

"Can you tell me how one would mix and then proof brioche overnight in order to make sure the dough is appropriate the next morning?"

I grinned. That was an early mistake I'd made in his bakery, but Philippe had helped me. "Because the dough has so much butter, it's best handled when it's cool, and then given enough time to proof, which would be overnight in a cooler. Then it should be worked carefully so as not to toughen the dough."

After I answered, he smiled. I'd hit it head on.

Looking around the room, I'd say we all made a good showing. The relief and fatigue were visible on all of our faces. Céline and Philippe went to taste something from Anne's table. Jean-Yves was at Désirée's table with his girlfriend. I noticed his girlfriend sample something, and was glad she was kind.

That left me and Monsieur Delacroix at my table.

"This is quite...unusual," he said. "The cake, of course, traditionally French. But the other items are a twist on what's expected. Especially something as fantastic as Cinderella's carriage, which I find clever and unusual. Creative. For Céline?"

"Mais oui," I answered. But which of us didn't dream of being Cinderella for a day? "These are for you," I said, pointing out the espresso cakes with foamy frosting tops.

"Ah, *bon*." He picked up a tiny spoon, began to eat one, and cracked a real smile.

I knew then that everything was going to be okay. I was so relieved I had made it, that I'd have my place, and that the bakers liked me and felt me to be one of them, that I went home that night and cried tears of joy and fatigue.

I'd made it.

Diplôme

This certifies that Alexandra Stuart has graduated L'École du Patisserie with Honors, performing in the Top Ten Percent of the class.

Chef Robert Desproes

The next day I had off, and I slept in. I called my mom and dad, and they were so excited for me. I uploaded some pictures for them, and for Tanya and my sister-in-law, Leah. Everyone called back with congratulations. Tanya made me promise I'd make her wedding cake.

Wednesday I got up early, whistling, and dressed warmly. I took the train into Rambouillet to work for the day. I'd be working there through the Christmas season.

When I walked in, Simone greeted me with a big grin. "So, Chef has arrived," she said, and I hugged her.

"Thank you, Simone," I said. "I feel really good."

I went to pick up my chef's jacket and to see what Patricia had set aside for me to work on that day, but I couldn't find it. I couldn't find either of my jackets.

"Ah, *bonjour,* Lexi," Philippe said. I'd forgotten he'd be there that morning. I was so used to working afternoons. "Is something wrong?"

"No, no," I said, looking through the various jackets and aprons hanging on the pegs. "I can't find my jacket or apron."

"You should ask Patricia," he said. He followed me to the back where Patricia worked. "Your employee has lost her jacket," he announced.

Okay, what was up?

Patricia came forward and handed me one. "Perhaps this will work instead," she said.

I took it from her and slipped it over my T-shirt. It fit perfectly.

"Oh!" I exclaimed as I buttoned it up. My name, Lexi, was embroidered neatly over the left breast, just like every other employee of the Boulangerie Delacroix.

"Thank you!" I said and flung my arms around her. Then I flung them around Philippe for good measure. Both laughed, but Patricia disentangled herself faster than Philippe.

"*Oui, oui,* now get to work," Patricia said. "In two hours, we will go to the café for a celebratory cup of café crème."

I spent the morning making the decorations for the Bûche de Noël we'd sell for the next week. Every couple of minutes I peeked down at my embroidered name and smiled.

"Ready?" Patricia asked a few hours later.

"*Oui.*" I wiped off my hands and slipped on my coat. We walked a few blocks to a café she preferred, and she ordered for us.

"So, you've done very well," Patricia said. "We were all most proud of you. I knew you'd do well. I asked Papa a week or two ago if I could get your new chef jackets and he agreed." She lit a cigarette. "Of course, making his special cakes last night didn't hurt. *Politique,* but smart."

I smiled and sipped my coffee.

"I want to talk to you about something *très serieuse.* I haven't made an announcement yet, but I am moving back to Provence. Xavier and I talked in November, and he said he'd like to marry me, but if it's not to be me, then he needs to move on to someone else. He put up with the absence when I was in Seattle for a year, but now that I'm home…" She shrugged and exhaled smoke rings. "It's time."

"Congratulations!" I said to her. "How exciting."

She waved her hand as if to say, *of course, of course.*

"So here's where you come in," she said. "I'd like for you to take my job at the bakery in Rambouillet."

"You would?" I asked. "But I could never do your job. You know so much, and I'm so new."

"I think you'd do fine, and there are enough people around you can ask questions of. But I have to tell you something. The job is going to change. Most of our cake baking, petits fours, and other pretty things will be made at the new bakery in Versailles and delivered. We are going to streamline the organization. You'd still be making mousses, custards, and a few chocolates, but most of the work will be breakfast pastries and breads. Things that are everyday staples for the village. The gâteaux will mostly be delivered."

"Oh," I said. Still, it was a job. In France.

"It would pay enough for you to get your own apartment, of course, and you never know where the future would lie. Perhaps after a few years, it would be Versailles for you. Who knows?" She shrugged and lit another cigarette. "Take a few weeks and think about it. I won't be leaving until after Epiphany on January 6. I'm telling the family at Christmas. Okay?"

I nodded. "Okay. I'll pray about it."

She rolled her eyes, but kissed my cheek in a very sisterly way. "You do that."

"Where are you going?" Anne asked. She'd called up on Friday night.

"To see Father Christmas with Céline and Philippe," I said.

"Have you ever noticed that you put her name before his most of the time?" she asked.

I didn't answer, but no, I hadn't noticed. Funny that she had.

"Then Philippe is taking me to a café where they have live music," I added. "Without Céline."

"Should be fun!" she said. "I'm working early tomorrow, so it'll be an early night."

"Any news on a permanent job offer?" I asked.

"Not yet," she said. I didn't want to share anything about mine until she heard about hers.

Céline and Philippe picked me up about an hour later, and I was ready to go. I had a tiny tree in my cottage with a few presents under it.

"Who are those for?" Céline asked, breaking away from her dad.

"One is for you, *jeune fille*!" I said.

She clapped her hands in delight.

"We'd better get going," Philippe said, "or we'll miss Father Christmas."

We drove to the village center and bought a chocolat chaud from a vendor. Christmas music filled the village square, and while there was no snow, it was frosty and delicious out. Céline and Philippe looked cute with their red cheeks, and I imagine I did too.

Soon a great cheer rose from the crowd as *Le Père Noël* arrived in a horse-drawn carriage. He got out and made merry noises to the children, who jumped up and down. Céline pressed forward with the other kids and got a bag of treats as her reward. She offered me a peppermint.

"Merci," I said, and she grinned. "Another tooth gone?"

"Yes, and this new tooth fairy is draining my bank account," Philippe grumbled.

After a few more minutes, we drove down the main street, with its twinkling with holiday lights, and delivered Céline to Patricia's apartment.

Then Philippe and I went to the café. A small quartet played jazz softly in the background, and the maître'd seated us.

"Table *à deux*?" he asked.

"Oui," Philippe answered.

I ordered the veal, as Philippe said it was very good. The café wasn't fancy enough for me to wear the red dress I'd worn with Dan—and that would have felt strange, anyway. Instead, I wore a cashmere sweater with a loose cowl neck, also red. I knew red was a good color on me.

"Congratulations on your schooling—the *diplôme*, the exhibition, everything," Philippe said. "You've done very well. I really enjoyed your exhibit." He grinned. "I knew you were a romantic."

"Yes," I said. "I am. And with my best friend getting married soon…" The conversation felt awkward. "I'm glad to be done. And to have the monogrammed uniform."

"Oui," he said. "They were delivered to the village, and Maman unpacked them. I imagine Odette was not too pleased when she saw it."

I sipped my wine and ate a stuffed olive before smiling. I was certain Odious was not happy.

"I meant to ask you," he said. "Do you have plans for Christmas?"

"No." I shook my head. "Not really. I plan to go to church."

"Bien sûr," he said. "Of course. Even my papa and Patricia go to church on Christmas. But after?"

"No," I said.

"Maman asked if you'd like to join the family at her house that night. Everyone will be there."

Finally! An invitation. I wouldn't have to celebrate alone. "I'd love it," I said.

"You'll get to see what Christmas is like in France," he said. "Of course, I am sure it is wonderful in Seattle too. You must be eager to get back."

I carefully set my glass of wine down and looked at the table. "I like France, and I like Seattle," I said. I was sure Patricia had talked to him about the job.

"There's no place for a woman like her own home," Philippe said. "Even Patricia is eager to get back to Provence. Dominique is glad to be home, and so is Marianne. It's okay to live somewhere else for a while, but after a time, one gets homesick. A woman misses her family, and then life is not so kind anymore. *C'est* natural." He shrugged. "It seems like a good idea to bloom in your native soil."

"Oui," I said, as the waiter delivered our main course.

Was he trying to push me back to Seattle?

Sixteen

Every region has its own specialties, and whether it was
Christmas Eve and the seafood dinner and the seven
courses, whichever family you were from,
it's a visceral part of your life.
Mario Batali

Christmas Eve morning was crazy, filling orders at the Rambouillet bakery. We worked like an athletic team. We talked little, but each of us knew what the others needed, and we stepped up to the plate and made it happen. Later, most of us would celebrate at Maman's house, so for now we focused on the work.

Philippe put some Christmas music on in the back, and it made the entire area festive. Céline played with her *fèves* in the office and ate cookies nonstop.

"Should I save one of the Bûche de Noël?" I asked Patricia. "For the dinner tonight?"

"*Non, non, non,*" she said, clucking her tongue and wagging her finger. "Maman makes the Bûche de Noël. She has always, every year. Even when my own maman was alive." Her eyes misted a little. "My maman was not a baker. Papa did it all."

"Okay," I said. "Should I bring anything?"

"*Non,*" she said. "And do not worry about gifts—no one expects you to bring any." She clapped her hands and flour flew into the air.

"I bought one for Céline…and one for Philippe," I said. "Is that all right?"

She grinned. "But of course!"

We went back to work, and after filling all of our orders, we closed the bakery at noon. We'd be off for a few days, at least some of us would. Patricia would be going back to Provence after January 6.

As we shut off the lights, I looked around the *laboratoire* and wondered if it should be my home. The bakery in Versailles would open after the first of the year. This was the last year Bûche de Noël would be made at Rambouillet.

Patricia drove me home, which was nice in one sense, because I got home much, much faster than I would have on the train. Much, much, much faster. As soon as Patricia screeched into the driveway, I leapt out, thankful for my life.

I saw Dominique, all dressed up, getting out of a car also. I looked down at my flour-and-chocolate-batter-splattered uniform, then at her neat, chic attire. Apparently, she hadn't been at the bakery in the village that morning.

She kissed a handsome young man who didn't bother to get out of his sports car, then she waved as he screeched out of the driveway. He would certainly catch up to, and possibly even overtake, Patricia on the way back to town.

I waved at Dominique, and she gave me a little Queen Elizabeth wave back before disappearing into the big house.

It reminded me that I had better start packing. No matter where I went, I'd be leaving her cottage soon.

I walked inside, looked at my chalkboard, and smiled. My low-tech French day planner. Jean 21 was listed as my Bible chapter. I would read it after Christmas. I wanted to read the Christmas passages this week.

I put on some music and hot water for *café presse*. Just as I settled into a chair and put my feet up, there was a knock on the door. I got up and opened the door. "*Oui?* May I help you?"

"Special delivery." It was the FedEx man. Or, should I say, Exprèsse Fédérale? I signed for the package and took it inside.

It was from Davis, Wilson, and Marks, with Dan's name as the return address. I sat down and opened the box. Inside the FedEx box was a perfectly wrapped gold package. I pulled the beautiful tie off the top and used my new letter opener to slit the tape on the side. The wrap fell away and in my hand lay a box. When I opened it, I drew in a breath and smiled.

It was the leather-bound volume of Jacques Prévert poetry I had admired—and bypassed—at the *bouquinistes* Dan and I had visited.

Inside was a card with a quote written in Dan's hand, followed by a note.

> *Any healthy man can go without food for two days—but not without poetry.*
>
> Charles Baudelaire
>
>
> *Thanks for bringing poetry of all kinds into my life. À bientôt?*
>
> Yours, Dan

I sank back into the chair, humbled and chastened by the fact that I'd thought Dan had overlooked me when really, he'd gone out of his way to remember just what I liked. I thumbed through the book, my heart rent by the words of Prévert as well as the feelings the gift stirred inside me. Part of me had wanted to believe he'd forgotten me, because if he had, he'd have made a decision for me. Now I was faced with making a decision on my own. Realizing the depth of his feelings pierced the thin sheath of self-protection in which I had held back my own.

And yet, my feelings on all scores were not exactly settled. Later, Christmas would start with a drive to church with Céline and Philippe, both of whom I adored. Then we'd head back for a middle of the night meal and gift opening after the rest of the family attended midnight Mass.

I needed a nap. I was already dog tired after the events of the past week and had pressing, unclear decisions just ahead.

As I was about to settle down, the phone rang.

"Hi, Lexi? It's Dan."

"I know who it is. Calling at home rather than work this time, eh?" I teased.

"Yeah." He laughed. "I wanted to wait until I could see through online tracking that my package had been delivered. A few days ago my assistant gave me a list of all the business gifts she'd sent out—and your name was on it! I'm so sorry. She got your address from a business card."

"What business card?"

"Sophie's," he said. "I dropped into L'Esperance to get your address, and she scribbled it down for me."

I'd have to tell her. She'd get a big kick out of it. She'd already e-mailed me that she planned to go to church in our Jetta tonight. The first time she'd ever celebrated Christmas at church.

"Well, thank you," I said, my voice softening. "I love the book."

"I'm glad," he said. "I like my suspenders too. Listen." He must have held the phone away from his ear and toward his body, because I could hear them snap.

I laughed. "I thought you'd enjoy something with the Eiffel Tower on it."

"I do," he said. "Well, anyway, I just wanted to be the first person from home to wish you Merry Christmas."

"You are," I reassured him. "Merry Christmas, Dan."

"Merry Christmas, Lexi."

We stayed on the phone for a few more seconds, neither of us wanting to hang up, but I finally did.

I went back into my room and lay on the bed, but I couldn't sleep. Cars were coming up and down Maman's driveway and people were talking. How did they expect to stay up all night? None of them were napping, obviously.

And then there was my racing mind. Dan. Philippe. Céline. Rambouillet. Seattle.

I rolled over on my side and just began to drift off when I heard a sharp rapping at my door.

I groaned. This nap was not meant to be.

I sat up, walked into the living room and opened the door. Luc stood on my doorstep.

"Bonjour," he said, kissing my cheeks warmly. "And *Joyeux Noël.* May I come in?"

"Bien sûr, of course," I said. "Please."

He followed me into the little living room. "This place is certainly cleaner than when Dominique is in residence," he said, looking around.

I laughed. "Dominique is five years younger than me. I was messy at twenty too."

"I have only a few minutes," he said. "I am on my way to Marianne's parents' house for Christmas. But there is something very important I want to talk with you about."

"Sure," I said. I sat on the edge of my chair.

"You know I plan to open a third bakery in Seattle, *non?*"

"Yes," I said, not sure how much of what I knew I should reveal. But he explained it all anyway.

"Well, I signed a lease on a shop in Fremont," he said, naming a funky section of Seattle. "I thought it would be a great dessert café, someplace for people to meet in the afternoons and late at night for dessert. Unfortunately, I am a better baker and businessman than I am a lawyer, and I didn't read the contract too well. There is ample baking and display room, but I cannot get an eating-in permit for that location."

"I'm sorry," I said.

"Yes, I was too," Luc continued, running his fingers through his hair. "So I consulted your friend Dan—of Davis, Wilson, and Marks, you know, the ones who do so many special orders with us?"

"*Oui.*" I glanced at the Jacques Prévert poetry book just to my side. "I know Dan very well."

"He has come to my rescue. I asked him if he could get me out of the lease, and he said he thought his friend could. But after his trip from France, he came to consult with me. He said that, after visiting Paris, he had a better idea. Why not make an upscale *pâtisserie* at the Fremont location specializing in wedding cakes and high-end catering, like a lot of the businesses he worked with wanted? 'There are quite a few places like that in Paris,' he said, 'but not Seattle.' He assured me that his firm would use the place and would mention it around. He even suggested you might enjoy working in such a place when your schooling was done."

Dan had suggested an almost irresistible way for me to return to Seattle. But did he know Luc would tell me who had suggested it? Knowing Dan, he'd probably wanted it kept quiet to allow me to choose on my own. I sank back in my chair, trying to absorb the conversation.

"So," Luc said, "I talked about it with Sophie and Margot and even Papa, and they all agree the idea is *fantastique!*" He smiled. "Now, Margot is staying to be chief pastry chef over all three bakeries, but if you like this job, you'd be able to do cakes and chocolates and tartes at the new place in Fremont. I think we'll call it Bijoux. Jewels. High end."

"You're offering me that job?" I asked. "Is that what you're saying?"

"*Oui,*" he said. "Full-time. Under Margot, of course, which could be a *problème…*"

"Oh, I like Patricia well enough now," I said, "and she used to intimidate me."

Luc grimaced. "Margot is not Patricia. But we only have a one-year lease. If the business is successful after that year, it will become a permanent Delacroix bakery. If not, then"—he kissed his finger tips and opened them into the air—"*pouf.* There would be no more job. You understand?"

"I do," I said. A risk.

"Good," he said. "I will need your answer in a few weeks. Many changes happening, you understand. Someone else will have to be hired soon if you do not like this job. You can always stay in Rambouillet and bake breads."

"*Merci,*" I said, dazed.

Luc looked at his watch and jumped up. "I must go, or I will not make it to Marianne's mother's house. I do not want to have the mother-in-law hit me with a broom for being late on Christmas, *n'est-ce pas?*" He grinned.

"Definitely not," I agreed, smiling.

"You think about this and let me know," he said. "Okay?"

"I will pray about it," I said. Saying that aloud was almost the only witness I had with them.

"Okay, pray then," he grumbled good-heartedly. "But let me know. I think it would be a good job for you, Alexandra."

I nodded. *"Joyeux Noël,* Luc."

"Joyeux Noël, Alexandra." He kissed my cheeks, rushed out the door, and then got into his car and drove off.

No wonder Philippe had been asking me about Seattle. He'd been testing to see if I would really want to stay here once there was a choice.

But stay here with him? Or just with the bakery?

I played French Christmas carols and let the tiny lights on my Charlie Brown tree twinkle as I waited for Céline and Philippe to pick me up. Our church was having a midnight service to mirror the midnight Mass much of France would attend.

I drank a mug of chocolat chaud to stave off my hunger. We wouldn't eat Christmas dinner until one-thirty in the morning, probably the same time as my family in Seattle!

At 11:20, Philippe's car pulled into the round driveway. Through the window I could see there was someone—an adult—in the passenger seat. Céline sat in the back.

I grabbed my coat and Bible and turned out the lights. By the time I'd finished, Philippe was at the door.

"Joyeux Noël!" he greeted me, kissing each cheek. He looked really nice, dressed up for Christmas, as was I, in my red dress. "You look *fantastique!*" he said.

"Joyeux Noël," I responded. "And so do you!"

He walked me to the car. "I'm sorry," he said in a low voice. "Gabby called me just before I left and said her car had engine troubles, and asked if I could pick her up and bring her to church. I didn't feel I could say no to someone on Christmas Eve. Her family does not go to church, and her Papa is nervous about driving in the dark anyway."

"No *problème*," I said, more amused by her manipulations than disappointed she was with us. I couldn't help wondering if Gabby had conveniently pulled a plug in her engine and would just as conveniently put it back after Christmas.

I got into the backseat, next to Céline. *"Joyeux Noël!"* I said and reached over to squeeze her hand.

"Merry Christmas!" she responded in English, I supposed because we were on our way to church. "First church, then food, then gifts!"

I laughed with her. Children were the same the world over.

"Good evening and Merry Christmas!" Gabby said brightly. "It's nice that you can join us. I imagine you would spend the whole evening alone, otherwise."

I said nothing about spending Christmas with the Delacroix family. "I'm glad I can join you too." I bit back a smile.

We pulled up in front of the church door, and Philippe let the three of us out while he parked the car.

We exchanged holiday kisses and greetings with others and then sat down. Philippe joined us, taking care to sit between me and Céline.

The church was semidark, with lit candles casting warm flickers all around. There were boughs of evergreen on every pew, and the cinnamon pine scent they cast throughout the church felt both warm and intimate. In the back, out of sight, a cellist played Christmas carols, and I sang along to them in my head.

We'd come early to get a good seat, and I opened my Bible to Matthew and read the Christmas story again while I waited. After doing so, I flipped to the end of the book and reread Matthew 28:19, the passage that had inspired me to come to France last year.

Therefore go and make disciples of all nations…

Have I done that, Lord? I asked silently. *I've made a quiet, occasional point of telling Patricia and Luc that I pray, and I do try to keep you in conversation naturally.* I looked over at Céline, who rested against her father's shoulder. *I've been kind to Céline. But making disciples?*

I looked around the room. My eyes were drawn to a woman sitting one row over and two rows ahead of me. How did I know her?

Of course! One of the women in Anne's English group. I spotted another. It was so wonderful of them to come to her exhibition. It made a big impact on her—an impact, I know, for Christ.

I smiled and bowed my head. I know what He was saying. Anne wouldn't have been here, with them, without me bringing her.

But just one person? I asked inside. It seemed so…insignificant.

I remembered another passage I had read in Matthew, before the one instructing us to make disciples of all nations. I flipped through Matthew until I found it in chapter 18, verse 12.

What do you think? If a man owns a hundred sheep, and one of them wanders away, will he not leave the ninety-nine on the hills and go to look for the one that wandered off?

Yes, Lord, you are the God that cares about the one. And so do I.

I closed my Bible and let myself get carried away by the cellist. We stood and sang Christmas carols—in English. I felt homesick and home-settled all at once. It made me even more confused.

After church, we dropped Gabby off at her house before returning to Maman's.

"I'm opening gifts tonight *and* tomorrow," Céline said. "We are going to my grandparents' house in London. More presents!"

"Well, if you have too many, I can forget about the one I got for you," I teased.

"Non, merci," Céline said in all seriousness. The three of us laughed.

I went into the cottage alone to grab the gifts I had for Céline and Philippe, and then walked up to the big house. I knocked on the door, and Maman opened it and greeted me with two big kisses on each cheek.

"Welcome! *Joyeux Noël!*" she said. She relieved me of my gifts, and after quickly checking the tags to see whom they were for, led me into the big kitchen.

I hadn't been in a huge French house before. This house, while updated, was at least three hundred years old. Large beams held up the vaulted ceilings, and windows were everywhere, with the shutters pulled back. The floor was polished hard wood, and the kitchen was, well, amazing. A beautiful, tomato red Lacanche oven. Normally, I wasn't an envious person, but oh, for that oven.

Because I'd worked with everyone there, I felt perfectly at home and comfortable. Having her family around her—even though

Dominique was nuzzling her boyfriend in a corner—made Maman happy. Only Luc and Marianne weren't there.

"So Luc and Marianne are at her maman's house?"

"Yes," Maman said. "For now, of course, her mother wants to be near her. And I can understand that," she said, indulgently.

I did too. I bet my mother would want me nearby if I'd been away for six months.

We gathered around the huge farm table and Maman and Patricia brought out the courses.

First, we had the *entrées,* what Americans think of as appetizers. Fresh shucked oysters, small platters of beautifully arranged fresh vegetables. Next came the roasts—turkey, duck, and beef. I stuck with the duck. I grinned. I was certain my father would not be serving duck in Seattle.

Then came the salade—fresh greens lightly tossed with vinaigrette. No Frenchwoman would dream of buying store-bought salad dressing, at least none I had met. Each woman mixed up an alchemy of oil, vinegar, seasonings, and mustard. Maman's tasted especially good. When I asked her about the secret ingredient, she told me there were two and whispered them into my ear—champagne vinegar instead of balsamic and yeast.

Then came the cheese course, and the beautiful Bûche de Noël. It was a large log—half a tree trunk, I'd have joked, if I thought a joke would go over well. It had been decorated with carefully sculpted marzipan woodland creatures and meringue mushrooms. There were piped icing leaves, weeds, and a sprinkling of ladybugs.

"It's gorgeous!" I exclaimed. Maman straightened in pride.

"Thank you," she said.

After dinner, we scattered through various parts of the sitting and living rooms and opened gifts. Since I had only two to offer, I brought them to Céline and Philippe.

"Me first?" Céline asked.

"Sure," her papa said. Céline took my box and very carefully opened it. Inside were dress-up gowns, costume jewelry, feather boas, and a false tiara left over from the Princess Diana age.

Her face went pale with surprise and then pink with pleasure. She put the tiara on her head. "Is it beautiful? Do I look like a fairy?" she asked after kissing my cheek.

"*Très jolie,*" Philippe assured her. "You look very pretty."

Next, I handed a gift to Philippe.

"For me?" he said, genuinely touched.

"Of course!"

He slowly opened his gift, *Georges Seurat, 1859–1891: The Master of Pointillism.*

"*Merci!*" he said, and leaned over to kiss my cheek softly.

Céline handed me a wrapped package. "This is from me."

I unwrapped a small tin, one I recognized from the flea market. Inside were some tiny Christmas cookies. "Did you bake these?" I asked.

She nodded.

"But I thought you hated baking!"

"I do," she said. "But I like *you!*" She smiled her gap-toothed grin, which betrayed her very grownup tone of voice.

Philippe cleared his throat a bit awkwardly and handed over a gift. "Here."

The package was square, but too light to be a book.

"What is it?" I peeled back the paper and opened a box. Inside was a watercolor of the Musée d'Orsay and the Bridge of the Arts with the sun setting in the distance.

"It's an original," Philippe said. "I saw you looking at them the Sunday we visited and thought you might like to have one of your own."

The colors were so vivid, the orange of the sun reflected and then slickly dispersed on the water of the Seine like oil.

"It's beautiful," I said softly. "It's my favorite part of Paris. In no small part due to you two." I gently kissed each of their cheeks in thanks.

"Enough kissing," Patricia said, coming up behind us, but she didn't sound as if she meant it. "I have a gift for Lexi too."

"You do?" She handed me a box, roughly but with affection. Her style. It was a small red case, like a cosmetic case, but I was certain there was no Lancôme inside. I unlatched it and opened it up. Inside, in perfectly formed compartments, were three offset spatulas with wide angles for more effective frosting of any size cake. There were decorating tips and nails, pastry bags and combs, and little knives for intricate sculpting.

"Thank you," I said, truly touched.

"It's nothing at all," she said, walking away. "You're welcome."

Céline went to open a gift from Maman, and Philippe and I sat by ourselves for a minute. He didn't bring up the job in Rambouillet—or in Seattle—so neither did I. I needed time to think.

"You're getting up pretty early," I said. "London?"

"Yes," he said. "We'll take the Chunnel and stay with Andrea's parents until early January. Then we'll be back."

His voice had an odd inflection to it, but I couldn't put my finger on exactly what it was.

"I'll look forward to seeing you guys then," I said. "Thanks again for the beautiful painting."

He smiled. "It was all my pleasure." A cousin pulled him away, and I went to find Patricia.

She was standing alone, smiling. I wondered if she was thinking that next Christmas she'd be in Provence with Xavier.

"I'm sorry I didn't get you anything," I said, truly remorseful at my oversight. "You've been so good to me, and so helpful. Your mentorship means a lot to me, and I thank you for that."

She patted me on the shoulder and looked at Céline and Philippe. "You have already given me the most marvelous gift," she said.

I wasn't sure what she meant, but not wanting to wade more deeply into that water right now, I let it slide. I did, however, begin to pray about a gift idea that had just sprung into my mind.

The next day, I talked my situation over with Tanya, who was officially an engaged woman.

"So, what are your choices?" she asked.

"Almost anything. It's hard to make sense of them all," I said. "I feel really confused. I almost wish someone had made the choice for me."

She laughed. "At least this way, if you don't like what you get, you only have yourself to blame." I heard some scuffling on the other side of the line. "Listen, here's what you do. Write out two lists. On one, put the pros and cons of staying in France. On the other, put the pros and cons of moving back to Seattle. Then pray over them for a few days. Call me on Sunday, and we'll talk some more."

"Yes, teacher," I said, teasing her for being her ever-organized self. After we hung up, though, I had to admit it was a good idea and might give me some focus. So with soft jazz playing in the background, I sat down and started making my lists.

Stay in France

Pros

1. Work at Rambouillet and Patricia, who has been so good to me, goes to Provence feeling confident about the whole thing.
2. Chance to see what develops between me and Philippe, and Céline
3. Ministry at the English church
4. Will get to know Anne better, possibly mentor her spiritually
5. Become more French
6. Might be able to work in Versailles in a few years

Cons

1. Will grow further and further away from my family
2. Will give up all chance of seeing if what I think is between me and Dan really is
3. Have to work breads and other boring baking for an unknown amount of time
4. Miss preparing for Tanya's wedding with her
5. Miss out on chance to help open Bijoux in Seattle

Go Home

Pros

1.   Closer to my family, whom I miss
2.   Can explore the growing involvement between me and Dan
3.   Focus on cakes, pastries, and other baking I love
4.   Totally involved in Tanya's wedding
5.   Challenge of opening Bijoux

Cons

1.   Miss working in France, which I enjoy, and where I am just starting to feel like I fit in
2.   Won't be able to see what might develop between me and Philippe, and Céline
3.   Will have to let go of ministry/friendship with Anne
4.   Lose chance to work at the flagship Versailles bakery in a few years, learning from a master

---

After writing it all out, I wasn't really any closer to a decision than I was before. I put the papers away. I decided to enjoy being in the village and in Rambouillet for a few days while I cleared my head.

That afternoon, Anne and I met in Paris for lunch and went shopping together.

"How is the job?" I asked.

"Part-time, still," she said. "But I have about a month left of money, and I'm looking elsewhere too. I saw Désirée."

"Really?"

"*Oui.* Working at one of her family bakeries in this Arrondissement."

"I guess she passed then," I said.

Anne nodded.

"I'm relieved for her," I said.

"Me too," Anne agreed. I wondered if she was thinking of her own father.

On Sunday, I went to church. It was kind of lonely. No Buki, no Philippe, no Céline. In a way, it was like when I came to France months ago. No one to prop me up. Just me and God.

I bowed my head. "Lord, help me make a decision."

I expected something solemn to pop into my mind. A Bible verse or an impression from the Holy Spirit, as I'd had before. Instead, I got a joke.

I started to grin as I went over it in my head.

An angel appears at a bakery and tells the chef that in return for her heavenly concoctions, the Lord will reward her with her choice of infinite wealth, wisdom, or beauty.

Without hesitating, the chef selects infinite wisdom.

"Done!" says the angel, and disappears in a cloud of smoke and a bolt of lightning. All heads turn toward the chef, who sits surrounded by a faint halo of light. One of her colleagues whispers, "Say something."

The chef sighs and says, "I should have taken the money."

I didn't want to laugh in church, but I smiled. It was as Tanya had said. I had a choice—God trusted me with a choice. No solution was perfect. I needed to choose the one I wanted.

I called her later that night, and we talked through the issues.

"Job?" she asked.

"Both have possibilities. Seattle is more immediate and rewarding," I said.

"Culture?"

"Hands down, France."

"Guys?"

I sighed. "I don't know."

"Do you like Philippe for Philippe, or for Céline?"

"I don't know. I know Céline needs a mother." I thought of how she'd held onto the hand of her school teacher at the bakery that one day, and how she clung to me and Patricia.

"Is it supposed to be you? You'd be with Philippe, not just Céline."

"I know," I said. "I like Philippe too. And I feel called to them in some way."

"And what about Dan?" she asked. "You said something was still there—maybe stronger than ever."

I nodded. "The truth is, Tanya, I just haven't had enough time to explore which one of them is 'it.'"

"Maybe it's neither," she said.

She couldn't see me, but I shook my head. "No. I think it is one of them. I'm just not clear which one."

Seventeen

The appetite grows with eating.

François Rabelais

A nne spent New Year's with her family, and I spent mine packing. Dominique wanted her cottage back and, no matter what I chose to do, I would have to move soon. I packed nearly everything except my clothes into boxes for the move. Then I met Anne in Paris for a day together.

There were a few things I really wanted to see and didn't want to do alone. We met near the Palais Royale and planned our day together. It was glorious not to have school or work for a few days after the past month of double-timing.

"So," Anne said. "What did you have in mind?"

"Sainte-Chapelle," I said. "I want to see the stained glass."

"Bon," Anne said. "I'd like to visit it too. I think it's the *cathédrale* that Louis XIII built to house the true crown of thorns."

I grinned. "I heard once that if you added together all the supposed pieces of the true cross, the supposed crowns of thorns, and other relics scattered across Europe, you'd have enough wood to build a large building. Still," I said, "it shows me that at their heart and in their history, the French people have always known there is a God."

Anne nodded. "You know what's next door to the Sainte-Chapelle, don't you?"

"Oh yes," I said. "I've been saving that for a good time. The Conciergerie. The last jail of Marie Antoinette before she was beheaded. Let's go there too."

We found our route on the map on the wall of the Métro station, and boarded the next train that came along. We sat and chatted in French, and I was so glad for our growing friendship. A year ago, I'd never have imagined I'd be living in France, have a close French friend, dream in French, and have a *diplôme* from a French pastry school. Almost like the cliché, I had to pinch myself to believe it was true.

We got to the Sainte-Chapelle, and it wasn't too busy. We hiked up a narrow, thin, curving stairwell seven hundred years old. It still took my breath away to think my feet trod the same ground as pilgrims half an eon ago.

Once we arrived in the chapelle, Anne exclaimed, *"C'est fantastique!"*

Indeed, it was. Light filtered through the thousands of panels that told the entire story of the Bible in stained glass, Genesis to Revelation.

"There is no place like France," I said. Anne, good French-woman that she was, heartily agreed.

Afterward we grabbed a hot crêpe spread with Nutella from a street vendor and sat on a bench, eating them together.

"How is the job going?" I asked her.

"Okay," she said. "I don't want to complain. It's a job, it's in Paris. And who knows? Maybe it'll lead to something better."

"But it's not *super*?" I asked. "Not exactly what you wanted?"

She shook her head. "Honestly, I don't get to do much. As you've probably noticed, most bakeries in France are family owned. I do a lot of decorating and prepping but not much baking. The family does most of that."

I nodded sympathetically.

"No job is a perfect solution, though, right?" she asked, looking for confirmation, I think. I didn't have the heart to tell her that I had two job offers.

"I have two Christmas gifts for you," I said. "I'm sorry I didn't get them to you before you left for the holiday."

"I'm sorry!" she said. "I didn't buy anything for you."

"Don't worry about it," I said. "Your company while I explore Paris and your friendship are great gifts. And these were not expensive."

She took the first box from me and opened it. Inside was a pair of white hoop earrings she'd admired at the secondhand designer shop we'd visited.

"Merci!" she said. "How kind of you to remember."

Then she opened the second gift, an envelope with a small piece of paper in it.

48 rue G. Lenotre
Rambouillet

"I don't recognize the address," she said. "Should I?"

I shook my hand. "I don't think you've ever been there. Meet me there on the seventh."

"Okay," she said, looking confused but too polite to press me.

We finished our crêpes and headed to the Conciergerie. It was eerie. The huge building had been run by the concierge, or keeper of the keys. Originally built as a royal palace, the royal family abandoned it when they moved into the new palace at the Louvre. Over time, it had become a prison. It was here that the most famous member of the French royal family, Marie Antoinette and her children, spent the last days before her death.

We walked around, our voices echoing off the yellowed walls, the flying buttresses silent witnesses to royal privilege and horror. We eventually came to Marie Antoinette's final cell. A picture of her, hair turned stark white by horror while in her midthirties, gazed out at me.

Live each day well, she seemed to say. *You never know how many you'll have.*

Anne and I—indeed, every visitor in the chamber—were hushed into silence.

Afterward, we ate a late lunch at a café.

"I'd better get going," Anne said. "Work tomorrow, you know."

"Me too," I said. "See you on the seventh?"

"See you on the seventh," she promised, looking confused and curious.

For irreligious people, the French have a lot of religious holidays. Certainly more than the United States. January Sixth was the Feast of Epiphany, the day that celebrates the visit of the three wise men to the Baby Jesus.

That morning I woke up and thanked God for the epiphanies He'd led me to over the course of the last year. One year ago nearly to the day, I'd been working in a dead-end job I hated, living with my parents, and had a vacuum for a romantic life. I'd been blasé, at best, in my relationship with God.

I grinned. He took me out of myself to find Him, and ultimately, I hoped, to find me.

Before I got out of bed, I opened my Bible to the last chapter of John. I grinned, thinking of the wise pastor at the English church.

Of course, the book ended with food! Jesus and his disciples were on the beach, and Jesus was making breakfast for them.

Lord, I prayed, *You sent me to France with a verse at the end of Matthew. Do You have a verse for me now?*

I read, and when one section caught my eye, I stopped.

When they had finished eating, Jesus said to Simon
Peter, "Simon son of John, do you truly love me more
than these?"

"Yes, Lord," he said, "you know that I love you."

Jesus said, "Feed my lambs."

Again Jesus said, "Simon son of John, do you truly
love me?"

He answered, "Yes, Lord, you know that I love
you."

Jesus said, "Take care of my sheep."

The third time he said to him, "Simon son of John, do
you love me?"

Peter was hurt because Jesus asked him the third
time, "Do you love me?" He said, "Lord, you know all
things; you know that I love you."

Jesus said, "Feed my sheep."

"I know You mean that for me," I whispered to God. "But what does it mean?"

I lay there for a moment, trying to listen, but heard nothing. I remembered I had not understood the other passage in Matthew until I got here. Maybe I'd understand this one later too.

I got out of bed, trying to ready myself for the huge day ahead. Céline and Philippe were coming for dinner. The thought of it drove me to a cup of coffee.

I walked to the village and bought supplies, and a chocolate croissant for fortification. I sat at the café and drank a café crème while I watched the village wake up. My village. I knew most of the men arguing across the morning's first cigarette. I knew whose kid was whining and whose dog was sniffing ankles. I knew which day the *charcuterie* would have the best, freshest salads. More than a few people smiled my way, though no one said more than *bonjour.* That was okay. I understood the French now and perhaps even had become more understated in my own way to accommodate and grow.

I went into the little shop and bought ingredients for puff pastry, almond paste, and some eggs. I bought a gold paper crown for Céline and a Coke for me.

At home, I lovingly created the nicest cake I'd ever made. I took out the bag of *fèves* I'd bought at the flea market and selected six—a baker, a journalist, Mary, Joseph, a fishmonger, and an angel. I placed them at even intervals in the batter and baked the cake. An hour later, it was perfect.

I went into my bedroom to pray and to nap. When I woke up, I finished preparing my cassoulet and my salade. At exactly six, Céline and Philippe arrived.

Philippe looked as nervous as I felt, which didn't make my life any easier. We walked around the tiny cottage with a bit more distance between us, holding back, I think. Céline, on the other hand, was her normal self.

"Ooh, what a beautiful galette de rois!" she said. "You are better cake baker than my papa."

"Hey, hey," Philippe said, laughing.

"But your bread is best, Papa," Céline acknowledged. Her joke broke the ice.

I wanted to eat dinner first. I didn't want anything to spoil it. Afterward, we sat at the table and had coffee, and I cut the cake while Céline went to the restroom.

"Don't say anything about your piece," I whispered to Philippe. He looked up at me, curious, but said nothing. "I've baked a *fève* into every piece to ensure Céline got one."

He grinned widely. "What a great idea!"

"She told me that every year Dominique always gets the *fève*."

Philippe grimaced. "Sometimes family is good, sometimes it's a little…too much. Dominique is in the 'too much' category."

Céline raced back to the table. She took a bite of her cake, but didn't find the *fève*. Philippe and I each took small bites, not wanting to reveal our small *fèves*.

Céline ate another large piece. "Why are you taking such small bites, Papa?" she asked. "Don't you like Lexi's galette des rois?"

Philippe laughed. "It's just that the meal was so good, *ma puce*. I'm eating slowly."

One more bite, nothing. On the fourth bite, Céline finally

found her *fève*. "Oh! Look!" She jumped up and down, and I pulled the gold crown from the table in the living room.

"Put this on," I told her. "You're queen for a day. Everything you wish will be yours."

Céline put the hat on her happy head, then took it off. "No, Lexi. You have it. I have everything I always wanted."

I put on the hat at her insistence. "What do you mean?"

Philippe gave her a warning look, but she paid no attention. "I'm moving to California!"

I nearly fell off my chair. "What?"

Philippe shook his head. "No, no, we're not moving to California. We're moving to Seattle."

This time I actually did stand up out of my chair. "You? You're moving to Seattle? You and Céline?"

I tried to process it. I went to the counter and got the coffee press, ground some fresh grounds, and put water on to boil. This bought me a minute to regain my composure.

"Yes," Philippe said. "It's true. Although Little Miss Secret Keeper wasn't supposed to say anything to you just yet."

I sat down at the table again. "What's going on?"

Philippe folded and unfolded his hands. "Well, you know Marianne is having a baby in two months."

"No," I said. "I didn't know." But it all made sense. That must have been what Sophie was talking about. She would never share anyone else's good news, she'd allow a person to do that themselves. Everyone else must have assumed I'd known. Or they'd talked about it after I left the village bakery. Then we got caught up in the Christmas rush.

That must have been what Maman meant when she said Marianne would want to be near her mother right now.

I couldn't help doing the math. If Marianne was seven months along, and they'd been married five months ago…

"Sometimes babies come early," Philippe said, looking at Céline.

"Ah, *oui*," I said.

"Marianne wanted to come back to France to have her baby, and live here, perhaps for a while, perhaps forever. Luc has been in Seattle for a while. I needed…some space from my father. Luc was tempted by the idea of baking at Versailles. I was tempted by the move to Seattle. And, *voilà*! Good news for everyone."

"I'm moving to California," Céline sang out again. This time, neither of us corrected her. We let her have her happy Epiphany Day. She got down from the table and played with my bag of *fèves* while I served Philippe more coffee.

"I didn't want to say anything until you'd made up your mind to move back or not," Philippe said. "And honestly, I had a lot of details to work out, and wasn't certain how, or if, it was all going to come together for me and Céline. What are you going to do? Have you decided?"

I nodded. "Yes, just recently. I've decided to move back to Seattle, mainly because of the satisfying—and challenging—job opportunity. I miss my family. And—and I have unfinished business there," I said. No more needed to be said.

No wonder Patricia had been so pleased when I told her I was moving back a few days ago. I thought she'd be devastated. Instead, she'd been as positively puffed as proofed dough.

"I thought so," he said. "You do well here, but it's not your home."

He took a sip of coffee. It was silent for a moment.

"I don't want you to think you owe us—me—anything when we move there," he said. "But I want to say that we'd never have been willing to make this jump if we hadn't met you. You showed us how very nice Americans can be. Céline feels much better moving there knowing a…special friend." He cleared his throat. "So maybe this will allow us to grow our friendship a little further in the US. I will look forward to it." He held my gaze for a moment while my insides flooded with confusion.

I'd already started to emotionally separate myself from them. Now, life seemed more complex than ever.

"I'm glad you're coming," I said, and I meant it. Whatever life held ahead for Philippe, for Dan, for me, it was good for Philippe to have some space from his father. He seemed so happy with the choice, as did the twirling, singing Céline.

"Maybe it's me who should wear this," he said, putting the gold crown on his head. "For the first time in years, I feel like a king on Three King's Day."

I grinned and offered him a refill. "Coffee, Your Majesty?"

The next morning I woke up still absorbing the shock of the news, but becoming more accustomed to it. If nothing else, my life the past year had taught me that I never knew exactly what was ahead, but that God had good plans, in the midst of pain, for all His children.

I got to the bakery in Rambouillet a little early. It was my last official day of work.

"So, you know the news, eh?" Patricia beamed. I beamed with her. She had the newlywed glow and she wasn't even married yet.

"Yes," I said. "And now I know about Marianne."

"You didn't know Marianne was having a baby?" she asked, shocked.

"Non," I said. "But I hope next year, when you're expecting, you'll tell me right away."

She whipped me with the towel she had tucked under her apron, and we both laughed.

I spent the morning decorating cakes and looking at my watch. Just a few more hours, and I'd have to leave for my appointment.

I got caught up in my work, and when I looked at the clock again, I only had five minutes to spare.

I dashed through the bakery, still in my uniform and without a coat, and told Patricia, "I'll be right back!"

She nodded, knowing where I was going.

I ran down the street and around the block, praying I wouldn't slip on the ice, and arrived only five minutes late.

"Look, it's Chef Nike," Anne said.

"Ha ha," I said in English, stopping to catch my breath.

Anne looked at me, then at the sign on the building in front of us. "Why am I at the office for work permits?"

"Because I didn't know any other address in Rambouillet, and I didn't want you to guess," I said.

"Guess what?" Anne asked.

"You'll see." I stood for a minute, catching my breath. The door to the office opened, and out walked someone I recognized. She stopped and looked at me as if she recognized me.

Oh, yes. It was the woman who had reluctantly given me my six months' work permit.

She looked at the name embroidered on my uniform. "Lexi. Yes, I remember you. Or at least your unusual name. American, right?"

"Kind of," I said. "I work for a French company, now."

She turned up her nose and huffed off, but Anne and I laughed together and I asked her to walk with me.

When we got in the door, Simone greeted us equally warmly. "*Bonjour,* mesdemoiselles chefs," she teased. "Patricia is in the back."

Anne and I walked back to the office, where Patricia waited for us. Anne looked at me questioningly as Patricia handed her a shirt-sized box.

"Your *vrai amie,* Lexi, has made a suggestion," Patricia said. "I hope you like her idea."

Anne opened the box, and pulled out a chef's jacket. A jacket with her name embroidered on it.

"You're offering me a job?" Anne asked. "Here?"

"*My* job," Patricia said. "If you want it."

Anne looked at me. "Is it okay?"

I gave her a quick run-down on what was waiting for me in Seattle, and she couldn't contain her grin.

"And Philippe is going? And Dan is there? And you get to do cakes and pretty pastries all day?"

I saw Patricia's brow wrinkle at the mention of Dan.

"Yes," I said. "It's a dream come true, for both of us."

Anne sat in the office chair. "But…what about France? You love France."

"I do. And I'm sure I'll come back. But," I said with a wry grin, "in America, they buy cakes at the grocery store. It's clear my people need me."

That was something we all agreed upon. Anne and Patricia joined me in laughter.

Simone came back to show Anne around, which left just Patricia and me. "Stay here," I told her. I slipped back to the walk-in and took out a layered box I had carefully hidden in the back. I brought it to the office and handed it to Patricia.

"For me?" she asked, surprised.

I nodded sheepishly. "A late Christmas gift."

Patricia undid the gold ribbon and carefully lifted off the box lid. "Oh, *c'est très belle*," she said, her voice softer than I'd heard it in quite some time.

"They are for your wedding cake," I said. "I won't be here to help make it, so I wanted to make these for you instead."

Together we peered inside the satin-lined box, and I smiled as I remembered the hours I'd spent at night, designing delicate gold flowers, grey kissing doves, pearls, and other marzipan and royal icing delights that would last, in the cooler, for months. Of course, I'd used the decorating tools she'd given me.

"They are beautiful," Patricia said. "I will place them with pride on my cake. But maybe," she teased, "you should have made some for yourself?" A wicked grin crossed her face.

"Maybe I already have," I teased back.

"*Touché,*" she said laughing with me. "You have learned well, my *protégée.*"

My heart swelled at the compliment. I'd do my part to make Bijoux a success if for no other reason than to honor her.

As for next week? Next month?

Life was uncertain. I'd eat dessert first.

Look for the final book in the

French Twist series

coming in the fall of 2009!

For more information visit www.sandrabyrd.com

Who ever said that growing
up and getting a life would be a **piece of cake?**

In book one of the French Twist series, journey to the
beginning of Lexi Stuart's adventures in getting out,
growing up, and discovering the life God has for her.

Available in bookstores and from online retailers.

WATERBROOK PRESS
www.waterbrookpress.com